PRAISE FOR MEREDITH SCHORR

SOMEONE JUST LIKE YOU

"*Someone Just Like You* has all of the wit, plot, clever banter, and a swoon-worthy ending of a Nora Ephron rom-com—I couldn't put it down!"

—Erin La Rosa, author of *For Butter or Worse* and *Plot Twist*

"These enemies-turned-lovers had such clever banter that I smiled throughout the entire book, enthralled by their differences that created off-the-charts chemistry." —Samantha M. Bailey, *USA Today* bestselling author of *Woman on the Edge*

"Brimming with heart and charm."

—Amy Poeppel, author of *The Sweet Spot*

"Schorr excels in creating genuine, relatable characters readers will fall in love with and root for." —Shauna Robinson, author of *The Banned Bookshop of Maggie Banks*

AS SEEN ON TV

"Adorable and steamy fun that's full of *Gilmore Girls* vibes."

—Abby Jimenez, *New York Times* bestselling author

ALSO BY MEREDITH SCHORR

As Seen on TV

Someone Just Like YOU

MEREDITH SCHORR

FOREVER

New York Boston

Forever
Hachette Book Group
1290 Avenue of the Americas, New York, NY 10104
read-forever.com
twitter.com/readforeverpub

First Edition: July 2023

Forever is an imprint of Grand Central Publishing. The Forever name and logo are trademarks of Hachette Book Group, Inc.

The publisher is not responsible for websites (or their content) that are not owned by the publisher.

The Hachette Speakers Bureau provides a wide range of authors for speaking events. To find out more, go to hachettespeakersbureau.com or email HachetteSpeakers@hbgusa.com.

Forever books may be purchased in bulk for business, educational, or promotional use. For information, please contact your local bookseller or the Hachette Book Group Special Markets Department at special.markets@hbgusa.com.

Library of Congress Cataloging-in-Publication Data

Names: Schorr, Meredith, author.
Title: Someone just like you / Meredith Schorr.
Description: First edition. | New York : Forever, 2023.
Identifiers: LCCN 2023003969 | ISBN 9781538754801 (trade paperback) | ISBN 9781538754788 (ebook)
Subjects: LCGFT: Romance fiction. | Novels.
Classification: LCC PS3619.C4543 S66 2023 | DDC 813/.6--dc23/eng/20230201
LC record available at https://lccn.loc.gov/2023003969

ISBNs: 9781538754801 (trade paperback), 9781538754788 (ebook)

Printed in the United States of America

LSC-C

Printing 1, 2023

To Howie (RIP), Doris, Jill, Mark, and Ronni.
Without the Solons, there would be no Starks.

Chapter One

I should have known something was up when my sister Nicole invited me to a random Tuesday night dinner with our other sister, Michelle, using Evite. Nicole had named the event "sibling dinner" as if we'd never shared a meal, and the occasion was too momentous to plan by simple email or text. Choosing the Dubliner pub in Hoboken, New Jersey, as the venue when two of the three Blum sisters resided and worked in Manhattan was another sign. Yet, despite these clues, I remained clue*less*.

I arrived at the rooftop bar the night of the dinner and immediately spotted my older sisters who, with long chocolate-brown hair and baby-blue eyes, could pass for my clones if it weren't for the age difference of thirty-four and thirty-two years to my twenty-seven. They'd snagged a prime table, blocked from the blazing sun by a royal-blue Corona Extra umbrella. But they weren't alone. Thrown by the unexpected appearance of our childhood neighbor Eddie Stark, I stopped short, causing the waiter walking behind me to spill part of a too-full cocktail down my back.

Before I had a chance to acknowledge the liquid dripping down my spine, Eddie vaulted off his chair and pulled me into a hug. "Good golly, martini-soaked Molly!"

Even as my mind spun with all the reasons why he could be here, I laughed and squeezed him back fiercely, inhaling his aftershave. It was a balance of Pretty Boy and Stern Brunch Daddy, which perfectly described Eddie.

"Good to see you!" I said, despite my concern that the circumstances for this "reunion" were ominous. Was his dad sick again? My uncertainty intensified at the delayed realization he was joined by his older sister, Alison. She also embraced me, but with a touch more restraint than her brother.

The Stark family had lived across the street from us growing up. More than three decades earlier, my mom and Laura Stark, with two little ones each, had become fast friends, and their bond only strengthened when, after a five-year break, they each had their third child in the same year. Back then, the households spent so much time together, it was sometimes hard to tell where the Blums ended and the Starks began. Both sets of parents still lived in the same houses, but the six offspring had all moved out years ago, most with their own spouses and children. Our dual-family reunions were now limited to special occasions, like milestone birthdays or the Passover seder we had three months ago. Which raised the question: what was happening here and why?

Nicole cocked her head and smiled indulgently. "It wouldn't be a family dinner if Molly didn't spill something."

My mouth opened, poised to argue the accuracy of her statement. This wasn't a *family* dinner. But I let it go. "You know I like to make an entrance," I said with a questioning look to Michelle, hoping my oldest sister would provide silent insight into the reason we were all here.

She mouthed, "No clue."

"Sit. Sit," Eddie said happily. "Unless you need to wipe down your dress or something."

"It's fine. Refreshing, if a tad sticky," I joked.

"Jude should be here soon and we can get started," Nicole said.

My face contorted into a grimace before I could stop myself. Jude was the youngest of the Stark trio and the bane of my existence growing up. He'd been absent the last several times the families had gotten together, either working or away with friends. Alas, my luck had run out. But I was less concerned about getting through an evening with Jude and more worried about the reason we were all gathered together in the first place. Surely Eddie wouldn't be smiling so damn much if his dad, who'd recovered from a heart attack the year before, had taken a bad turn.

"He's here!" Nicole waved in the direction of the stairs leading to the roof. "Jude!"

"Lower your voice," Michelle hissed. "It's a bar, not our private backyard party." Ignoring her own command, she called out, "Jude! Here!"

I followed my sisters' line of vision to where Jude was approaching our table. His wavy dark hair was, as usual, mussed up like he'd run his fingers through it moments before, and he had at least two days' worth of stubble. The just-rolled-out-of-bed head was in direct contrast to his tailored uniform of black dress pants paired with a black vest over a white button-down shirt. He must have come straight from Hillstone restaurant, where he worked as a bartender.

Four sets of eyes (all but mine) crinkled with delight, and four sets of legs (all but mine) stood to greet him. Taking their cues from experience, my muscles immediately tightened. I rolled my shoulders back and subtly shook out the stress in an attempt to relax. We were all adults now. Reverting to old habits was a choice we didn't have to make.

"Sorry I'm late," he said. "I just got off my shift." He hugged his own brother and sister and both of mine, then gave me a nod of acknowledgment. "Mole."

I nodded back. "*Rude.*" *So much for making the mature choice.* I caught one side of Jude's mouth quirking before I turned my attention to the happy hour drink specials on the menu. At twenty-seven, the name-calling was as natural as it had been at seven and seventeen. At least "Mole" (his oh-so-clever nickname for "Molly") was better than Buck Tooth Blum, which lost its validity when my braces came off at thirteen. Then again, Jude certainly wasn't privy to any skin markings under my clothes.

After a round of drinks had been ordered and delivered, Nicole clapped us to attention. "I'm sure you're all wondering what we're doing here."

"Not all of us," Eddie said, and the two exchanged a knowing glance.

My curiosity was piqued. This…whatever *this* was…appeared to be a team effort between the two middle children.

"As you know, this year marks a big anniversary for both sets of our parents. Thirty-five years for the Blums and forty for the Starks." Nicole paused. "Can I get a woot-woot?"

Michelle wolf-whistled. "Parents getting it *done.*"

Eddie covered Jude's ears. "Not in front of the child. He still thinks Laura and Randy *got it done* exactly three times."

Jude wiggled out of his older brother's hold. "Too late. I walked in on them getting it done at least one more time. Remember, Mole?"

I nearly choked on my drink at the unsightly memory of when

we were about ten and exiled by our brothers and sisters for fighting, only to discover Laura on her knees in front of a naked Randy in the Starks' finished basement. Thankfully, Jude's mom blocked our view of anything other than his dad's hairy chest. Seeing Randy's twig and berries at such a young age might have scarred me for life. "I'd rather forget." I shuddered.

Nicole clinked a knife against her wineglass. "Simmer down, siblings. Given the difficult year both families have had, Eddie and I thought it would be nice to do something special to honor these momentous marriage milestones."

I assumed on our side she was referring to the death of our maternal grandfather earlier that year. "I'm all for it," I said, sneaking a peek at the original invitation on my phone, where it was confirmed the guest list had included not only the Blum siblings but the Starks. *Note to self: Read more carefully next time.*

Nicole beamed. "Of course you are!"

"Same."

She clapped. "Yay, Jude!"

On autopilot, I sang, "Don't make it—"

"As always, your originality is awe inspiring," Jude said, cutting off my crooning the legendary Beatles song "Hey Jude" and pointing his fork at me. "I'm legitimately shocked this party wasn't your idea, if only to prove you're the *best* Blum daughter and the *best* neighbor of all."

I rolled my eyes at the jab—uttered one degree above a whisper, but loud enough for me to hear—even though there was a bead of truth to it. I was a people pleaser by nature, especially when it came to my parents, and no one knew this more than Jude. My usefulness in volunteering to set or clear the table, taking out the trash, putting away the toys, etc., when we were kids tended to shine a light on Jude's use*less*ness, and he hated it. I swirled my cocktail straw around and around my glass willing myself not to engage.

"Anyway." Eddie raised his voice. "We were thinking about reserving a restaurant for a co-celebration. We'll limit the guest list to close family and shared friends to keep it reasonable, but let's make it special."

"And we'll split the cost six ways," Nicole said.

Jude drummed his fingers along the table to the beat of the song playing over the speakers. "Not for nothing, but is it fair for me to contribute the same amount of money as Alison, Michelle, and Eddie when you all have kids who will eat the food too? And what about spouses? I assume I can bring a date, but if not..."

"We'll figure out the cost later. Wait..." Nicole grinned. "Are you seeing someone? Spill the tea."

Jude blushed, looking like the "sweet" boy my sisters knew him to be and nothing like the devil he only showed when no one was around to witness except me. Like when he offered me what I thought was a piece of chocolate but was really a Purina Fancy Feast beef-flavored treat for Gizmo, the Starks' cat. In hindsight, I should have questioned the uncharacteristically generous Jude's motives, but in my defense, it looked like a square of a Hershey bar. Regrettably, it tasted more like... well, cat food.

"It was a hypothetical question, but if you must know, I *am* seeing someone," Jude said. "Whether I'll *still* be seeing her by the party remains to be seen."

"Jude's dating a lawyah," Eddie said, the proud brother.

"Impressive! Maybe Molly knows her," Nicole said.

"Yes, because all lawyers know each other," I mumbled into my Tom Collins.

"And Molly's not a lawyer anymore," Alison, whose file digitization company worked with my old law firm, said.

"I'm still a lawyer, just not a practicing one!" I cringed inwardly. Why was I so defensive? Upending my legal career to prevent a lifetime of misery hadn't been my plan, but I was so much happier as a legal recruiter.

"Molly's boyfriend is a major league baseball player," Nicole said.

Jude's dark eyes widened, and his jaw dropped as if dumbstruck. Too bad Nicole was wrong. "*Minor* league." Stan played for the Brooklyn Cyclones. "And he's not my boyfriend. We've only hung out a few times."

Eddie raised a hand. "Hold up. Let me get this straight: Jude's dating a lawyer and Molly's hanging with a baseball player?"

The siblings exchanged glances and...wait...were they snickering? "What's so funny?"

"Nothing," they responded as a group.

"All your interest in *our* love lives makes me wonder how unsatisfied you must be with your own," Jude said.

"Exactly," I said, daring a bonding glance at Jude.

He peered at me through his beer glass. "What's this about you not being a lawyer anymore? You would have made a great prosecutor."

A compliment from Jude? "Yeah? And why is that?"

He smirked. "Because you like to see people punished."

Having walked right into that one, I released a long, slow sigh. "Clever." I *had* witnessed Jude get into trouble on the regular. From his perspective, I probably appeared to revel in it, but he had only part of the story.

"I figured you'd have made partner by now in world-record time. Did you quit to run for city council?"

I scoffed. "Why? If I say yes, will your disinterest in politics suddenly be replaced by an unquenchable thirst to run as my opponent again?" I'd been the easy pick for student council president senior year of high school until "Mr. Popularity" Jude decided to throw his hat into the ring at the last minute because he knew how badly I wanted to win. His debate speech promising free pizza every Friday afternoon as an incentive not to cut out of class early was more persuasive than my anti-bullying campaign, and it sealed his victory. Even ten years later, the memory made my blood heat to a simmer. "I suppose your experience choosing the snacks for the school vending machines really primed you for your current position of serving drinks at a bar, huh?"

The initial gratification as the jab left my lips was immediately replaced with stubborn and enduring guilt. I knew bartending hadn't been Jude's first choice for a career.

"Not exactly, but the satisfaction of beating you is the reward that keeps on giving." Jude flashed a cocky smile and locked his arms behind his head. The swell of his arms from this posture proved that despite being the youngest child, he was no longer the rug rat in the group.

I barely avoided snarling. As if anyone at this table would be impressed by his triceps.

Eddie cleared his throat. "Are you two done?"

His voice pulled me back to the present, and I was determined to stay there. No matter how hard I tried, in the words of Michelle Obama, to go high when Jude went low, he brought out the worst in me.

Eddie continued. "We were thinking of having the party the third weekend in October, which gives us three months to plan and send out the invitations."

"Will we use Evite?" I couldn't resist.

"We'll use proper invitations." Nicole wrinkled her nose. "In case some of the older guests don't have computers."

Over the course of the next hour, our large party of six morphed into mini soirees of two or three. Jude and I managed to avoid overlapping conversations. After dinner, Nicole insisted the three of us share a cab back to the city rather than take the PATH train, and the driver dropped her off on the west side first. Jude and I both resided across town on the east side in Murray Hill. Our apartments were six blocks apart, because apparently eighteen years as neighbors wasn't enough for us. Nicole had called shotgun, a relic of our youth, which left me alone in the back with Jude, and neither of us switched to the front when she got out.

I curled myself as close to the door as possible. If, God forbid, it opened, I'd roll onto the street. But the fear of falling to my death wasn't strong enough to lessen the physical distance between us. And we hit traffic because...well...*of course* we did. I was listening to *This American Life* when he nudged me in the arm.

I removed my earbuds. "What?" Were we home? I glanced out the window, expecting to see one of our apartment buildings in the distance.

"Why aren't you a lawyer anymore? What was it? The long hours? The pressure? The lack of control?" Jude's voice seeped condescension.

I glared at him. "Did you read a top-ten list on BuzzFeed or something? None of the above." *All of the above and then some.* "I'm still a lawyer. Like I said, I'm just not practicing." I was surprised this was news to him, although it had probably been at least a year since we'd seen each other and I wasn't so self-absorbed as to think my career path was a topic of conversation at the Starks' dinner table.

"What *do* you practice?"

I squeezed my flaring nostrils. "I'm a legal recruiter."

He made a sound I assumed was supposed to be a laugh. "So, you quit the law to find jobs for other lawyers?"

I gritted my teeth. "Yes. And paralegals and other legal administrative staff too. Any 'law-related' positions, really. The majority of recruiters are former lawyers or paralegals. It's not an unprecedented move." I wasn't the first to make the transition, nor would I be the last. My eyes narrowed. "What's it to you?"

"Just curious," is what he said, but his dubious expression screamed otherwise.

Don't press him for more. Let it go. But I couldn't. "You're dying to say something. Just say it."

"Wasn't your dream of being a lawyer why you worked so hard in high school...why you were so determined to be in student government in the first place?"

I might have actually hissed at the audacity of his reminder, given that the inclusion of student council president on my college applications might have gotten me off the wait-list and into the acceptance pile of an Ivy League school. But it was true. My goal of being a lawyer motivated my placement in the top twenty in my high school class of 365, graduating summa cum laude from the University of Michigan, and attending a top-tier law school. My hard work earned me my pick of summer associate programs before I accepted a first-year position at Fitzpatrick & Green, one of the largest global law firms. "Reality didn't live up to my dreams."

"It's not like you to quit."

My lips pursed. "I didn't quit."

Jude cocked an eyebrow.

"Okay. Technically, I quit, but not because I couldn't hack it. I just wasn't happy. I get more satisfaction from assisting others in finding jobs that make *them* happy." I clenched my jaw. Why was I trying to justify my choices to my childhood rival? Jude's opinion meant nothing to me anymore. I'd given up trying to prove myself worthy of his friendship or, at the very least, his kindness around the fourth grade.

It didn't matter. Life was good. Legal recruiting suited me more than being a lawyer ever had. I had a fabulous apartment, with the exception of its close proximity to Jude's, where I lived alone but in walking distance from both work and my best friend, Esther. And I'd just started dating a minor league baseball player, which was a way more glamorous job than that of Jude's "lawyah" girlfriend. I would know. In fact, the only source of my discontent was being trapped in this car with Jude right now. He could suck it.

"Understood." He turned to face the window and muttered, "Quitter."

The blood rushed to my head. I'd done nothing to deserve his disdain. I closed my eyes as a montage of activities contradicting that statement danced in my head. I had, in fact, done *plenty* to Jude over the years, but only after he made it his daily goal to make me cry first. He'd given me no choice but to become a worthy opponent or play victim indefinitely. Since graduating high school, I'd made an effort to avoid hostility, but he seemed determined to rattle my chain every chance he got.

It hadn't always been that way. I had a fuzzy recollection of us playing together long, long ago without fearing he'd destroy my toys or make me the subject of public ridicule—when we were pals. There were even embarrassing pictures to prove it, including one of us at three years old smiling and holding hands, both topless in bathing shorts, in a baby pool in the Starks' backyard. The eight-by-ten photograph was hung prominently along the stairwells in both families' houses. It was bad enough *my* parents hung a photo of me topless, but the Starks too? "You were a toddler, Molly," my dad said when I complained. "You two were adorable," added my mom. "It's not like you had tits yet," my sisters said. Still...it was embarrassing.

I gave Jude side-eye. He was now texting someone. The lawyer? If the traffic kept up, we might be stuck in this car for another twenty minutes. I could use the time to ask how we'd gone from holding hands while joyously splashing in a kiddie pool to him telling our mutual friends I had the farts after he sprayed a class-mate's bathroom with liquid gas at a birthday party, me taping a note with the words "I wet the bed" on his back, and other misdeeds we could never retract. Except there might be a statute of limitations on questioning a lifelong rivalry. And there were certain ghosts in our history I wasn't prepared to conjure up. So instead, I put my earbuds back in and directed my thoughts to something positive.

Throwing a co-anniversary celebration was a thoughtful gesture. My mom had been so sad since Papi had passed. Hopefully, the party would bring her joy and give Mr. Stark incentive to lay off the fried food. Jude and I could certainly set aside our issues for one night. It wouldn't be the first time. And until then? Well, it wasn't like we'd have to plan the party as a duo or anything. We could all agree *that* would be a bad idea.

Chapter Two

A few days later at work, I tapped the hardcover résumé in front of me. "I'm so glad you came in. You're even more impressive in person than you are on paper," I said.

"Thank you." Patrice, the late-fifty-something Black woman on the other side of my office desk, gave me a wry smile. "Does that mean you have a job for me?"

Ignoring the beep of my iPhone, I scrolled through the list of job openings on our company's internal database again. There were available positions for senior paralegals, for sure. But were any of them suitable for Patrice? The in-house legal department of a television station was seeking a legal assistant, but the head of the department was notorious for not supporting other women. There was also an opening for a paralegal at a midsize firm that claimed to prioritize life balance while simultaneously pressuring employees to work weekends and holidays.

Patrice had told me she was needed at home most nights to care for her young grandson. She was warm and friendly and deserved a collegial working environment. How could I connect her to a job with full knowledge it either didn't fit her lifestyle or countless people had held it before her and quit out of sheer misery? She'd be back seeking a new job in a few months, likely with a different recruiter, one who hadn't pocketed the commission for sending her to hell, and I'd have to return a portion to the client anyway. It wasn't worth it.

"Not at the moment, unfortunately. But an amazing opportunity will come around and I'll be excited to share it with you when it does." This, at least, was true. Patrice was a referral from someone I'd staffed a few months before, and I'd called her for an interview without having any particular job opening in mind. She was my first referral, and I was especially motivated to get it right.

When she was gone, I checked Gmail on my phone. After reading Nicole's message, I wished I hadn't.

Both sets of parents love the city, so what better place to have the party than Manhattan? **Jude and Molly:** We're putting you in charge of choosing the venue because you both live there. It's a big responsibility, we know, but consider it a compliment and a tribute to our faith in you! Besides, your time is the most flexible since you're both single and childless. I've attached a list of places you should consider.

My skin itchy with irritation, I emailed a response.

I'm happy to help with the venue, but since you (Nicole) also live in Manhattan and don't have children, perhaps you can join us too.

Three was *not* a crowd with a threatened twosome of Molly and Jude.

I went to the pantry to refill my coffee. When I returned to my office, there was a response from Nicole.

I'll be too busy overseeing the planning but will be available for consultations and tiebreakers if you and Jude can't agree.

I spat my coffee. *If* we can't agree? There was no *if.* And consultations? Really?

While I was still contemplating my reply, an email from Jude came in.

Thank you for organizing everything, Nicole. I know how the restaurant business works and my connections are far-reaching. I'm happy to take care of this.

I stared down at my phone. Well, that was unexpected. Thank you, Jude! I didn't share his confidence in his party-planning abilities despite his so-called knowledge and connections, but I was grateful he'd volunteered. The less time we spent together, the better for everyone. Period.

And then another email from him landed in my inbox.

In case my last message wasn't clear, I don't need Mollyanna to come along if she's too busy recruiting lawyers to help plan the party.

I squeezed the paper cup in my hand, forgetting it contained coffee—hot coffee. Howling, "Son of a bitch!" when the liquid seared my skin, I leaped off my chair. After wiping my arm down with leftover napkins from my lunch, I sank back down. The pain subsided but my rage didn't. After all the years of Jude teasing me for being helpful, now he was insinuating I was trying to get out of doing my fair share of the work? That he didn't *need* me? Well, thanks to his inability to know when to stop, we were now partners. Though I couldn't stand the idea of the two of us touring restaurants alone together, there was no way... *no way*... I was handing the reins over to Jude now. He would take all the credit and milk every second of it. And he'd hold it over me for a lifetime. Not happening.

That's so sweet of you, Jude, but I'm not too busy at all. In fact, with my background in law, I'm a master in negotiations, which could come in handy in terms of pricing. Let's combine our skills. Unless you'd prefer to sit this one out and let me handle it myself.

Left unwritten was "as usual." For all I knew, it was Jude's plan all along to get out of doing any work while looking like a hero in the process. I'd probably end up choosing the venue solo, but it was better than the alternative.

His response came thirty seconds later, and I braced myself for his obnoxious retort, probably something about my no longer practicing the law.

Combining our skills works for me.

"Ugh!" Trying to maintain the peace with Jude was pointless. He was impossible! When I was agreeable, he was contrary, but when I struck first, he was as amenable as a server at a luxury resort. Spinning my chair around and around, I counted all the reasons I hated him. I stopped at ten, but only because I was dizzy, and my brain could no longer focus.

Chapter Three

Two days later, I was on my tri-weekly phone call with my mom. We used to talk twice a week until Papi died and I unofficially changed it to three. Today's catch-up also served as a convenient break from mentally preparing myself for my first restaurant viewing with Jude. As always, Mom asked what I had planned for the night.

"I'm meeting...um...someone for an...um...drink." I rolled my eyes to my kitchen ceiling and put the phone on speaker. Then I tugged aggressively on a lock of my hair. The party's "leadership committee" (Nicole and Eddie) hadn't decided yet if we should tell our parents what we were planning or leave it as a surprise. This meant I couldn't tell her the truth, but I hated to lie to her. Jude was technically *someone*, and I predicted I'd need at least one alcoholic beverage to get through the evening.

"Is it a date?" Despite my being her only single child, her tone was less hopeful and more matter-of-fact. Mom knew and accepted I wasn't in a rush to settle down. I had no desire to jump from one casual relationship to another indefinitely, but until I found someone who not only *accepted* my Molly-isms but *adored* them and the other way around, I was in no hurry to forsake others until death did us part. I didn't bother to tell her about the men I dated casually, like the new baseball guy, Stan. "More like a business meeting." My hands now free, I emptied the dishwasher.

"Look at my baby girl networking after hours."

My cheeks warmed at her pride, even though she had it all wrong.

While Mom updated me on her life since the last time we spoke, I Swiffered the sandcastle oak floor of my decent-sized, at least by New York City standards, living room. I'd used my sign-on bonus at the law firm for the down payment on a one-bedroom apartment in a co-op, but without the generous paycheck that came with the high-pressure job, making the monthly mortgage and maintenance required me to stay within a precise budget. I was happy to contribute to the anniversary party, but the added costs meant I needed to place someone at a decent-paying job and earn the accompanying commission soon.

My parents didn't need to know this. Nicole was the flake in the family, not me. After graduating college, she earned certifications in real estate, travel, *and* cosmetology before finally finding her bliss as a preschool teacher. Michelle was the risk taker. A few years back, she and her husband, Patrick, quit their jobs and threw all their money, and some of my parents', into a start-up app development company. With the state of the economy in constant flux, the past years hadn't been easy on them. But me? Stable was my brand. I was the solid one—the one with the sure-thing career plan. Or I had been until I left the practice of law after only a year and a few months.

Being a lawyer had been my plan since freshman year of high school. Besides a budget and a pro/con list, it had taken a lot of soul searching to make the change to recruiting. Even after I was convinced it was the right decision, I hated putting my parents in the position of paying off a portion of student loans for a degree I was no longer using. Unfortunately, my budget only worked if I accepted their generous offer. But at the end of the day, we agreed my quality of life was more important than the partner status I might have achieved in a decade, and they'd practically insisted. I was grateful they were in a position to help and still have enough money to retire in comfort.

"You don't want your *High School Musical* DVD game anymore, do you? The garage sale is next weekend, and I'm collecting items," Mom said.

I returned the Swiffer to the pantry. "You can have it. But another yard sale already? Didn't you just have one?" My family, the Starks, and another couple, the Lesigs, held a group garage sale every few years to force them to dispose of possessions they might otherwise hoard: once-coveted handbags none of the Blum women had actually used in years, extra casserole dishes taking up space in the kitchen cabinets, etc. It wasn't for the money, and most of the items went to charity at the end of the day. But my dad and Mr. Stark enjoyed racing to make three figures first. It was a lot of work, though.

"Do you need me to come over?" Since I was little, I'd helped organize items for sale, minded the lawn the day of, and played mediator between my parents in case they didn't agree whether to let go of an item. I could almost hear Jude say, "Because you're the *best* child of all," and something sour swirled in my gut.

"You were so cute, guarding our possessions, like anyone would be intimidated by a pre-tween with pigtails and braces, but it's not necessary. We don't have enough merchandise this year. We're just doing it for our own amusement."

I was about to insist when my phone alerted me with a calendar reminder about my and Jude's appointment. I told her to let me know if she changed her mind, and we ended the call. Then Jude texted.

> **Jude:** Leaving straight from work. I'll have to meet you there.

I gave my phone the middle finger. Did he honestly think I wanted to commute with him? I grabbed my purse and headed out with dread seeping through my bloodstream. *Stop it. This is for Mom and Dad.* The milestone had not come without struggle. They'd temporarily separated when we were kids, and it was miserable. My father tried to make our weekend visits to the Holiday Inn Holidome, where he was living, fun. *There's a pool! Room service!* But I'd cried into my pillow every night until he moved back home two months later. Now they were within spitting distance of their thirty-fifth anniversary. It was worth celebrating for sure, even if it meant forced proximity to Jude to make it happen.

I reminded myself of this until I arrived at the Walker Hotel near Union Square, where Society Cafe was located in the back of the lobby. I was ten minutes early to ensure I arrived before Jude. I sat at the bar, where the bartender promptly placed a glass of water and a drink menu in front of me. *Good service: check.* I noted the polished wood décor and the gold-plated ceiling. *Ambiance: check.* With any luck, this place would be "The One" and my partnership with Jude would end as quickly as it had started. I cursed the stubbornness that hadn't allowed me to accept Jude's gracious...*snort*...offer to handle it on his own.

As if he was reading my mind, my phone pinged with a text message from him.

> **Jude:** Like I said, I don't need your help, but as long as you're here, wanna join us? Or were you planning to get hammered at the bar instead?

I whipped around and scanned the restaurant for a moment until I spotted Jude at a booth in the back. He was with another man. *R*ude had not only beat me here, but he'd started without me. I inhaled deeply and let the breath whoosh slowly through my lips. *Do it for Mom, Dad, and the Starks.* With my head held high, I joined them. Jude was wearing his Hillstone uniform again. Either he'd been telling the truth about coming straight from work rather than lying to sidestep a suggestion from me to travel together...*as if*...or he had no other clean clothes.

"This is George," he said by way of introduction to the restaurant's banquet and private events coordinator. "And this is Molly. She's a singer in a band."

George, a handsome Black man probably a handful of years older than us, widened his eyes. "Really? What kind of music do you play?"

I shot Jude a searing look then turned to George with a more pleasant one. "I'm actually not a singer. Jude likes to tease me about the Beatles song 'Ob-La-Di, Ob-La-Da.' You know, Desmond and Molly Jones." I gestured with my hands. "He has a barrow in a marketplace. She's a singer in a band. *Blah blah blah.* I teased him first about 'Hey Jude,' and he copied me."

"I didn't copy you."

I murmured, "Um hmm" and directed my attention back to George. "Let's talk party, shall we?"

George, who looked amused—or confused; it was hard to tell—nodded his agreement, and we got to business.

"How many guests can you accommodate?" I asked, reading from a list of questions on my phone.

Jude threw his head back in a laugh. "Did you stay up late last night researching what to ask? Let me guess—anniversaryparty-planning.com?"

I smiled politely at George even as my cheeks tingled with heat. "I figured one of us should be prepared."

"I have it all in here," Jude said tapping his head.

I rolled my eyes.

George carried on like a true professional. "Our private room accommodates sixty, or we can do a standing cocktail reception for eighty-five. How many guests will there be?" He glanced from Jude to me and back to Jude.

Jude said, "About a hundred" at the same time I said, "Sixty should be plenty." Eddie had said close family and mutual friends.

"It won't be that large a party," I said simultaneously with Jude's statement, "Sixty is cutting it close."

George laughed. "You should take your show on the road."

I sighed. "We haven't nailed down the guest list yet." It wasn't like me to leave such an important question unanswered, but my focus was off…probably a result of Nicole pushing this whole partnership with Jude.

"That's fine. We might be able to make a hundred work as well. The party we hosted recently for Jason and Jeremy Giambi came pretty close." George darted his glance between us. "They're former major league baseball players."

Jude laughed. "Trust me. I know who they are. I played first base partially because of Jason."

"You're a baseball player?" George asked.

"Not anymore." Jude drummed his fingers against the table to the beat of "Ob-La-Di, Ob-La-Da."

George waited, seemingly expecting Jude to elaborate, while I did a mental count of the guest list to counter the awkwardness of the conversation. Jude had been on his way to a full baseball scholarship until he tore his ACL his senior year in high school. Afterward he'd needed surgery and knee reconstruction as well as physical therapy. He lost his scholarship, and his athletic career was over before it got started.

"Freak bike accident back in high school." Jude gave me a quick look before turning back to George.

My breath hitched. What was the *look* for? Did he think I'd take advantage of the topic of conversation to say something mean about the end of his would-be baseball career? Or was it something else?

"Sorry," George said, fiddling with the iPad in his hand.

Jude waved him off. "Don't be. It's not like I was as good as Jason anyway."

My head jutted back. What was with the humble pie? Jude was very good…great, in fact. Even I, his number negative fan, could concede that much.

"You and the rest of the general population," George said with a chuckle.

Conversation returned to the party, and Jude continued to ask questions at random, as if my list didn't exist, but I was too distracted to care. His tone when talking about baseball had been as dry as a California forest, but I wasn't convinced. Jude had lived and breathed baseball. Now he wore a bartender uniform instead of Yankee pinstripes.

Either his impassiveness at the death of his athletic career was an act or he'd truly put baseball behind him. Maybe he was even happy as a bartender. Despite our contentious relationship, I prayed for the latter.

"These are pictures of other events we've held here." George placed his tablet faceup, equidistant between Jude and me.

"After you," Jude said.

As my hands reached for the device, Jude smiled and grabbed it right out from under me.

I scowled. He was so childish.

"Kidding," he said, raising his hands in surrender. "Take it."

I huffed then reached for it, only for him to pull it back at the last second . . . *again*.

I dropped my arms to my sides. "I'm out. You win, Rude."

"Quitter."

My nostrils flared. *Oh, no, he didn't.*

The air grew thick. Voices in the background were fuzzy.

We locked eyes.

It was on.

My hand touched the device first, but Jude's clamped on top of mine like a claw. I slid the iPad closer to my side, but Jude was too fast for me and reversed my progress. We were back to center. "Ladies first," I grunted, trying to free my hand while maintaining my grip on the tablet.

"Show me a lady and I'll let her go first." He tightened his hold.

"Give it to—"

"I'll take it." With the grace of a pianist, George retrieved the tablet from beneath our double grip and stood. "Why don't you call me when you have a head count." He gave a curt nod, turned on his heel, and mumbled, "Or better yet . . . don't."

Jude and I watched him retreat with open mouths.

"I guess we can cross Society Cafe off our list," I said.

"No thanks to you."

I'd been shaking out my hand but froze. "*Me?* What about you?"

Jude ignored me.

"What now?" I asked.

Jude was silent for a moment, as if momentarily thrown by the question, then finally said, "I set up another meeting for tonight at Bistrot Leo on Thompson." He chewed his lip. "Sorry I didn't run it by you first, but my manager used to work there, and he just suggested it today. The guy I spoke with said to drop by after our meeting here."

"Let's do it." I wasn't thrilled with the late notice, but his apology appeared sincere, and I liked the idea of sealing this deal before I went to bed tonight. I stood to go.

Jude stood too. "Actually, do you mind if I meet you there? I need to stop at the pharmacy to pick up meds for Yogi."

I hitched a breath. "Is he okay?" I'd only met Jude's puppy— a goldendoodle named for baseball icon Yogi Berra—once, but it was love at first sight.

"Digestive issues," Jude said with a wrinkle of his nose. "But he'll be okay."

My shoulders dropped an inch in relief that it was nothing serious. "How about we meet there in..." I glanced at my Apple watch. It was five after seven. "Is eight good?"

He grinned. "Perfect."

Since I had time, I enjoyed a leisurely stroll through Greenwich Village. The sidewalks were crowded with people spilling out of the many bars and restaurants. I breathed in the air of Manhattan in the summer—a combination of garbage, sweat, and cigarettes, but also a dizzying mix of aromas from the many different kitchens in the area—pizza, Mexican, fried everything. Starving, I stopped for a slice at Joe's and sat in Father Demo Square across the street.

A few minutes before eight, I arrived at Bistrot Leo and waited for Jude outside, where potted plants surrounded the semi-open restaurant. I reviewed the questions on my phone determined not to let Jude bulldoze me again. When he still hadn't shown up by the time I was finished, I considered going in without him. He might be pissed, but with Jude it was also quite possible he wouldn't care. Also, it wasn't like he'd waited for me at the last place, so I owed him no consideration. Stan had sent a text with a funny baseball meme, and after responding with the skull emoji and confirming our date for the following night after his game, I entered the restaurant.

The space was softly lit with an intimate ambiance. I approached the hostess, a white woman around my age with a long, sleek blond ponytail and huge brown eyes. "Hi there. I'm supposed to talk to someone about holding an anniversary party here in October." When she looked at me blankly, I realized I didn't have a name for the *some-one* in question. "My friend..." I gulped at the misnomer, but what else could I call him? My enemy? Business partner? "He spoke with someone earlier today who said to come by tonight."

She smiled politely. "Of course. Give me one minute and I'll check with my manager."

While I waited, I brought up Yelp on my phone to see if any of the reviews mentioned parties. I hadn't found any by the time the hostess returned.

"Unfortunately, there's no one here to talk with you tonight, but we can definitely set something up for a later date," she said in an apologetic tone. "But do you happen to have the name of who your friend spoke with?"

I glanced over my shoulder. "He should be here already. Let me text him."

> **Molly:** Are you on your way? I'm here and they asked the name of who you spoke with.

While we waited for Jude to respond, I stood awkwardly while she said good night to an older couple on their way out.

My phone pinged.

> **Jude:** Don Messwidme.

I turned back to the hostess with a smile. "The guy's name is Don Messwidme." I froze. *Wait.* I repeated it slowly hoping I was wrong. "Don Mess-wid-me." I wasn't wrong. *The little fucker.*

The hostess's lips quirked.

Embarrassment seeped through me. "You know what? We'll call to set something up. Sorry for wasting your time."

I scurried out the door, my chest heaving with anger, and plopped myself on the nearest bench.

Molly: There's no meeting, is there?

Jude: Gotcha.

Chapter Four

At 1:40 a.m. the next night, I was finishing a pitcher of beer with Esther on the outdoor back patio of Tuttles, a bar across the street from my apartment. The communal picnic tables that had previously been filled with twentysomethings were now mostly unoccupied aside from us. Our other friends had left, but it was in the unofficial friendship handbook that anyone who lived within walking distance of a bar wasn't allowed to take off if someone else wanted to stay. There were limited exceptions to this rule, including puking and hooking up (hopefully not at the same time), but being tired wasn't one of them. I was exhausted like I'd just disembarked a red-eye flight, and my buzz was all but gone, but since Esther wasn't ready to leave, neither could I.

"You are pathetic," she said.

I lifted my head, previously buried in my hands. "Say it again." I pushed out my lips. "Please?" Four years of being her college roommate, and I still found her British accent irresistible, even more so after several beers and two Superman shots.

She rolled her big brown eyes. "*Pathetic.* Why are you so tired?"

I blinked. "Because I worked all day, waited until my date with Stan at close to midnight, met you out, and it's almost two in the morning!" After cutting my date with Stan short, I had joined Esther and a few of her colleagues from the communications agency where she worked as a medical editor supporting their healthcare clients. The whole minor-league-baseball thing was a turn-on initially, and I liked his thick head of dark, messy hair, but I realized at some point during our first drink that we had nothing in common and no real chemistry beyond the first blush of physical attraction. I decided it was kinder to set him free than prolong our third date out of mere politeness, only to make two stops on a shared cab ride home at the end of the night. I'd texted Esther as much from the bathroom, and by the time I returned to Stan, a group of post-college girls had surrounded him like a swarm of flies. We parted ways with no hard feelings.

"Pitiful. I spent all day proofreading and fact checking data on clinical studies. I was seeing double before my first drink, yet I'm still fabulous company." She poured the remains of our pitcher of Blue Moon evenly between both of our glasses.

I crossed my fingers she wouldn't order another. It was last call, so it was now or never. "You're living on European time."

She blew a raspberry. "Nice try. I've lived in the States since college. I'm just cooler than you. And one month younger."

"Oh, yes, I lived centuries in those four weeks while you were still swimming in amniotic fluid." I would turn twenty-eight a month and three days before her, to be exact. The bar staff cleared away the empty tables around us. "They probably want to go home," I whispered.

"Take your time," a velvety deep voice said from behind me, so close the hair on the back of my neck stood up.

My head swung around. I found myself staring at the voice's

crotch. I looked up at the barback, a white guy with messy (sexy) dark hair wearing head-to-toe black.

"For the next thirty minutes at least." He winked.

"You have great hearing."

"You have a loud whisper."

I pressed my fingers to my lips to suppress my giggle.

He gestured at our empty pitcher. "You finished?"

"We are."

We locked eyes for a moment. When he was out of earshot, I turned back to a smirking Esther. "What? He's cute. His forearms in that tight t-shirt are delicious."

She tut-tutted me. "He looks like Stan, whose poor body hasn't even gone cold yet." Esther had met Stan the same night I did, when he and his friends had approached us at a bar earlier that summer.

"I'm sure the college girls at the bar are keeping him warm." I changed the topic of conversation to our plans for the weekend. Esther was visiting her uncle and twin nieces. When her aunt-in-law had died tragically from a brain aneurysm the year before, leaving behind her husband and three-year-old twin girls, Esther became a source of support since the rest of their family lived in England.

"I'll be there three days to help with the *Oh Crap! Potty Training* method. I'm too young for this shit...no pun intended...but if I leave it to Uncle Colin, those girls will be wearing diapers at our age, and not as part of a drinking game. But I'm paranoid my automatic cat feeder will malfunction and Poppy will starve while I'm gone."

"I'd say you were being paranoid if you didn't already say it yourself." Poppy was Esther's rescue tabby cat.

"It happened to my assistant's best friend's cousin." Esther's eyes widened, and her trimmed eyebrows formed an upside down U.

I chuckled. "She'll be fine. I'll check in on her while you're gone...make sure she's been fed and hasn't trapped herself under the couch again." It wouldn't be the first time. Esther would have taken Poppy with her to Connecticut if her uncle and both twins weren't allergic to cats. But I, her trustworthy best friend who was also allergic to cats and needed Benadryl for extended contact, could handle this much.

"I hoped you'd say that. Thanks." Esther ruffled the blond, nearly white bangs of her pixie cut. "I assume your plans are more scintillating than mine, and hopefully don't involve excrement?" she asked.

I cringed at the phantom foul smell of her nieces' poops, then groaned, remembering what a nice buzz had allowed me to tuck away temporarily. "I'm checking out a restaurant with Jude on Sunday." Nicole had confirmed the head count for the party was between fifty and sixty depending on RSVPs. A far cry from Jude's "about a hundred" estimate. But did he admit he was wrong? Of course not. If he'd been right, though, knowing Jude, I'd never hear the end of it. I wasn't holding my breath for an apology for being sent to Bistrot Leo to meet Don Messwidme either.

I took a gulp of beer. It was almost too embarrassing to share with Esther, but I did it anyway. When I was finished, I said, "I can't believe I didn't see it coming."

"Don't blame yourself, hon. He's a grown man acting like a wanker." She pushed her empty beer to the side. "What's the deal with you two anyway?" Esther didn't know my history with

Jude since it hadn't come up until we were thrown together for the party.

"Besides hating each other since birth, nothing." I back-tracked. "Well, not since birth. He was my first friend, but things changed sometime around the first grade."

She leaned forward in interest. "Changed how?"

"He stopped liking me out of nowhere." I took a sip of beer as a vague memory sprang to mind of coming over to the Starks' house after school to play with Jude and him telling me to get lost before slamming his bedroom door in my face. I'd run back across the street in tears. Things got worse from there. "He made a career out of embarrassing me in front of our classmates. He once told them my lemonade was actually pee because I drank from a clear thermos instead of a juice box like everyone else. And he called me names like Bucktooth Blum and Mollyanna. Mole is the most utilized these days."

Esther slapped her hand against her mouth. "Mollyanna! That's brilliant."

I glared at her.

Her eyes softened. "Sorry. Poor Molly. He sounds like your classic bully. It's hard to picture sweet Molly having an actual nemesis."

"Ha! I doubt he'd ever describe me as sweet unless it was an insult." Before the dinner in Hoboken, the last time I'd seen Jude had been at the hospital to visit his dad. When I showed up in the waiting room with a box of See's Chocolate for his mom, he'd muttered, "kiss-ass" under his breath.

"I give myself major props for maintaining any social stand-ing under the circumstances." I ran a finger along the rim of my beer glass. "Eventually, I stopped missing him as my friend and accepted him as my enemy. For every prank he initiated, I retaliated."

Esther rested her head on one hand and grinned tiredly. "For instance?"

"Once, I snuck down to the Starks' basement during a co-family movie night and placed flower stickers on all his toys for his friends to see the next time they came over."

"I like this Molly," Esther said, her mouth quirking on one side. "What else?"

I tapped my chin in thought. "Another time, I replaced his regular loose-leaf notebook binder with an *American Idol* branded one." I chuckled. "We had homeroom together, and the look on Jude's face when he pulled it out of his backpack and saw the faces of that year's Top Ten smiling up at him...priceless. I constructed my pranks as if they required FDA approval."

"I'd expect nothing else," Esther said affectionately.

"*Jude*, of course, gave almost no forethought to his whatsoever, still somehow managing to knock them out of the park every time. Spontaneity never worked for me." I frowned, remembering my one and only impulsive play.

Esther mirrored my expression. "Where'd you go?"

I sat up straight as the not-yet-digested drinks swished uncomfortably in my stomach. "Nowhere. Anyway, it was all relatively harmless through middle school. Almost like a performance for our classmates."

A wrinkle appeared between Esther's eyebrows. "What happened after middle school?"

I sighed. "The older we got, the higher the stakes became. He ran for class president for the sole purpose of beating me. But he missed out on a ski trip because of...well, because of *him*, but also because of me. It's complicated. Anyway, the list goes on. Just lots of blame thrown around. I even blame *myself* for things, but…"

Thing. I blamed myself for one thing. I swallowed hard. I couldn't bring myself to tell Esther the full story. "In any event, we're adults now. I want to move on, but based on Jude's recent behavior, it's safe to say he doesn't."

"So what do you have planned for your retaliation this time?" She rubbed her hands together.

"Nothing."

It wasn't as if the idea hadn't occurred to me. Like muscle memory, enacting revenge was my first impulse. While stewing in anger, I'd even quietly brainstormed ideas in the Lyft home from Bistrot Leo. But no good would come of it. Jude *wanted* me to play his game. "Retaliating would be eating out of his hands. If I ignore him, he'll lose interest. Then we can find a venue and go our separate ways as God intended."

"*Pfft.* Are you really that naïve, Mollyanna?"

I wrinkled my nose. "I'm going to regret sharing that nickname until you're too senile to remember it, aren't I?"

"Probably." She chuckled. "Either you're right, or he'll consider it a big fat win in his column. My money is on the second option. Could you live with yourself?"

I scooched my chair back as if ready to stand. "Believe it or not, I think I can."

Esther clucked her tongue. "It's your funeral. But I bet he's planning his next heist right now."

"That would require him to *plan*. He just *does*." I sighed dramatically. I hated to admit it, but she was right. Somewhere, possibly just a few blocks away, Jude was probably engaging in a similar conversation with one of his friends. *Bragging*. I chewed my lip in thought.

What kind of sucker just sat there and took it? Jude wouldn't let me off the hook even if I played the role of mature working woman with no time for hijinks like a movie star. No, he would keep poking the bear. Only that phrase suggested I was more powerful than him. I sat up straighter. I *was*. And I wouldn't let him get away with thinking otherwise.

I downed the rest of my beer and slammed the empty glass on the table. "I changed my mind. Let's do it."

Chapter Five

*J*ust like when we were kids, striking back at Jude wasn't a choice. It was a survival mechanism. But it had been a long time, and I was *way* out of practice. Sunday afternoon I walked down the stairs to Sakagura with a light quiver in my stomach. I paused at the entrance and breathed deeply. As always when dealing with Jude, my body chemistry was a mixture of giggly anticipation and sweaty apprehension. A glance at my knees peeking out from under my floral-printed miniskirt confirmed they were wobbling even though I was standing still. I shook out my shoulders to dry out the dampness that had gathered under my arms despite the uncharacteristically cool July day.

I wiped my clammy hands on my skirt and entered the restaurant. Sakagura had been my addition to the list of possible venues for the party. On my first day at the law firm, my assigned mentor had brought me there. Its hidden location in the basement of a random midtown office building had me worrying it wasn't really lunch on the menu but some terrifying first-year-associate initiation, but I quickly discovered the cloak-and-dagger address only added to the charm of the Japanese restaurant tucked into the cellar. I'd been back many times since for the sashimi, soba noodles, and impressive sake menu. I thought we could hold the party in one of the private dining areas set apart from the main room and bar with shoji screens. Surprisingly, I got no argument from Nicole, Eddie, or Jude. The latter was the most surprising of all.

Esther thought my prank for today was uninspired—sending Jude to the appointment an hour late was too similar to him sending me to a restaurant that wasn't expecting me at all. But my lack of creativity was by design. If Jude also assumed I would come up with something more innovative, my messing with the appointment time wouldn't even cross his mind. Well, that was the idea, at least. Experience had steered me away from overconfidence when it came to Jude.

I gave my name to the hostess and told her I had an appointment with Mari. I held my breath waiting for her to say the other member of my party had already arrived, but she said no such thing. *Good.* Jude hadn't beaten me there and started without me like the last time. If everything went according to plan, he was still at his apartment putzing around with Yogi and his two roommates on the assumption he had plenty of time. *Ha! Take that, Rude!*

I bounced on my toes, tempted to clap my hands in glorious anticipation. The chuckle lodged at the bottom of my throat worked its way out of my mouth. I was still giggling when an older Japanese woman wearing a midnight-blue robe walked through the string curtain separating the hostess station from the dining area and smiled at me. "Molly?"

I sucked back my laughter and held out my hand. "That's me."

"I'm meeting with two of you, correct? Jude?" She glanced to my right and left as if expecting another person to magically materialize.

Adopting a fake regretful expression, I said, "Unfortunately, Jude isn't going to make it."

"Actually, I'm right here," came a deep voice from behind me. I froze. Was that...? *No.* How did...? *No.*

"Jude Stark," he said, now at my side with his hand extended to Mari.

Mari grinned and shook his hand. "Let's begin. Follow me." She led us single file beyond the curtain through which she'd come a minute earlier. I labored to walk like a normal person, all the while picturing Jude's victorious-with-a-side-of-smug smirk directed at my back.

How had he known? Was it actually an hour later because Jude had snuck into my apartment and changed the time on all my clocks? Or had he planted a tracking device on my phone during our last meeting to keep constant tabs?

I clenched my fists. What if Esther had consorted with the enemy and told him everything? I loosened my fingers. Of all the ridiculous scenarios running through my head, I ruled out only the last one. Esther was fiercely loyal.

Guessing at an explanation was pointless. Historically, Jude's stunts had a 99 percent success rate whereas mine hovered at around 85 percent. Bottom line: this one fell in the 15 percent failure column. It hadn't worked, but the world hadn't ended, and no one had gotten hurt. It could have been so much worse. Now I just had to get through the meeting and keep my head held high during his inevitable "I'm so much better than you" speech before I could go home and mope in private. I'd confide in Esther if I had any confidence she'd refrain from saying, "I told you so." I had no such confidence.

Once settled at a table, Mari told us about the various prix-fixe menus for the party and private room options. I was only half present. Singularly focused on the success or failure of my prank, I hadn't read through my list of questions ahead of time, and my shaky voice evidenced my lack of preparation. This time, Jude didn't make jokes about my preparedness (or lack thereof). But I knew the perfect insults would materialize at his whim as always. He was so unlike me, who tended to rehearse my arguments ahead of time, imagining different scenarios so I'd be prepared no matter what my opponent tossed my way.

He was playing it so cool, even asking for my thoughts as if we were truly partners. I worked to look everywhere else but at him. My reward was one of those annoying eye twitches. Perhaps another nickname for Jude to adopt. *Eye-twitch Molly.*

A half hour later, we told Mari we'd be in touch after conferring with the rest of our families and made our way to the exit. Once outside, no words were exchanged. If, like me, Jude was going straight home, we were both headed in the same direction. I waited for him to brag about my prank-gone-wrong. Minutes passed, although it might have been painfully long seconds, and he said nothing. We continued to walk, step by step by step. Our silence made all the surrounding noises seem louder: car engines, kids playing, the hum of third-party conversations. I mentally willed him to get on with it. But no, he was *whistling*...to the tune of "Ob-La-Di Ob-La-Da"...just waiting for the right moment to sock it to me. If this were a movie, the background music would build as if warning viewers of approaching drama. Finally, I couldn't take it any longer. "What did you think?" I gulped. "About the place?" Anything to break the awkward silence.

Jude stopped whistling. "I always call ahead to confirm.

You told me the meeting time, but I double checked. Years of working in the restaurant business, I guess." He shrugged, the words falling from his lips so nonchalantly, he could have been pointing out a crack in the sidewalk and not explaining how he'd managed to escape the practical joke played on him by his near-lifelong nemesis.

I stopped in place and gazed up at him from about seven inches below. "That's it? That's all you have to say?" His posture was relaxed, and in his pale yellow drawstring shorts and black t-shirt, he could pass for a guy on a casual walk, not an angry victim of a prank, preparing his inevitable next move. He was so unpredictable. Sometimes his gloating was loud and obnoxious, and other times he took his victory softly and with no fanfare at all. It was impossible to prepare for it.

"It was a solid effort, Mole." A breeze blew in, sweeping a dark hair into his eye. He brushed it away and kept walking.

I doubled my stride to catch up to him.

He stopped in front of my building and looked up. "This is you. The Churchill."

Was he really going to let me off the hook that easily? I didn't buy it.

His phone rang. "Hey," he said to whoever it was before holding up a finger and mouthing, "One second" to me.

I nodded my assent.

"What's wrong?"

The question caught my attention, but I stared down at my bubblegum-pink toenails and pretended not to eavesdrop.

"That's because you're too nice. It's not your job to make everyone else happy. They don't even appreciate it."

Without thinking, I raised my head in keen interest. Jude's

forehead was scrunched with concern. Was this the lawyer? Or had he moved on to someone else?

"Do you mind?" Jude's eyes, directed at me, were rounded in annoyance.

My cheeks flamed, and I stepped backward, nearly colliding with a pedestrian. "Sorry." I paced the sidewalk in front of my thirty-two-story building a few times, then stopped. Why was I outside waiting for him to finish his call when I was already home? I cleared my throat to get his attention. "I think I'll just"—I pointed at the entrance to my lobby—"go inside. We can talk about the party...um...later." I started walking.

"Let me call you back." He ended the call. "Wait."

I froze. *Crap.*

"Do you have a minute?"

I turned back around. "What?"

"About this rivalry." He pointed between us as if there were any question who the rivals were. "Can we stop?"

My mouth formed an O. These were the last words I expected to fall from the lips of one Jude Stark.

"I thought we ended these pranks in high school. We're pushing thirty, Mole...Molly. It's boring. Don't you agree?"

Slightly dizzy with disbelief, I planted my feet firmly on the ground. "Are you serious? You started it! Did you not? You used my love of dogs and concern for Yogi against me, knowing I'd fall for your lies."

"I didn't plan it."

Tell me something I don't know.

Jude shrugged. "After George stormed off at Society Cafe, my mouth opened and before I knew it, it was on. It wasn't like I could say, 'Never mind' after the fact."

I cocked my head. "Why not? There were fifty-five minutes between us leaving Society Cafe and our planned meeting at eight. At any point during that window, you could have sent a retracting text, but you didn't."

A momentary flash of regret washed over his face, and I held my breath, wondering if he might finally apologize for being the worst version of himself around me. "It was so much more fun to let it play out, though," he said.

"For one of us." I gave him a pointed look.

"You're right." He scrubbed a hand through his messy hair, making it messier.

I pulled on my ear. "I'm what now?"

"You're *right*," he mumbled. "But it's been a rough year for both of our families. What do you say we focus on the party and only the party starting now?"

I searched his face to gauge his sincerity. There was no twitch to his lips, quiver of his chin, or laugh lines around his eyes. I scanned the length of his body for evidence of suppressed humor, like bobbing shoulders. When it occurred to me it might look like I was appreciating his strong neck and muscular calves...I most certainly was *not*...I lifted my head. "Okay," I said, taking him at his word. My voice sounded like it came from someone else's mouth—in an alternate universe, one where Jude Stark had actually turned into a grown man.

"Let's do this for our parents," he said. "By the way, nice job throwing me off the scent by choosing something similar to my prank. I honestly would have fallen for it if I hadn't called to confirm. Like I said, it was a solid effort." He smiled, and for a split second, I saw the little boy with a mop of dark hair and golden cheeks from all the time he spent outside riding his bike and playing SPUD in the backyard.

"It was, wasn't it?" The knowledge that he saw the wisdom in my choice of prank sparked a lightness in my belly completely unfamiliar to me in Jude's presence. I returned his expression—matching smiles—and allowed myself to imagine a reality where, despite everything, we could be friends again. Or at least civil.

Chapter Six

Later that week, my mood was bright despite discovering an empty container of half and half in the office pantry. Settling for whole milk, I poured it into my bitter coffee while humming "Karma" by Taylor Swift. Coffee creamer was small stuff, and I had bigger, more pleasant, things on my mind. Earlier that morning, I had secured an interview for Patrice—the candidate who'd left my office disappointed the week before.

Still singing to myself, I returned to my office and stiffened at the sight of my managing director, Michael, hovering over my desk with his back to me. Michael, also a former lawyer, had replaced our previous managing director, Jill, a month earlier when she retired. It was safe to say I missed Jill.

Our one-on-one meeting was scheduled for ten-thirty in *his* office, not—I glanced at my watch—9:14 in mine. This was weird. But weirdness would segue into creepy if I continued to observe him from behind. In his late thirties, Michael was white with short, spiky brown hair, blue eyes, and a slightly oversize forehead. He was decent-enough looking, but carried himself in an entitled douchy way, and his ass wouldn't make any top one hundred lists. I straightened the collar of my chambray shift dress and cleared my throat in greeting.

He turned and flashed a smarmy smile. "Molly. I had a cancellation this morning and thought we could meet earlier."

I waited for him to follow up the suggestion with something along the lines of "if it works for you," but it never came. It wasn't a suggestion. Lucky for me, my calendar was open. "Do you want to talk here?"

"Here is good. Have a seat."

"That's my line." I chuckled, humored by his hospitality in someone else's office.

Once we were both seated, me with my legs crossed and hands resting on my thighs and him on the other side of my desk with his legs spread and arms clasped over his head, I opened up the dialogue. "I don't think I've had an opportunity to officially welcome you to Gotham. Welcome!" Getting right down to business without small talk would make me appear unconfident or nervous. It was important to send the right message. *I am capable! You can trust me!*

"Thank you. I wanted to discuss your performance at work."

I pasted on a smile. "I'm happy to." Who needed small talk?

"Tracking of your computer shows you spend as much time on sites like Vault and Above the Law as you do on the internal job database, LinkedIn, Leopard List, and other attorney databases." He leaned forward and squinted at me.

My pulse raced. I was well aware all work conducted on a firm computer was subject to surveillance, but why would Michael monitor my activity personally? "I wouldn't say *as much* time, but yes, I utilize both sites regularly." Vault was a website that ranked law firms and their attorneys based on reviews by verified employees. Above the Law was another great source to secure dirt on firms.

Michael removed one of the many picture frames I kept on my desk and studied it. "Why?" His gaze remained on the photograph. It was one of me, Nicole, and Michelle dressed up and smiling against a view of the Hudson River at Michelle's wedding.

"It's part of my due diligence. There's always more to a firm or company than what the hiring manager shares with us." I smiled knowingly—recruiter to recruiter. "Candidates appreciate that I go above and beyond and feel confident that when I send them on an interview, it's a big step toward getting their dream job." Remembering my coffee, I took a sip.

Still holding the photo, Michael poked his tongue into his cheek. "The employer *pays us money* to match them with employees. That payment constitutes any review we need. You shouldn't be wasting your time vetting existing clients or even potential ones." He placed the picture back on the desk facedown.

I touched a finger to my cheek. The skin was hot. His interrogation suggested I was a suspect in a crime as opposed to a thorough recruiter. Placing the photo back in its rightful position, next to one of me and Esther on a booze cruise in Turks and Caicos, I said, "Our clients also appreciate that I don't waste their time sending them candidates who are wrong for the position. Is it such a bad thing to want *both* parties to be happy? I scheduled an interview just this morning with Abraham & Painter. They called me personally for this opening because they trust me to bring them good candidates. I'm very confident it will be a match." My skin still buzzed with excitement.

I continued. "The departing paralegal is retiring after eight years in the position, which speaks volumes about the work environment, as does the firm's general low employee turnover rate. And the candidate has twenty-five years of experience, a well-rounded résumé, and an easygoing personality I think will mesh well with the rest of the department." I beamed at him. Surely, my enthusiasm would transfer.

He sneered. "It's very sweet how nurturing you are. You're almost maternal toward your candidates."

Sexist son of a... I felt my blood pressure rise and squeezed my flaring nostrils. *Keep your cool.*

"Recruiting is a competitive career." Michael clasped his arms behind his neck again. "Competition between clients, candidates, and recruiters alike, but it's what drives us all."

Not *all* of us. What drove *me* was making the best match between client and candidate. I forced my gaze away from the sweat stain beginning to form on Michael's right armpit and waited for the imminent mansplain.

"Have you ever heard of the Triple-A method? Not the American Automobile Association"—he snickered—"but Alpha, Aggressive, and Ambitious. In the real world, Molly, not all work environments are congenial playgrounds. But people still need to work for those companies. *We* need to work for those companies. We can't turn down a client or leave an opening ignored indefinitely while you wait for some unicorn position to come available that ticks every single box." He stood. "It's in your best interest to take on more clients. Be more of a team player."

My breath hitched. Did cherry-picking my clients mean I wasn't a team player? I assumed the autonomy in this position meant my work had no bearing on my colleagues. Jill had encouraged individuality and finding your own path. But Jill wasn't here anymore.

I'd quit my job at the law firm in large part due to a hostile working environment. Each time I imagined placing a candidate in a position my gut screamed was wrong, wrong, wrong, my imagination exploded with visuals of them waking up each morning with dread in the pit of their stomach and a single goal: to get through the day. The way I had. Except it wasn't only one day. It was day after day *after day* with no reward except a paycheck I had no time to spend.

Finding the perfect match between employer and employee was my mission statement—my *brand*. It took research, meticulous attention to detail, and a lot of patience, but when it all came together, the reward was *chef's kiss*.

"Closing more deals also means more money for you, in case you've forgotten," Michael said.

I worked on commission, which meant I only got paid when I successfully connected a prospective employee to an employer. Michael had a point in that I could probably make more money if I sent candidates out on more interviews and encouraged them to take less than ideal or even *adequate* jobs. But it wasn't how I worked. It wasn't who I *was*. I didn't want more money if it came at the cost of selling out my candidates.

"Think about it, Molly. Alpha. Aggressive. Ambitious." He knocked three times on my wall and left.

I turned my chair to face the East River outside my window and let my head fall back. More like *Quadruple* A: Alpha. Aggressive. Ambitious. *Asshole*. I opened my eyes.

Michael was gross, but I couldn't afford to get on his bad side or, worst-case scenario, be pushed out. And what if the complaints came from higher up? Gotham Recruiting got a cut of my commission. The less I brought in, the less money they made. The plan was to stay with the company for a minimum of two years, hopefully longer with promotions. A history of switching jobs every year wasn't a deal breaker, but as a recruiter, I knew it raised a red flag.

I closed out of Vault and vowed to keep off it and other similar sites from now on, at least for openings already in our system. Once I saw a bad review of the firms who employed us, I couldn't unsee or ignore it. The only remedy was to stop looking. A hostile environment was the exception, not the rule. What I *didn't* know couldn't hurt me, and if I was being honest, earning more money wasn't a bad thing, for me or for my candidates. I just needed to find a compromise to up the pace without selling them out. Besides, it was unhealthy to lose sleep over their continued job satisfaction.

Keep telling yourself that, Molly.

I clicked the attachment on an email sent from the human resources coordinator of Pro City Sportswear and read the job specification form again.

The sportswear company was looking to fill the legal counsel position in their in-house legal department. They sought someone with two to three years of law firm experience in entertainment or intellectual property law. Since this was a repeat client for me, I'd already run my due diligence in terms of work culture earlier that year. Hopefully, nothing had changed since then. Before my conscience got the better of me, I sent three résumés of qualified candidates.

A text message from Jude popped up on my phone. We were seeing another restaurant that night.

> **Jude:** Sotto 13 is closed for renovations. Meeting place has changed to office space at 328 Broome Street. See you there at 6:30.

My fingernails dug into my palms. I read the text again only to confirm it said what I thought it said. The likelihood this was not pure and utter bullshit was probably too low to qualify for calculation. Rude was way off his game. It was laughable if not a little concerning.

I copied and pasted it into a text to Esther.

> **Molly:** See below. Is he for real? Does he think I'll just take him at his word without confirming with the restaurant? Especially given that's how he outed me only a few days ago?

I called the main number for Sotto 13, and when a woman answered the phone said, "Hi. This is Molly Blum. I'm scheduled to meet there tonight about a possible party."

"Oh, yes," she said, her voice upbeat. "It's in the calendar. The Blum and Stark party."

"Correct."

"We're all set."

Just as I thought. Surely she'd volunteer the change in location if there was one. So much for "renovations."

Oh, how Jude must have delighted at my naïveté at accepting

our newfound peace at face value—together with all his similarly obnoxious friends. He might have even used it to show his "too nice" lawyer girlfriend what happened when you trusted someone with absolutely no good reason. I blamed him, but I was equally at fault. It was Jude we were talking about; I should have known better.

"Did someone tell you about the address change?" the woman from the restaurant asked.

"The address..." My voice cracked, and I cleared my throat and tried again. "Address change?"

"The restaurant is temporarily closed for renovations...paint fumes don't go well with pasta...but we have office space on Broome Street: 328 Broome."

"Okay, 328 Broome. Got it." We ended the call. *Huh.* I stared at my phone in a daze. I'd been so certain Jude calling a truce only to pull another prank right away was all part of his ongoing evil plan to drive me bananas. It wasn't. Yet even while being earnest, he still managed to turn me inside out. It took a special kind of talent. I shook my head in wonder as my phone pinged an incoming text.

> **Esther:** Wow. He really doesn't think much of you, does he?

Way to sugarcoat it, Esther.

> **Molly:** You should sit down for this. He was telling the truth. The meeting is at a different location!

I closed my eyes while I tried to make sense of what I was feeling. At the forefront was guilt for jumping to conclusions about Jude's motives. But who wouldn't be skeptical after years of being the most popular pawn in his game of tricks? There was, of course, happiness and relief that the change of address was legitimate. Now we could continue planning the party sans combat—a positive for sure!

But along with guilt, happiness, and relief was another pesky emotion I tried to dismiss but couldn't.

Disappointment.

Chapter Seven

*W*eird.

I was standing in front of 328 Broome Street. But the only business name listed on the buzzer was Bang Bang Tattoos. I peeked inside the building through a set of glass doors. There were at least two male patrons with their shirts pushed over their shoulders ready to be inked, and one woman with her back to me mid-branding. *Yup.* Definitely a tattoo parlor.

I scratched my head with one hand and double-checked Jude's text with the other. It confirmed I was at the right address. The woman on the phone at Sotto 13 had also said 328 Broome Street. Into my phone, I asked, "Siri. How many Broome Streets are there in Manhattan?"

There is one Broome Street in Manhattan.

I worried my lip. A tattoo parlor sharing space with an Italian restaurant in New York City wasn't out of the realm of possibility, I guessed.

I stepped inside. It was a narrow space, but what it lacked in width, it made up for in length. *That's what she said.* I chuckled to myself. The décor was minimalist with white walls and black workstations. A white man in a black baseball cap with stylized letters B.A.N.G., latex gloves, and a neck tattoo peeking out of a black t-shirt approached me. "What can I do for you?"

I kept my voice low to avoid disturbing the concentration of artists holding needles. "This is a weird question, but I was given this address to meet someone about planning a party."

"A tattoo party?" His reply was delivered in a much louder tone than mine, drawing attention to our conversation.

My head jerked back. "No...an...uh...dinner party... anniversary party for my parents."

The guy's eyebrows shot up to his forehead. "You want to hold your party here?" He rubbed the patch of hair on his chin. "It's not something we've done before, but I guess we can close to the public for a night. How many tattoos do you think you'd need?"

"No. Oh, my God. No!" My face felt like it was held over a fire like a marshmallow on a stick. My mom was *not* a fan of ink. When Michelle finally exposed the long-kept secret of the snake tattoo she got in college, Mom went on a loud rampage about how Judaism prohibited body art. Never mind we were reform Jews, and I suspected my mom was covertly agnostic. The Starks, however, kept kosher in the home. Holding a surprise wedding anniversary celebration for conservative Jews at a tattoo parlor where all the guests got inked was the stuff of television sitcoms, not upper-middle-class suburban reality. "I'm sorry for the confusion. I was told Sotto 13, the restaurant, had an office at this address. Do you know anything about that?"

"Can't say I do." He glanced over his shoulder and took a step back as if trying to make an escape without my noticing.

I had one more ace up my sleeve before I lost him completely. "Is there an upstairs space maybe?"

He faced me again, this time with a smirk. "Upstairs is for the more *delicate* areas of the body."

A phantom pain shot through my nipples and between my legs. His lips curled up knowingly.

My gaze dropped to the floor. "I'm sorry to have bothered you."

"No problem." Handing me a business card, he said, "If you change your mind about having a party here...or upstairs...let me know." He walked away laughing.

By the time I exited the building a few seconds later, embarrassment had turned to amusement. It wasn't every day one tried to plan a party for four sixtysomethings at a tattoo parlor. Too bad Jude had missed it.

Wait.

Why had Jude missed it? Assuming this was the address where we'd *both* thought the meeting was being held, shouldn't he have been here by now too? I leaned against the brick exterior of the building. *Unless*...unless Jude knew the meeting wasn't being held here. Was it possible it was a trick after all? But how? I'd spoken to the restaurant directly. Then again, this was Jude. He must have had someone on the inside and called in a favor.

Maybe I should have been impressed by the lengths he would go to—flattered he'd use up a favor to beat me—but I was mostly angry. Angry at having my time wasted yet again. Angry at Jude for winning yet again. Angry at myself for falling for his trickery *yet again.*

My heart pounded harder with each beat until I remembered how I'd whipped myself into a similar frenzy only a few hours earlier. Jude might infect my mental health, but I'd be damned if I let his nefarious ways send me to an early grave by way of cardiac arrest. And maybe...just maybe...he had a legitimate excuse for being late. The answer came in a text delivered at that precise moment, once again raising my suspicions that he'd somehow planted a tracking device on my phone.

> **Jude:** Never underestimate me, Mole.

My fingers danced over the keys to tell him to go fuck...no, NOT duck...*stupid spell check*...himself when another text popped up.

> **Jude:** I'll see you at the restaurant. The meeting doesn't start until 7.

I put on my game face and resigned myself to another confrontation. Would he laugh in my face or act like it was no big deal again? It was hard to say. I took two steps toward the restaurant, thought better of it, and walked back into the shop. *It's not over till it's over.*

When I arrived at Sotto 13 purposely ten minutes late, I smelled no paint fumes whatsoever. *Shocking.* I figured Jude would assume I'd be mortified in the aftermath of yet another defeat at his hands and put effort into appearing calm and collected, like I had at Sakagura. So I played my part well. I apologized for being tardy—said I was held up at my last appointment—then I laser-focused on the restaurant's party planner and pretended the "other guy" at the table was there on unrelated business. Jude needed to believe I was too embarrassed to make eye contact so that when I had the last laugh later, it would be all the more satisfying.

After the meeting ended, we stepped outside the restaurant and faced off on the sidewalk.

Jude crossed his arms over his chest and snickered. "Any new tattoos you care to share? I don't see anything, but maybe you went upstairs?" He skimmed the length of my body.

My cheeks heated up when he lingered an extra second on my breasts. "I didn't get a tit tattoo, *Rude.*"

The insinuation he was checking me out appeared to startle him, but he recovered quickly. "Face it, Mole. You might have made the grades, but I'm shrewd."

I groaned. "I never said otherwise. In fact, I was just telling my friend—"

"You were talking about me to a friend? What about?" His eyes danced. "My charm? Intelligence? Oh, I know…my moves." He checked the coast was clear over his shoulder before doing the moon walk for a few feet.

Don't laugh. Do *not* laugh. I tapped my foot in impatience, my mood somewhere between anger and awe.

A petite blond around our age exited the restaurant and pulled him into a hug.

"Don't be a stranger," she said after they separated. Then she turned to me with a sheepish grin. "Sorry, but he made me do it."

I nodded at his person on the inside. "He's very persuasive." As she walked down the street, I turned back to Jude to find him smirking. *It's on.*

"I won't pretend I didn't fall for it," I said, keeping my voice as even as possible. "You knew I'd call the restaurant to confirm and set it up perfectly. But once I recovered, I realized the brilliance of actually holding the party there."

Jude opened his mouth, presumably on the verge of bragging, when my last sentence sank in. He snapped his jaw shut. "What?"

I nodded eagerly. "You were being shrewd without even trying! A tattoo party is genius!" I flashed the tattooist's business card. "I said we'd be in touch. What a great way to show our parents that sixty is still young... feed into the whole 'midlife crisis' idea. You know?"

Jude blinked, then shook his head like a dog after a bath.

I pulled down the strap on my yellow sundress to reveal a tattoo in the shape of a jar of honey on my shoulder. "It's why I was late. The best reviews are from personal experience, right? And I'm too sweet. Like you always say." I gazed at the ink like a mother with a newborn baby on her chest then beamed up at Jude.

The smirk had disappeared, replaced with shock. "That's not... you didn't actually... wow."

His face! I wished I could bottle it. Like I'd told Esther, it wasn't easy to pull one on Jude, but when it worked, it was glorious. This one was risky, since there was a decent chance he'd immediately know it wasn't a fresh tattoo, but I got lucky for once. In a perfect world, I'd maintain the ruse for as long as possible, but I was incapable of keeping it together another second. A laugh tickled the back of my throat, forcing me to put him out of his misery. "You're not the only shrewd one in this partnership. In other words..." I paused dramatically. "Don

Messwidme either." I lost it, cracking up while Jude stared at me looking momentarily bewildered.

It took a second before he joined me in howling. When we finally stopped laughing, Jude said, "It's not real, is it?" He touched the ink lightly, sending a weird jolt of electricity up my arm.

"Of course not. It's temporary." I wiped a tear from my eye.

"Phew." He swiped his forehead exaggeratedly. "I should have known."

"Yeah...you should have." It felt good to be the one smirking.

"Falling for one of your pranks is one thing. Molly Blum getting a spontaneous tattoo is another. It seems like a decision worthy of one of your famous pro/con lists." He chuckled.

"I don't do rash decisions." *Except once.* And just like that, I wasn't laughing anymore.

"Why do you look so sad all of a sudden? You won. You should savor this rarity."

"I'm not sad. This was fun. It's just...I believed you...about making peace."

"That's on you." His eyes softened for the briefest of moments. "You wouldn't want that anyway. Fighting with me gives you an excuse to let your mean flag fly. You like it. Case in point, the victorious look on your face less than five minutes ago. I haven't seen it in ten years."

"Don't flatter yourself. I don't like it...this *war* we've been fighting for a lifetime. Where you're concerned, I act out of necessity, not for my enjoyment. Any amusement on my part is a consolation prize."

His response was a facial expression I could only describe as cynical yet bordering on entertained. It screamed, "Bless your heart," and for a moment, I wondered if he'd follow it up by ruffling my hair. But he just smiled. "It's okay. I like it too. Especially since I'm better at it than you. Most of the time." He typed something on his phone, more interested in whoever he was texting than continuing our conversation.

I watched in interest as he worked the thumbs of both his hands on opposite corners of his phone. He wasn't texting after all. But what *was* he doing? I leaned forward until his screen came into view and froze. It looked like a 3D video baseball game. For someone like Jude, who once brought the stadium fans, albeit mostly students and parents, to their feet when he hit real home runs, could the virtual version ever compare?

With no interest in asking him this question and even less prepared for the answer, I stepped back, before he could snap at me for hovering, and revisited what he'd said. Was he right? Despite my denial, did I like fighting with him?

I'd always used Jude's behavior to justify my own—I had to defend myself—but the look of surprise, defeat, and sometimes awe on his face when my plans had gone off without a hitch had been priceless. I couldn't deny the twinge of disappointment I felt when I thought he'd been telling the truth about the restaurant's address change.

If I was being honest, I'd more than *liked* taking Jude down a notch; I'd reveled in it. Until one day, when I'd been so angry with him, I reacted rashly instead of planning my actions with painstaking detail as per usual. The incident, one I'd kept bottled up for a decade, had changed everything, not only for Jude, whose dreams were stolen in one pivotal moment, but for me.

Chapter Eight

Ten years earlier, I'd been stuck at home on a Friday night, grounded because the video Jude had filmed of me drunk and puking at a classmate's party had found its way to my parents. It couldn't get worse than being homebound for the entire weekend. Or so I thought until I received back-to-back rejections from both Cornell and U. Penn that same night—TGIF, my ass!

My hatred of Jude burned hotter than lava. If he hadn't run for student council for no other reason than to rub his popularity in my face, the election would have been mine. With senior class president on my applications, those emails might have begun with "We are pleased to welcome you" rather than "We regret that we cannot offer you admission."

I'd glared out the window at where his bike sat on the Starks' otherwise empty driveway, grabbed the wire hanger left by the trash from my dad's dry cleaning, and snuck across the street. Then I stabbed his back tire once, twice, three times. It wasn't a prank. It was rage. I regretted it instantly and ran home with a plan to slip money into his locker to pay for a new tire the following Monday at school.

Only I didn't know Rude was still inside his house at the time. I thought he was already at the high school warming up for the game against the Spring Valley Tigers. I had no idea he never actually made it because he rode his bike and the tire blew out on the way.

I only learned about the accident later that night, when I heard my parents whispering about how Jude would be okay eventually, but the damage to his knee would likely take him out of commission for the rest of the season. Except it wasn't just the rest of the season. He lost his baseball scholarship and suffered sustained injuries that crushed his dream in one fell swoop. And it was my fault.

I never told anyone what happened. I was way too ashamed and, if I was being honest, terrified my parents would force me to come clean to Jude and his family. But the guilt ate away at me. For months, I woke up in cold sweats after dreaming about Jude being thrown from his bike and falling to the ground, leaving his limbs raggedy like a doll's.

Even though I couldn't change the past, what happened next was in my control. I'd made a vow: end this war with Jude. No more pranks. It was easy enough once I went away to college. Slowly, the guilt and nightmares subsided.

Until now. Being around him so much these days was a constant reminder of what I'd done. But, lacking all the facts, Jude provoked me at every opportunity. I'd tried not to let him get to me. I really had. But he had made it clear the wheels were in motion for Jude and Molly Wars 2.0. My choices were to play along or get played.

Which meant there was no choice at all.

And so it went. Jude and I continued our reindeer games.

When I produced the sound of human flatulence from sitting on the whoopee cushion Jude had snuck onto my chair at The Writing Room, he declared with a straight face, "Better loud and proud than silent but deadly, right, Mole?" At Allora, I switched out the restaurant's ball point with a "trick" pen I'd made with the help of a YouTube video and laughed as the ink leaked all over Jude's hand.

It was as if, by unspoken agreement, we stopped trying to outsmart each other, and instead lowered our emotional age by about fifteen years. Two weeks later, we had quite possibly been banned from more than one restaurant, but the favorites bar on my computer was loaded with pages and pages of practical jokes and pranks. I had enough ideas to last me through the party and beyond.

And then Nicole scheduled The Call.

It was a mandatory video call for the six Blum and Stark siblings with only one item on the agenda: the party. Unfortunately, the only time we were all available that week was Saturday at seven o'clock—*in the morning*.

I set my alarm for 6:27 and snoozed twice before dragging my ass out of bed at 6:45. After pairing a bra and hot pink exercise tank with my pajama shorts—no one would see below my waist anyway—I smoothed my hair into a ponytail and applied skin-brightening moisturizer and slightly tinted gloss to my face and lips respectively. Then I made a cup of coffee, got settled on my beige fabric couch, and joined the Zoom meeting at exactly 6:59.

Nicole was already there, wearing a floral bathing suit coverup and a smile too bright for a pre-breakfast meeting. Next came Eddie. He wore a sweat-stained t-shirt and held a bottle of

Gatorade like he'd just finished a workout. Then Jude appeared. Based on the indentations from his pillow still on his face, he had just woken up. Yogi lay across his chest like a blanket. Alison, who was showered, made up, and ready for business, had set up her computer by her kidney-shaped pool. Michelle was last and connected only by audio. This was against Nicole's "rules," but according to Michelle, rules didn't apply to oldest sisters.

After a few minutes of awkward greetings and talking over each other, Nicole called the meeting to order. "Status update: We've set the date for October twenty-first. Considering how much trouble we had scheduling this call, choosing a date for the party so efficiently is something worth celebrating."

Eddie and I clapped on camera while Michelle sang, "Applause. Applause," behind a black screen.

Nicole bowed as if solely responsible for this accomplishment. "Alison ordered beautiful invitations."

"I'll drink to that," Alison said as Dana, her wife, leaned over her shoulder and poured from a bottle of La Marca prosecco into her glass of orange juice.

Once we said a collective hello to Dana, Nicole continued. "Michelle is almost finished compiling addresses for all the guests, Eddie found a photographer, and I met with the florist. We're going to re-create both sets of parents' bridal bouquets. Which leaves one item... and it's a doozy." She made her angry face—which I hoped she'd improve if she ever had children, because it was currently more likely to elicit giggles than fear—at one of us... or possibly all of us. It was hard to tell with Zoom. "We don't have a venue."

Two of us. I glanced at Jude to gauge his reaction. He was roughhousing with Yogi and...oh my God...*that dog*. I was besotted. Too bad the cutest dog had the meanest man on the planet as his human daddy.

"What do you have to say for yourselves, Molly and Jude?" Nicole asked.

Michelle's voice piped in. "This is about the juniors? I don't need to be on this call. Later." She left the meeting before anyone could argue.

"Juniors? Haven't heard that one in a while." Eddie chuckled.

Nicole huffed. "Yes, *juniors*. You hate when we treat you like children, then stop acting like children!"

"I never said I hated it." Jude laughed as Yogi licked his face. Between licks, he said, "It's not our fault you gave us the hardest job."

Nicole said, "This isn't like you, Molly. I'd think you'd be the first person to complete your assigned task, especially since the party is for Mom and Dad." Her lips pinched together in frustration.

"Jude's distracting her," Eddie said as his two-year-old son, Miles, a chubby, angel-faced boy, crawled onto his lap mumbling, "Dada."

Jude scowled. "Because it's always my fault, right? Mollyanna couldn't possibly be led astray without my influence."

"It doesn't matter whose fault it is. The point is, we need a venue," Eddie said.

"If you can't handle it, don't worry about it," Nicole said. "We can take over."

It was classic reverse psychology, and it worked...on me anyhow. Nicole and Eddie should have known better than to pair us together, but we *were* behaving like children. Without a venue, there was no party. If our parents didn't get the celebration they deserved, it would be our fault... *my* fault.

"You'll still be *invited* to the party, of course," Nicole confirmed. "And we'll just tell everyone you helped."

"Jude should be used to this," Alison said.

I set my mug on the table. "No! I want to be part of the planning. We can handle it. Right, Jude?"

"Hmmm?" His attention remained on Yogi.

I answered for him. "We'll get it done." I instantly regretted my phrasing but hoped no one would pick up on it.

Eddie wolf-whistled. "Molly and Jude getting it done."

Nicole giggled. "Cover your stump before you hump."

"No glove, no love!" The addition was uncharacteristically immature for Alison, but drinking at dawn could have that effect.

"Stop it!" I braced myself for Jude's snide protest of any suggestion the two of us would ever *get it done.*

"We'll handle it." Jude looked at me, or at least I assumed he was looking at me. "I'll call Mole to discuss. And to those who accused *us* of acting like children: can you spell hypocrite?"

The meeting ended, and I called Jude. It went straight to voice mail. My instincts screamed that Jude was extremely anti–voice mail, which made leaving a message all the more tempting. Except I was trying to keep my priorities straight. Party planning—yay. Aggravating Jude for the pure pleasure of it—nay. But just as I opened up our text exchange, my phone rang—Jude. "I just called you. It went to voice mail."

"Because I was calling you. Did you not hear me say I would call you? Must you always go first?"

"It depends on what activity you're referring to." I squirmed. Jude and I did not do sexual innuendo.

"I'll leave that between you and your baseball player."

"We're not seeing each other anymore." I brought my coffee cup to the kitchen sink. "Not that it's any of your business...or that you care. What did you think about the call?" *Priorities.*

"I haven't received a scolding like that from my siblings...or yours...since before puberty."

Back in the living room, I flumped onto my couch. "So, since last month?" Jude made a noise that sounded like laughter, and it did something strange to my belly.

"There's that mean flag I was talking about," he said. "Remember the truce I pretended to propose?"

"Vaguely."

"Let's do it for real. Make peace, that is."

I bit my lip. "Can I trust you?" *Fool me once, shame on you. Fool me twice...*

Silence filled the phone waves as if the question required substantial thought. Finally, he answered. "At least until we decide on a restaurant."

"Fair enough. Have you given any thought to the ones we've seen already?"

"Not really. Did you? Keep in mind, saying yes will not endear you to me."

"In that case, yes. Haha." I cleared my throat. "But no. I haven't. I took notes, though. We could go over them together... if you want."

"Tell me when and where."

"Are you around this afternoon? We can do it at my place." I jerked my head back. Did I just invite Jude Stark to *do it* at my apartment? "Or somewhere else?" Yes. Somewhere else would be better.

"Your place is great. Is two okay?"

"Perfect." Not really, but since I'd offered my digs, it would be weird to renege now. "And Jude? Can you bring Yogi?" It was a spontaneous request, but if there was anything about Jude I *did* like, it was his dog.

Jude agreed, and we ended the call. Since I was already dressed…mostly…I treated myself to Daniel's Bagels around the corner from my apartment.

While I waited for my bagel and an iced coffee, I people-watched. There was no better spot for it on a Saturday morning than a bagel shop in twenty–thirtysomething Murray Hill. It was a little early for the post-hangover crowd, but there was a trio of guys who looked like they hadn't gone to sleep yet, a woman leaning on her husband (or someone else's husband—he wore a ring but she didn't) whose green complexion suggested she might not be able to keep down even one bite of a bagel, and a—

"Loud Whisper Girl."

I jerked out of my people watching and smiled at the cute, messy-haired guy in front of me. "Good Hearing Guy!" It had been weeks since I'd bantered with the barback at Tuttles at closing time, yet despite the hundreds of women who frequented the bar on a given weekend, he remembered my loud whisper! I was determined to play it cool on the outside even while dancing on the inside.

"My friends call me Timothy. Early morning or late night?"

I smoothed my palm along my ponytail. "Early morning." I'd stayed in the night before to review a new recruiting strategy passed down from Michael. Then I finished off a bottle of wine to forget everything I'd learned long enough to fall asleep.

I'd been trying to escape Michael's radar by pausing my

pre-interview vetting practices, but I worried I was betraying my candidates, most of whom were more concerned with salary and benefits than work environment. I considered it inherent to my job to think beyond the quantifiable questions asking, "How much?" and dig deeper, even if Michael disagreed. Each time I skipped that all-important step, the guilt burned through me like Satan had taken up residence inside my conscience.

"What about you? Just wake up or out all night?" The answer was in the pillow-and-sheet markings on his face similar to Jude's from earlier. In a "who wore it better" contest, Timothy won by a landslide.

The guy at the counter called out, "Cinnamon raisin bagel with raisin walnut cream cheese and an iced cinnamon coffee with half and half!"

"That's me!"

Timothy cocked an eyebrow. "Someone likes raisins and cinnamon."

"Guilty. Do you?"

"Only when there's a gun to my head."

"Different strokes." I shrugged.

"Everything bagel with cream cheese, tomato, and lox, and a small coffee, black!"

"That's mine." He gestured toward the counter. "Ladies first."

After I paid, I waited uncertainly for Timothy. If our conversation wasn't over, it would be rude to leave without saying goodbye, but hanging around might make me look desperate. I didn't do desperate. I took a step toward the exit and stopped. I didn't do rude either—conundrum.

"Raisin Girl!"

I smiled with my back still to him.

"Hold up."

I turned around.

"You didn't tell me your name."

"It's Molly."

"Molly, like Molly Jones!" He cringed. "Beatles reference. I do that a lot, sorry," he said, removing the New York Giants cap from his head and covering his stubbled face with it.

A delicious warmth flashed through me. "I don't mind."

He dropped the cap. "Do you not mind enough to want to hang out sometime?"

"I don't mind the exact right amount." Now outside, I tucked my bag under my arm and bent to pet an adorable goldendoodle chained to a pole. "Hi sweetie. *Hi!*" I cooed. "What a cute pupper!"

"Meet Eli."

"This precious creature is yours?" I asked, while Eli slobbered all over my hand.

"Sure is."

I stood and tried not to swoon. Not only was Timothy sexy, with his bedhead and scruff, but he had an adorable dog to boot. "I hate to randomly run into you and run, but…" I glanced in the direction of my apartment. "What's your phone—"

"Can I get your number?"

We laughed together.

With goofy grins, we exchanged digits. Then, with one more scratch of Eli's ears and a tentative promise to hang out soon, I headed home to eat, clean, and shower before Jude came over.

Ugh. Jude is coming over.

Chapter Nine

I was seventeenth-guessing the wisdom of inviting Jude to my home when the doorman rang to tell me he'd arrived. While I waited for him to make his way up the elevator to my ninth-floor apartment, my doubts propelled me to take photos of every surface in my six-hundred-square-foot apartment as insurance in case he did anything sketchy, like change all the clocks to the central time zone, rearrange my hanging paintings, toss my throw pillows out the window, and other Jude-like hijinks. I'd also be sure to turn down my sheets before sliding into bed later in case he left a fake—or heaven forbid real—tarantula under the covers. After all, this was the Jude Who Cried Truce.

A dog barked from the hallway outside my door.

Yogi! My spirits lifted. With all my misgivings about Jude, I'd forgotten about the doggie.

My doorbell rang. "It's Yogi!" a voice called out.

I opened the door to find Jude in cargo shorts and a dark gray t-shirt. In contrast to my jitters over this get-together, his relaxed posture and soft features had the air of someone who'd practiced the look in the mirror.

He went to loosen Yogi's leash, but hesitated. "Do you mind if he runs free?"

I waved him off. "Of course not. Come in."

Jude tugged on his Yankees baseball cap. "So, this is Molly's place."

I followed his line of vision and tried to see my home through his eyes. My mom was the decorator—I just paid the bills—but I'd approved all her selections, including my beige fabric sofa, weathered gray pine coffee table, light blue faux fur oval rug, white office desk, and collection of bright floral watercolor paintings hanging along the wall. "What do you think?" It was an impulse question, but I might as well have invited him to insult me. The pain in my palms where my fingers dug in had me seeing stars.

"It's very...um...tidy. You make your bed every day?"

"Of course." Then I followed it up with another dumb query. "You don't?"

He answered nonverbally with a "Yeah, right" expression. "My parents used your childhood bedroom as an example of what mine *should* look like. In other words...clean." He shook his head. "You were such a delightful, well-behaved child, weren't you?"

In other words, I was a goody-goody kiss-ass. *Mollyanna.* "And you were Rosemary's Baby."

Jude's lips quirked. "Nah. I was Groot. I made a mess. I danced. I was moody. I rebelled. I was your typical teenager." He leaned forward and swiped his finger along the surface of my desk. "No dust," he said, waving it at me. "Impressive."

I placed my hands on my hips. "Are you suggesting I was *a*typical? By whose definition?" Yogi danced at my feet with a hairband in his mouth. "Is that mine?" I looked at Jude questioningly. Where had he gotten it? They'd been here less than two minutes.

"Yogi Berra, drop it now!"

The dog whined and cocked his head at us.

"It's okay. I don't want it anymore." I laughed as Yogi ran circles around us.

"He has a thing for hairbands...has accrued quite the colorful collection at home. Haven't you, buddy?" Jude said, pulling on the red band in Yogi's mouth in a dog vs. man game of tug-of-war.

"You and your roommates wear your hair up often, do you?" I joked. Jude lived with two guys. When it hit me Yogi likely stole the accessories from the women they brought home, I felt myself blush.

Probably thinking the same thing, Jude did too. "Anyway. Sorry."

"No biggie." I sat on the couch. "Sit." Assuming the invitation was for him, Yogi jumped onto my lap.

"But you weren't nearly as chaste as you let on to your parents, were you?" Jude said, joining me on the opposite side of the couch and continuing our earlier conversation.

I eyed him suspiciously. "Is there a point to this line of questioning, and if so, can you give me an ETA, please?"

"I'm just saying...I was there when you barfed on Sanjeev's expensive rug after drinking—"

"I don't need a reminder of your presence," I said, referring to Jude catching the incident on video to use against me later. I curbed my residual anger, finding it not as challenging as it used to be, maybe because Jude getting me punished for my first (and only) offense when he got away with *everything* was what had spurred my anger and led to the biggest regret of my life.

He winced before carrying on his speech as planned. "I was also in attendance when you finished off all of Erica's French onion dip with your fingers after smoking weed. And I was under the same roof when you gave Seth..." He coughed. "Dated Seth. My point being teenage Mollyanna dabbled in her share of alcohol, drugs, and sexual experimentation."

I buried my heated face into Yogi's curly apricot-colored fur and silently cursed Jude's long memory. His teammate Seth was the recipient of my first blow job. The possibility... probability... *certainty*... that Jude possessed this information made me want to dig a hole to China. "Thank you for the walk down memory lane. So nice of you to keep track of my debauchery."

"We hung out in the same crowd and went to the same parties. Remember?"

At least the second half of that statement was accurate. My friends were more academic than Jude's, but we were well liked and attended most of the more popular students' parties. "If you knew I was a *typical* teenager, why'd you ask?" I lifted Yogi off me, stood, and walked to the kitchen. "Something to drink?"

"Just making conversation. Although I'm surprised you engaged in such rebellious activities at the risk of getting caught and blemishing your model-child persona at home."

Not realizing he'd followed me, I jolted at the feel of his breath on my neck. "Teenage hormones are a powerful thing, *Rude*," I said with my head in the fridge.

The real reason I was so obscenely well behaved growing up, at least as far as my parents were concerned, was none of Jude's business.

Unlike me, a seven-year-old Jude hadn't overheard his mom complain that parenting three girls was overwhelming. Jude's father hadn't shouted about the cost of raising him and his siblings only a few days before packing up his things and moving out. *Mine* had.

After Dad moved back in, I silently assumed responsibility for keeping him there. One of us had to. Michelle, the rebellious one, had just gotten caught shoplifting. Nicole, the needy one, suffered from bad dreams and had taken to crawling into their bed every night. Which left me to be the peacemaker—the perfect little girl who morphed into a well-behaved teenager. As long as I colored inside the lines, there would be no unpleasant surprises. Little had changed since I'd entered adulthood.

That said, the call of boys and drinking was too loud to resist completely. But it was only on rare occasions I did anything to potentially get on my parents' radar. The night I snuck home drunk after Sanjeev's party, Michelle met me at the front door and laughed her ass off when I hoofed it straight to the downstairs half bathroom to puke again. She was living at home temporarily after graduating college, and I gave her my Tory Burch sunglasses in exchange for not telling our parents. She later confessed she'd had no intention of ratting me out, but who was she to refuse a bribe? I ended up getting grounded anyway when the video Jude took came out.

Back in the present, I poured us each a glass of water and returned to the couch with Jude and Yogi at my heels. Yogi made himself comfortable on a butterfly-patterned throw pillow.

"Are you okay with this? Yogi and white couches don't mix. Kind of like..." His eyes crinkled at the corners. "You and me."

I didn't comment on the comparison. "It's fine. I invited him. And contrary to your assumption, I don't treat my apartment like a museum, which means Yogi can sit wherever he wants." I scratched behind his ears, and he wagged his tail in pleasure.

"I'm sure you were thrilled when my parents got wind of the video you made," I said. "I'm surprised you didn't use your first-hand knowledge of my less angelic moments against me more often. Not only to take pleasure in my punishment, but to get Randy and Laura off your back."

"The video was only meant to embarrass you in front of our friends. I had no idea they'd call your parents about it. I might have hated your 'I'm so perfect and pristine' act, but I was no narc." He gave me a pointed look.

Unfortunately, I couldn't say the same. I dropped my gaze.

Jude sat. "While we're on the subject, I know you think I only ran for student council to watch you lose."

I focused my attention on his fingers, drumming along his thighs to an imaginary beat. "You won, didn't you?"

"I did. But despite my gloating, my decision to run had nothing to do with wanting to beat you."

I lifted my head. "I find that hard to believe."

"I can't say I didn't enjoy the victory." He smirked. "But the reason I ran was to beef up my college applications. Ms. Rogers warned my parents at the parent-teacher conference that baseball alone might not be enough to make up for my average-at-best GPA. Student politics sounded fun, especially when Haley agreed to be my running mate."

I'd forgotten Haley and Jude had dated. Haley and I were in most of the same classes, had the same GPA by less than a percentage point, and she graduated twenty-first in the class to my twentieth. She wanted to be a doctor as much as I wanted to be a lawyer. I'd always thought she and Jude were a strange pairing. Studious wasn't really Jude's type. "Thanks, um, for telling me." Except I almost wished he hadn't. I'd accused Jude of intentionally using his popularity against me—had almost convinced myself his accident was karma for deliberately trying to mess with my future by running despite no interest in student politics whatsoever. Knowing his decision wasn't personal after all only made the flame of my guilt burn hotter.

"Anyway, I'm sorry if losing the election cost you the Ivy League experience after all your hard work. If it's any consolation, winning wasn't enough to make up for my shitty grades anyway, especially when baseball was no longer an option."

My body went still. An actual apology? I looked around the room for a hidden camera and back at Jude. The sincerity reflected on his face was humbling, and I forgave him right then and there. "It turned out okay in the end." I'd loved U-M and would never have met Esther if I'd gone to Cornell or U. Penn.

Jude nodded. "For me as well. No regrets."

I wanted to ask if that was true. Was he happy with the way his life had turned out? Or did he think about what could have been every time he watched a baseball game? But since I liked the answer he provided, I took him at his word.

"You mentioned something about notes for the party?" he said.

Oh yes, the party. I handed him a pile of loose papers. "Nothing too detailed, but let me know what you think."

A few minutes later, we agreed the space at Sotto 13 was too small, the menu at Sakagura too limited, and the atmosphere at The Writing Room too casual.

"Society Cafe had the best ambiance," I said.

"And they have a private room for sixty."

"Too bad we've probably been banned from the place, because I'd like to see their catering menu." I chewed my lip. "Maybe Nicole or Eddie can talk to George directly?"

"No." Jude vaulted off the couch and paced. "There's no way I'm giving the fucking *seniors* any material to use against us."

"Seniors. Ha!" So, Jude was equally annoyed by our older siblings' patronizing attitudes. I always assumed nothing got to him.

"He's not going to turn down our money. We'll just set up another meeting like nothing happened and be on our best behavior." He stopped pacing and turned to me. "Can you do that? Behave?"

I blinked. "Can *I*?" I asked, pointing at myself. "Of course. Can *you*?"

Conveniently not answering my question, he flopped back onto the couch. "It's settled then." He dropped a paper on my lap. "Was this supposed to be with the others?"

I glanced at the document and groaned before aggressively tossing it across the room where it landed, instead, at our feet. I was never good at throwing paper airplanes or frisbees either.

"Gerrit Cole you're not. He's a—"

I finished the sentence. "Pitcher."

Jude laughed. "Did you memorize the Yankees roster to impress your ex or something?"

"Or something," I said with a snort. "I've been following the sport since I was a kid."

"Ah, yes. You came to a lot of the games, but I assumed it was to watch the boys." He waggled his eyebrows. "Seth had quite the curveball."

"It was not for the boys!" Under my dad's tutelage, I'd watched every season of professional baseball since grade school. I'd also attended all the games in high school until Jude's accident. Seeing our classmate Matty Torres in what used to be Jude's position at first base would have been a painful reminder that when I failed to think through my decisions, people got hurt. I shifted my position on the couch. *No regrets.* "Anyway…"

Jude picked the paper off the floor and read out loud. "Tips for reaching out to potential applicants. Lead with a personal greeting. Make them feel special by complimenting their résumé and solid experience. Mention exclusive opportunities and openings available only through us. Promise to connect them to law firms with sign-on bonuses, generous lifestyle concessions, and fast partnership tracks. Keep it low pressure by asking them to refer others who might be qualified and seeking employment." He looked up. "What about this makes you want to toss it across the room? Emphasis on the *want to*," he added with a chuckle.

I slouched against the couch cushion. "Cold-calling people makes me feel gross."

Jude narrowed his eyes. "Isn't that your job?"

I gave a noncommittal shrug. "I feel guilty sometimes."

"Again…it's your job."

"Stop it with the eye rolls," I said, pointing at his face. "My company works for the law firms and corporations, not the individuals. I hate the idea of approaching someone who's happy in their present position to dangle another one…a potentially worse one…in their face only for them to take it and wind up miserable when they didn't want to quit in the first place!" I shuddered at the scenario.

I was aware of my privilege and understood that not everyone in need of a job could afford to be picky, but I couldn't turn off the desire to connect the right person to the *right* job—not just *any* job. "Obviously, cold-calling candidates is one of my responsibilities, but my manager's practices don't always sit well with me." I told him about Michael's "pep talk" and the Triple-A method.

Jude sighed. "You're not forcing people to interview, Mole. They have free will and can say no. Michael sounds like an asshole, but who says you have to listen to him? What he doesn't know can't get you in trouble. I'm well aware you have a latent rebellious streak. Just pretend you're dealing with me." He smiled sheepishly.

"Hmmm." As always, Jude made things sound so simple, but I packed it away to consider later. "Will you call George or shall I?" *Meeting adjourned.*

"I shall," he parroted.

This time *my* eyes rolled.

"Speaking of George, most people say their favorite Beatle is George, John, Paul, or Ringo, but I like Pete best."

I froze in confusion. "You've lost..." *Oh.* I burst out laughing. "Oh, my God. You are such a massive dork! How were you so popular in high school?"

Jude shrugged, biting back a grin. "Just because you can't appreciate a good Beatles pun doesn't make me a dork."

"If you say so." If we continued this dialogue, my rolling eyes might get stuck in the back of my head like my parents warned me back in the day.

We stood and said, "Where's Yogi?" at the same time.

We quickly determined he wasn't in the living room or kitchen, hiding under a chair, or behind a bookcase.

Our next stop was my pint-sized bedroom.

Jude studied the room—the bed, the blue stained-wood

nightstand, space-saving wall-mounted sconces, built-in book-shelves, *the bed*. Why did my face feel so hot all of a sudden? *Get a grip, Molly. It's a bed, for heaven's sake.*

"It's a good thing my parents haven't seen this room or they'd compare it to mine. It would be 2010 all over again," Jude said.

I lifted my bright floral-printed comforter and checked under the queen-size bed, happy for an excuse to hide the weird flush on my cheeks, confirmed by a glance in the mirror hanging on my door. "Yogi?" I rose to a standing position. "Not here."

Which left the bathroom. "Mystery solved," I said, spotting the dog's wagging curl tail at the foot of the cabinet. Completely oblivious to our search mission, he didn't even look up when we entered the room.

"Time to go, Yogi." Jude stopped short. "What the…"

At Yogi's feet was a colorful array of rubber and plastic bands, scrunchies, headbands, and tie clips. I threw my hand against my mouth.

"Maybe I should have named him RuPaul." Jude laughed, then turned to me and grimaced. "I swear I didn't put him up to any shenanigans."

"He takes after his daddy, I guess." I bent to pet him. "Lucky for him he's so cute." I glanced over my shoulder at Jude. When our eyes locked, my heart raced stupidly. I turned away and slowly stood. We silently walked to my front door with Yogi leading the way.

"I'll text you after I speak to George."

As the mistrust crept in, I opened my mouth to request assurances.

Jude put a finger to my lips.

My breath caught.

"I promise not to fuck with you." He removed his finger.

I swallowed hard. "Can you blame me for being skeptical?" The words came out choppy.

Jude's lips split into a crooked, knowing grin. "Not at all."

We stared at each other unblinking until Yogi broke the silence with a yip. Jude cleared his throat. "Later, Mole."

"Bye, Rude." I closed the door behind me and exhaled. As far as face-to-face dealings with Jude went, it could have been worse... *so* much worse.

And I hoped the humidity would hold up, because I was all out of hair bands.

Chapter Ten

Two days later, I was on my first date with Timothy. Rather, we were both at Tuttles, where I nursed a glass of rosé and he poured drinks behind the bar. He'd asked if I preferred to wait until we were both available for a *real* first date, but I was happy to drink for free while watching him work. Besides, it was a slow Monday night, and so far, he'd had plenty of time to talk to me.

He'd just told me how he worked as a barback/bartender at Tuttles part-time while securing a certificate at the Institute of Culinary Education.

I beamed at him. "I love that about New York City—so many people pursuing passions outside of their day jobs. The struggling waiter-slash-actor, uninspired lawyer-slash-novelist, mysterious bartender-slash-chef."

"Mysterious, huh?" He raised an eyebrow. "Is that the same as sexy?"

I ran a finger along the stem of my wineglass. "For sure."

We both turned our heads toward the flat-screen on the wall as a commercial for the new Marvel movie came on.

Timothy looked back at me and pointed to the screen. "You a fan?"

I nodded. "A fan, but not a fanatic. I love the Avengers franchise, but haven't watched all the separate movies."

"Who's your favorite character in the Marvel universe?"

"Hmmm. Thor? Storm? I don't really have one. You?"

Without hesitation, he said, "Groot."

I froze with my wineglass halfway to my mouth at the second mention of this character in three days. What a strange coincidence.

"Especially teenage Groot," Timothy continued. "All that angst. I was Groot. We were all Groot." He drummed the fingers of both hands along the bar. The movements were hypnotizing and somehow familiar.

Before I could reflect further, the front door of the venue opened, and a gaggle of thirsty customers made their way to the bar.

Timothy shrugged apologetically. "Duty calls."

I shooed him away. "No worries." My phone pinged a text from Esther asking what I was up to. I wrote back I was out with Timothy.

> **Molly:** Well, I'm not really out
> WITH him, but we're both here.

Her response came immediately.

> **Esther:** Sounds dodgy.

I laughed.

> **Molly:** It's not. He's working, but it's not crowded so he can hang out with me.

Across the bar, Timothy was busy making drinks for people who weren't me.

> **Molly:** Except right now. I'm bored.

One could only appreciate how well her date's ass fit into his brown cargo shorts for so long.

> **Esther:** Don't be bored. Talk to me.

My phone rang—Esther.

"Hey. Give me a second." I waved until I got Timothy's attention, then pointed toward the exit with my phone. "What's up?" I said once outside.

"You like this guy?"

"He's cute, has an even cuter dog, and I'm drinking for free. It's enough for now."

"I'm sure he'd be thrilled to know he ranks second to his dog," she said dryly.

"He's a goldendoodle and precious." I'd only seen Eli the one time so far, but could easily picture his cute wet nose and soft brown eyes partially hidden under curly peach-colored fur.

"Another goldendoodle?"

"Huh?" I paced the narrow sidewalk in front of the bar as pedestrians passed me in both directions.

"Didn't you say the best thing about Jude is his golden?"

I stopped in place. "Oh, right." Yogi was also a golden-doodle. "Ha! Small world. But don't wreck my buzz with Jude talk." The meeting at my apartment had gone surprisingly well, but it didn't erase almost a lifetime of hostility. I was afraid to trust our newfound peace. "What's going on with you?"

"I'm off to Connecticut."

"Again? That's so nice of you." It had only been a few weeks since the last time she had visited her uncle and the twins.

"It's also an excuse to avoid Killian."

My muscles tensed. "Is he still bothering you?" Esther had dated Killian off and on in college—"off" when he wanted to fuck someone else and "on" the rest of the time. He was a prince in his own mind because at least he never cheated. They'd recently run into each other at the Dunkin Donuts in our neighborhood, and she hadn't been able to lose him since.

"I told him I wasn't interested in dating him again, but he insists it would be as friends. Even suggested we go out in a group. I'm not sure it's a good idea."

I twirled a hair around my finger. "Because it's not." Esther was badass, but Killian had been her Achilles heel, and I didn't want her to revert. "Can you block him?"

"It's a bit premature for such drastic measures. At least while I'm in Connecticut, I have a built-in excuse to say no. Hopefully, he'll get the hint and lose interest when he realizes he can't bench me anymore."

"While you're away, I'll—"

"Check on Poppy, I know. And thanks."

"What are friends for?" I peeked through the window and caught Timothy's eye. He waved. "I should go back inside the bar. But call if you need me!"

"Will do. Enjoy your date. Make sure he wears a French letter."

I laughed. The British lingo for "wear a condom" was certainly more cryptic than *cover your stump before you hump* and *no glove, no love.* "Bye!" We ended the call, and I went back inside, just as a familiar tune played out of the speakers.

Timothy drummed his fingers against the bar to the beat of the song: "Ob-La-Di, Ob-La-Da."

"You like the Beatles?" I shouldn't have been surprised given he'd referenced Molly Jones at the bagel place, but I was. You rarely heard their music in bars catering to people my age. My dad and Mr. Stark had played their vinyls at most of our family parties growing up, which was how I'd soaked up my knowledge.

Timothy nodded assuredly. "I'm obsessed with buying Beatles albums. My friends say I need help, but I have that one already." He halted his drumming in dramatic fashion and grinned.

It took me a moment, then I snorted. "Hilarious."

"I had tons of Beatles puns, but that was yesterday. Now they're hard to get back."

I pressed a fist against my lips and laughed.

We continued to exchange witty banter until closing. At one point, it was so quiet, we played jacks with peanuts. Later, he walked me to my lobby. He kissed me, and he kissed me well.

I wasn't ready to take things to the next level, but I practically floated all the way to my apartment.

There was just something familiar about Timothy. I couldn't pinpoint why, but it was almost like I'd known him my whole life.

Chapter Eleven

Despite Jude's multiple assurances there would be no more antics, I had my guard up before our second meeting at Society Cafe. He had shifts at Hillstone most evenings, so I skipped out of work during my lunch hour later that week. I half expected to arrive at the venue to find it empty aside from a skeletal staff setting up for dinner or a lone patron having a midafternoon drink at the bar. I was already planning my revenge as I approached the entrance. When I heard someone call my name from behind me, I was caught off guard and tripped, nearly losing my balance. *Cha Cha Real Smooth, Molly.* I turned around and hoped Jude hadn't witnessed my literal false step.

He wore relaxed-fit blue jeans, an olive-green crew-neck t-shirt, and a twinkle in his eyes. He clapped. "It takes skill to trip over a flat surface. You're not there yet, but practice makes perfect."

I glowered. "I wasn't expecting you."

He raised an eyebrow. "Why not? Our appointment's in five minutes." Handing me a CVS bag, he said, "This is from Yogi."

I looped my index finger through the plastic handles and extended my arm as far from my torso as it would go. What if I was holding a bag of dog shit? Or a bomb?

"It won't blow up."

Easy for him to say. I harrumphed but opened the bag. Inside were Goody Ouchless elastic hair ties, Conair Scünci no-slip jaw clips, and butterfly hair barrettes. My jaw dropped.

Jude shrugged. "Yogi says sorry for eating all your hair shit."

I willed my mouth to work and managed to squeak out, "Did he really?"

Pink dotted his cheeks. "Not at all. I picked those up on the way here because if I brought them home first, he'd seize them for his kingdom."

"Th...thank you, but it was totally unnecessary." For one thing, I never wore jaw clips or barrettes, and second of all...who was this guy and what was happening here?

"It was the right thing to do." He jutted his chin toward the restaurant. "We should go."

Momentarily entranced, in a way I refused to analyze, by the barely visible chest hair peeking through the over-stretched neck of his shirt, I nodded absently and tucked the bag into my purse. Then I followed him inside while mentally readying myself for the meeting. It was time to lock this shit down. I could wrap my head around the alien who had taken over Jude's body later. And I might wear the barrettes because...butterflies. But for now...party.

George was ready for us, and even though Jude wanted to pretend the last meeting never happened, I couldn't do it. I looked George in the eyes and apologized for our immature behavior. "We were really impressed with this space and hope you won't hold our prior antics against us."

"There's nothing to forgive. In fact, I don't remember any prior antics." George followed up the statement with a facial expression worthy of an Oscar award for worst performance by someone with no memory of our antics.

Behind his back, Jude mouthed, "Told you so" while rubbing his thumb and index finger together in the "money" gesture.

I bit back a laugh. But seriously... who *was* this guy and where was the real Jude?

George led us into the private room where the party would be held.

My eyes swept over the shiny medium-brown wood floors, bronze ceiling and chandeliers, working fireplace, wine cellarettes, and pops of greenery. "It's perfect," I whispered. If rustic and elegance had a baby, it would look like this.

"Do you have a special wine selection for parties or can we choose à la carte?" Jude asked.

Partnering with Jude made my prepared list of questions useless, so while he went over the liquor options with George, I half-listened while reading a text from Timothy asking when I wanted to go out again. Then Jude dropped a comment about being a certified sommelier and I nearly dropped my phone. I'd had no idea. I responded, "As soon as possible" to Timothy and closed out of my texts.

"For sparkling, would you rather go with Champagne or cava? We also have prosecco," George said.

"What's the difference?" The room grew silent like a proverbial record had scratched. My neck grew warm. "Sorry?"

George smiled kindly. "It's a common question. All three are sparkling wines, but Champagne is only made in the Champagne region of France, cava is made in Spain, and prosecco is made in Italy. There are also differences between the three in flavor and bubbles and even within each category."

"Thank you!" You learned something new every day.

Jude coughed into his hand. "Ignorant."

I jutted a hip. "Excuse me for not being a *sommelier* like *some* people. Do *you* know the difference between a patent, trademark, and copyright? Didn't think so." Despite my sharp retort, I was smiling on the inside. Mean Jude was back, and I could handle him. It was the Jude bearing gifts and uttering apologies who rattled me.

After we told George he had our votes and we would circle back once we ran it past our siblings, we said our goodbyes and headed outside.

"Damn, it's humid." I raised and lowered my elbows to air out my sweaty pits.

"Do you always do the chicken dance when it's hot? Is that your thing?" He mimicked my "dance" moves.

"Fuck off." My multicolored plaid dress was adorable. It was also polyester—a hot-weather "don't."

Jude chuckled. "Let's grab a beer and text the others. We can watch the Yankees. There's a day game today, and you've been following the sport since you were a kid, right?" He raised his eyebrows.

"Some of us have to work."

"I promise you'll be back at your desk in plenty of time to lure happy people into taking horrible jobs."

My stomach clenched. "A beer would be good."

Johnny's Bar was a tiny neighborhood dive that smelled of sour beer and possibly mold, but a four-dollar pint of Rolling Rock probably tasted the same no matter where you drank it. "I love these zebra-printed stools." Unfortunately, cute didn't mean comfortable, and I wiggled my butt from side to side for the perfect fit.

Jude looked up from his phone and caught me mid-wiggle. "You would."

My phone pinged. It was a group text from Jude to our siblings laying out the details for holding the party at Society Cafe. The last sentence read:

> **Jude:** Mole and I agree we should have it there.

Reading the words "Mole and I agree" was almost as weird as the actual agreeing part. Keeping those thoughts to myself, I said, "I didn't even see you typing that."

"I'm stealthy." He took a sip of beer and watched the game on the flat-screen television above our heads.

Back-to-back texts came in from Alison and Michelle.

> **Alison:** It works for me. And by the way, Molly and you agree? Isn't that something?
>
> **Michelle:** You two agree? I'm dead. DEAD.

I choked on my beer.

Jude gave me a quick glance before dropping his gaze back to his phone. A moment later, another text landed.

> **Jude:** We also agree that you guys are annoying as fuck.

I chuckled.

Another text popped up.

> **Nicole:** It's a miracle! Eddie and I will review this information and get back to you.

Jude grunted. "Your sister."

"The same sister you crushed on hard in junior high." Jude would call me a troll while simultaneously drooling over Nicole, who looked exactly like me aside from being two inches shorter with a slightly rounder face.

"Don't project your crush on my brother with my imaginary crush on your sister."

After he said the words, I watched as a film of red crept up his neck onto his cheeks and he pressed a fist to his lips in the inception of laughter. *Uh oh.* Where was he going with this?

"You told everyone that Eddie was your brother..." His shoulders shook. "*And* how much you wanted to kiss him." He wiped his eyes.

"And *you* told everyone I had a fetish for incest." Jude was always there to take my most embarrassing moments to the next level.

Jude howled. "I totally forgot about that."

I mumbled, "That makes one of us." I was done *reminiscing* with Jude but wasn't about to leave an unfinished drink on the bar. While he watched the game, I scrolled through Instagram. It was the usual content—pictures of my friends' pets and lunches, celebrity selfies, and witty/uplifting quotes/memes. And, of course, advertisements from Etsy, Friendship Cottage Cheese, and Ceiling Crashers. Wait. What was Ceiling Crashers? I froze with my thumb on the screen then did something I almost never did with ads: I clicked "Learn More."

"Mole!"

I jolted. "What?"

"I was talking to you. What has you so mesmerized?" Jude held up a hand. "Never mind. If it's a dick pic, I don't want to know."

I screwed up my face. "It's not a dick pic. It's nothing."

"Bullshit." He removed the phone from my hand and looked at the screen. "Ceiling Crashers. Never heard of them before."

"Until I was today years old, I hadn't either. They're a career counseling and coaching company for women."

"And you find them fascinating, why exactly?"

"When did I say I found them fascinating?" I said, even as my fingers itched to regain possession of the phone because I was... well, fascinated.

Jude studied me intently.

I frowned. "Do I have something on my face?"

His eyes moved from my forehead down to my chin and back up again. "Two eyes—check, nose—check, mouth—check, mole—check."

My hand flew to my cheek. Then it sank in. "When will I ever learn?"

Jude flashed a crooked grin. "If history is any indication, never." His face turned serious. "Why did you really quit the law?" He coughed. "The *practice* of law?"

Not this again. "Why do you care so much?" I gestured toward the television. "The game is on."

Ignoring the game, he said, "I don't care. It's just..." He

shrugged. "You studied so hard in high school. I assume that same work ethic followed you to college and law school. You had all these *plans*."

I squirmed, still not quite comfortable with the reality that the calculated course of my professional life had changed so drastically. Jude didn't need to know this. "Sometimes plans are forced to change based on the circumstances. You of all people know that." I was fairly certain *his* plans had involved studying baseball strategy, not wine and food pairings, until that option was taken away. I stared down at my feet. *And whose fault was that?* But he'd said so himself: no regrets.

"We're not talking about me."

I considered his question. Answering honestly was the least I could do to make up for putting my foot in my mouth. "The law firm environment was too hostile for me. Between the pressure of billable hours from the firm and unreasonable expectations from clients, I woke up sick every morning." I took a sip of my beer. "And I had an abusive client."

Jude's eyebrows pinched together. "Abusive how?"

I swallowed hard, not sure I wanted to dredge up the bad memories and share them with Jude of all people. What if he sided with Maxine and accused me of being a crybaby? But there was no twinkle in his eye or any indication he was itching for material to use against me. "So many things. She regularly questioned or criticized my work in front of my supervising attorneys, even when they weren't already on the email string. She refused to let our paralegals touch her work, then complained my billing rate was too high. The next day, she'd charge me with an assignment so beyond my experience level, because she didn't want to pay for a senior associate or junior partner's work, then complain when I didn't finish it in ten minutes."

Jude made a sound from the back of his throat. "Damn."

"And the thing is, I did everything she wanted, the way she wanted it done, but she would change her mind with no warning and then complain that I wasn't a mind reader." I wiggled a finger at Jude. "Trust me. I worked my ass off to anticipate her needs."

Jude nodded. "No doubt."

Moved by his certainty, I continued. "It wasn't repeating the work that bothered me—shit happens—but her refusal to ever take ownership of anything maddened me. She gaslighted the hell out of me until I wondered if maybe I *did* misunderstand her and it *was* my fault, or maybe as a first-year associate, I *should* have been more comfortable with partner-level work."

I gripped my glass. Shielding my candidates from people like Maxine was why I so painstakingly researched work environments before setting up interviews. I downed my beer and wiped my mouth. "The worst part was everyone knew it was her issue, not mine. They all thought she was a monster. But it didn't matter, because she was the client and I had to bend over and take it up the ass if that's what she wanted."

Jude's eyebrows shot up and his eyes danced.

"Metaphorically!"

His lips twitched.

"Even if I switched law firms, there would always be another Maxine, and if I ever wanted to make partner, I'd be expected to pick up more clients, even nasty ones like her. And sure, I could move in-house to the legal department of a corporation and *be* Maxine...only with a heart...but I kind of hated being a lawyer." I took a deep breath. "And now I'm babbling."

Jude pointed at my phone. "Maybe you should work for Ceiling Crashers."

"And switch careers again?" I scoffed.

He scoffed back. "Why not? You did it once. And career coaching is similar to recruiting, right?"

"Adjacent, but different." I knew little about coaching, but I imagined it was everything I loved about recruiting without the politics or questionably skeevy practices of those who applied the Triple-A method. *Cough...Michael.* I gave an indifferent shrug. What did I know?

"It doesn't matter, because I already have a job." I glanced at my phone. "One I need to get back to." I had a few things to finish up in the office and would then continue my work from home. I'd started doing my due diligence again, only from my personal computer and on my own time, and was already sleeping better as a result. Hopefully, the handful of interviews I'd set up while pretending to be a "team player" was enough to satisfy Michael for now.

I stood and dropped a twenty on the bar. "There's enough here for another beer. Enjoy, and don't say I never gave you anything."

As I pushed the door open and stepped into the sun, I heard him say, "You've given me a headache my entire life, Blum."

Chapter Twelve

A week later, ten of us sat around a large conference table, Michael at the head, for our weekly meeting in one of the company's boardrooms. I was sandwiched between my colleague Cindy on one side and one of the male directors, Pranav, on the other. Michael had spent the last fifteen minutes repeating his mantra to collect as many résumés as possible, cast them out to a wide net of clients—who should be touted as the "Shangri La" of firms—and whenever possible, encourage candidates to take the highest-paying job in order to make the highest commission.

His greasy practices left me itchy all over, like an army of ants was using my body as a battlefield. Why he had left the practice of law—and a firm famous for hiring sharks out for blood—was a mystery.

"Before we go, I'd like to call out one of your team members as an example of what can happen when you listen to critical feedback, take it in, and apply it. Let's hear it for Molly." Michael smiled in my direction. "Since my pep talk earlier this month, Molly doubled her productivity, and just yesterday, one of our corporate clients extended a job offer to her second-year associate candidate." He clapped, urging the others to join in.

As heads spun my way, some from the left, a few from the right, others straight on, I resisted the urge to use my long hair as a curtain for my burning face. I prayed they wouldn't break out into "For She's a Jolly Good Fellow."

"Nice going, Molly!" Pranav said, with a thumbs-up.

I forced a smile at those around the table. "Thank you, everyone!" I had no objection to being called out for "good behavior," but it was awkward and unnecessary. I suspected Michael was more interested in feeding his own ego than mine. Little did he know my increased productivity had nothing to do with his "pep talk." It was purely coincidental.

"That's all for this week. Happy recruiting," Michael said.

Everyone gathered their water bottles, notepads, and phones and stood to go.

"Molly?"

I groaned inwardly, but pivoted to face Michael, who was leaning against the edge of the table, his gray dress pants and matching sweater blending almost perfectly with the room's carpeting.

"You have a minute?"

"Sure."

"I wanted to congratulate you again on your deal. That makes two this month. I see you're employing the Triple-A method!" He lifted his chin, pleased with himself.

"I am." I left out the word "not." *I am not.* I'd found this candidate, Anna, by running a list of junior associates from Manhattan's biggest law firms notorious for overworking their attorneys. Many lawyers straight out of law school coveted positions in Big Law for the money and prestige, but after a year or two grew unsatisfied and depleted and longed to make the move in-house. I hit the jackpot with Anna, who was tired of the long hours, high billing quotas, and low-level mundane tasks. I'd found a way to seek out only those candidates likely to be unhappy in their present positions. I also searched for dirt on the corporation from the comfort of my couch at home. Both practices were decidedly anti-Triple-A.

"Keep it up and I'll put in a good word for a promotion to director at year end. No guarantees since you haven't been a legal recruiter for very long, but it will get you on their radar."

I widened my eyes. "Wow. Thanks." A promotion to director now was four years ahead of my five-year plan. For an oily guy, Michael was supportive—as long as you did things his way. I hoped he wouldn't try to make me his apprentice. I shuddered at the thought.

"Cha-ching!" His blue eyes danced.

Right. With a promotion came a higher rate of commission. *Focus on the positive.*

Checking his watch, he said, "Gotta bounce."

On my way back to my office, I stopped by Cindy's. She was arguably my closest work friend, despite our nearly twenty-year age difference. We'd met on my first day a year earlier when she'd been assigned by Jill to take me out to lunch, and she'd become a mentor of sorts. Although we worked very differently, we talked shop and compared notes often.

I knocked twice on her open door.

She looked up, brushed a golden curl away from her forehead, and grinned. "Molly. The prodigal recruiter!"

"Go me!"

"You happy?"

With that simple question, my smile flattened, and my belly

tangled with knots. Happy wasn't the word I'd use. Sneaky was more accurate. But I saw nothing wrong with using the resources at my disposal to uncover anything unpleasant and possibly harmful at a place of employment. Obviously there was no way to know for sure without a crystal ball, but I had to try. In my opinion, it was neglectful not to. I just resented being forced to go undercover to do it. Because I couldn't tell Cindy I was going behind Michael's back, I forced my lips to curl back up and gave the only acceptable answer. "I am *so* happy!"

Back at my desk, I had one thing on my mind, and it wasn't a potential promotion. I typed **Ceiling C** into Google on my phone. Before I even finished spelling out the full company name, the dropdown read my mind—both convenient and terrifying—and offered several options:

Ceiling Crashers
Ceiling Crashers Rosaria Martin
Ceiling Crashers Instagram

I clicked on the first link, which brought me to the company website. In a nutshell, their mission was to help cis and trans women set and meet career and business goals, whether finding a job at someone else's company or forming their own. They offered different ranges of coaching so that cost wouldn't be a barrier to women who couldn't otherwise afford the assistance. Rosaria Martin, the founder, spent a decade climbing the corporate ladder because it was part of her life plan, but career fulfillment had eluded her until she realized her passion was to help *other* women find *their* passion. Her story touched a personal nerve, and my interest was piqued.

I switched to the home page, where right at the top was an announcement of a talk she was giving about the club and its membership at the 92nd Street Y the following night. What were the chances? My second date with Timothy was later in the week, and I had no other conflicts. It had to be a sign.

I wanted to meet Rosaria Martin…pick her brain for tips and tricks for gleaning a candidate's true workplace desires and helping them find the perfect employer match. Placing the phone facedown on my desk, I spun around in my chair. The nerves in my stomach tightened with stress.

Was it too much? Doing some research from my home computer behind Michael's back was one thing, but initiating a relationship with a career coach who took my personal mission to a whole new level was…I assumed the first adjective that would spring to mind would be "defiant" or "insubordinate" and accompanied by the familiar sting of apprehension. Instead, it was what my nani would call *bershert*. In other words, meeting Rosaria Martin felt inevitable. Without thinking, I stopped spinning, resumed hold of my phone, and sent a text.

Molly: So…Ceiling Crashers?

I buried my face in my hands. *Jude? Really? Why?* Was there a way to recall texts?

Ping.

Jude: ??? Sentences are supposed to have a subject AND predicate.

I had known he'd throw shade and reached out anyway because he was next to me when I first discovered the company's existence. Asking Esther, or even Timothy, would have required a full recap. Jude's response was to be expected, but I'd come this far. Jude was, after all, the reason I decided to continue my pre-interview vetting process without Michael's knowledge. What he'd said in my apartment had sunk in. Of course, I'd never feed his ego by telling him so. But if anyone would applaud this mission, it would be him. Although he'd never be quite so direct about it either.

> **Molly:** The founder is giving a talk tomorrow night. I'm debating going.

I chewed a knuckle while I waited for his reply.

> **Jude:** We've completed our mission. Your nights are free to do what you want.

I cringed. I had no business asking for his validation like a thirsty cream puff. I was hit by a fuzzy memory of long, long ago, before I'd accepted that Jude was my enemy. In the early years of elementary school, I'd tried everything to regain his approval, whether it was taking my first jump off the high dive at the town pool despite fear I'd crack my skull or getting a home run at kickball during recess. But that was then, and this was now. We were on a break from our rivalry, but we weren't friends. And I didn't need his or anyone else's permission anyway.

He was right, though. After *consulting* with Eddie, Nicole had authorized us to finalize the reservation for the anniversary party at Society Cafe, which meant my evenings were free to do what I wanted again, even if that included attending a seminar hosted by a woman who inspired me. I wasn't the only one who stood to benefit from the connection. If any of her members were interested in the legal field, I could be a trusted contact...someone who would always have her client's best interests at heart. I stared at the framed quote from Ruth Bader Ginsburg hanging above my desk: "Women belong in all places decisions are being made." *Damn straight.*

With a little help from RBG, my own decision had been made. I slipped my phone into my purse as another text came through. With an exasperated sigh I pulled the device back out and read the message.

> **Jude:** Most people regret what they DON'T do more than what they do. In other words, what have you got to lose?

I smiled as the remaining tension left my body and I completed the registration.

Chapter Thirteen

The following night, my attention was riveted on the stage as Rosaria Martin, who looked to be in her mid to late thirties, spoke to the crowd about Ceiling Crashers.

"With a little push and some encouragement from me and my team, each of you has the potential to forge your own career path." Rosaria's eyes sparkled with passion as she scanned the crowd. "Whether through résumé building, practice with interviewing, questionnaires designed to help pinpoint your interests, and more, we can help you. I offer both online seminars, where I share my proven plan in simple steps, as well as one-on-one opportunities for those who want more intensive coaching."

From my seat at one of the banquet tables, I tore my eyes away from Rosaria on the small stage of the Warburg Lounge at the 92nd Street Y and gauged the reaction of the approximately one hundred other women in attendance. They appeared to be equally captivated. I guessed most of the women, who ranged in age from twentysomething, like me, to late fifties, were either current or prospective members of Ceiling Crashers.

Rosaria concluded her speech by inviting us to join her online community to get started. "Thank you all so much for coming. I'll stick around for a few minutes in case anyone has questions."

After a rowdy round of applause, there was a scramble to the podium. In no rush, I took my time, simultaneously checking my emails, returning texts from Esther and Nicole, and listening to what those ahead of me in line said to Rosaria. A few asked for more specifics about the various membership tiers. Unsurprisingly, I was the only recruiter. A few minutes later, I was at the front, eye-to-chin with Rosaria—the woman had height.

"Your speech was so inspiring," I said, with complete sincerity. She'd described the anxiety of her first career as a financial analyst for a global consulting firm—the lack of personal fulfillment, pressure to perform, and near constant ache in her gut—and how she was unable to enjoy her weekends knowing that Monday morning was looming. It was all so relatable! When her health and personal life suffered as a result, she finally stepped off the path she was on and worked with a coach to forge a new road, ultimately launching her own coaching company.

Rosaria smiled warmly. "I'm so glad to hear that. I hope you'll consider joining the community."

I licked my lips. "When you spoke of turning your passion into a career? The thing is...what *you* do is my passion."

She cocked her head of silky honey brown hair.

I took it as a silent urge to continue. "I'm not looking to join the community. I'm actually a legal recruiter, but I take a very personal approach with my candidates. I'm sure you're really busy, but I'd love to take you to lunch one day and pick your brain. Your questionnaires, especially, speak to me."

I'd already jotted down a few questions in the notes app on my phone to include in my own questionnaire: *What sounds better to you: working extra hours each week for more money to spend at holiday time or getting home to eat dinner with your family at six? Do you prefer working independently or a more collaborative approach?* Presently, I asked these questions during my interviews, but it would be more efficient to have candidates answer them in advance. They might be more honest with more time and without me sitting across from them.

Rosaria's mouth opened, but I kept going before she could shoot me down. "Although you obviously work within a broader range of careers"—her alumni included CEOs, teachers, florists, flight attendants, and more—"and mine is limited to legal work, my strategy is very focused on job satisfaction and matching employee to employer to the optimal satisfaction of both parties. My manager says I'm supposed to focus on employer needs first, and he's correct on one level, but it's not enough for me."

Realizing I was meandering, I changed direction. "Although there isn't total overlap between what we do, I genuinely think I can learn from you, if you can spare the time and are willing, of course. I have thoughts on Ceiling Crashers as well, assuming you have any desire to hear them."

I'd spent two hours the night before reading everything I could about the company. I came up with a two-page list of marketing suggestions designed to expand their reach. I would never offer advice unsolicited, but if I was going to ask Rosaria for hers, it was only fair to have something to give in exchange besides a free lunch. The truth was, once I started scrolling their IG feeds, I didn't stop until I'd read all five thousand posts.

Rosaria glanced over my shoulder and held up a finger.

I turned around and saw there were more women waiting.

I adjusted the strap of my purse. "I don't mean to monopolize your time. I just... I'm super inspired by you and your company and—"

She handed me her business card. "Call me tomorrow. We'll set something up."

My eyes widened. "Really?" I'd planned a backup argument in case the first one failed to convince her.

She laughed. "It's always nice to talk to someone like-minded. And my interest is piqued over these ideas of yours."

Happiness bubbled up inside me. "Tomorrow. Thank you!"

I headed toward the exit, stepped outside, and bounced up and down in excitement. I hadn't been this exhilarated about my job since before my first one-on-one with Michael more than a month earlier.

I was dying to tell someone. Unfortunately, the only *one* who knew about Ceiling Crashers was Jude, and he'd probably ping back a snarky retort like, "Is there a reason you're telling me this?" Or "Get some friends, Mole." A safer recipient of my good news would be Esther or even Timothy, who I barely knew yet... just about anyone other than Jude. But I lacked the patience to go through the entire story. I wanted to race right to the ending, and only Jude knew the beginning. That was, for sure, the only reason. *Oh, what the hell.*

> **Molly:** I went to the seminar and I don't regret it!

Send.

I chewed my lip and kept writing.

> **Molly:** You're probably drafting a clever way to insult me right now. But I'm too high on life to care.

I dropped the phone in my bag. It didn't matter how he responded...*if* he responded. He was just a vessel through which to express my delight. Done.

I removed my phone, not quite as done as I thought, and sent another text.

> **Molly:** That message was for Yogi btw.

On the subway downtown, I listened to Rosaria's latest podcast. *Maybe* I'll *do a podcast one day.*

A text came in as we reached my stop at Grand Central/ 42nd Street.

It was from Jude: a photo of Yogi wearing a doggie t-shirt with the words "Too glam to give a damn" with a pile of hairbands at his front feet.

Chapter Fourteen

> **Molly:** I snagged the last two seats at the bar!

I sat on one, plopped my purse on the other to reserve for Esther, and grinned at a bunch of strangers with a mixture of guilt and satisfaction. The bar scene at Hillstone was notoriously crowded, and scoring even one barstool was a coup.

> **Esther:** Almost there. Still in a wee bit of shock you chose Hillstone.

My lips uncurled. It was true I typically avoided the restaurant given its star bartender—Jude. But like I'd told Esther, they had the best sushi in town, poured a generous glass of wine, and Jude and I were getting along better than we had since we both wore topless bathing suits. Being around him didn't fill me with dread like it used to. I wasn't sure how I felt about that, but the sushi *was* delicious. Speaking of Jude, I spotted him halfway down the circular bar. He was leaning over to talk—I blinked—make that *kiss* a customer. I dropped my eyes to the menu the other bartender had placed in front of me along with a glass of water. *Professional, Jude. Real professional.*

A few minutes later, someone tapped my shoulder, and I turned around and smiled at Esther. Patting the empty stool next to me, I said, "I had to basically stalk a couple as they finished their drinks, and I had a showdown with *him*." I motioned to a man standing behind the bar a few feet away who was glaring in our direction. *You snooze, you lose.* If he hadn't stepped on my foot in his rush to claim it for himself and refused to apologize, I might have let him have the second stool, but his aggression overrode my impulse to share. "Scrappy, right?" I noted the ruddiness of Esther's normally fair skin. "Did you stop at a tanning booth on the way over?"

"Not quite." She snorted. "Funniest thing. When I got here, I thought I saw you face smashing the bartender and ran right over to see what had gotten into my best friend. Besides the bartender's tongue. Less funny is that now I'm sweating like cheddar at a desert buffet and it wasn't even you." She swiped her brow.

My eyes bugged out. "Of course it wasn't me! The bartender in question is Jude and his tongue was in *her* mouth, not mine," I said, pointing to the girl who *had* been kissing him. I was legit shocked the mere *suggestion* of Jude's tongue in my mouth didn't make me dry heave.

"I realize that now, but...wow." She whistled. "She looks exactly like you from far away."

"Yes, because all brown-haired and blue-eyed women look the same." I checked Esther from head to toe. "Are you planning to sit, because the very bitter man over there would gladly take your seat."

"Fine. Fine." She sat and hung her black Baggu purse with mine on the hook under the bar.

Jude appeared with his trademark smug expression. "What brings Mole Blum to my bar?"

I feigned confusion. "But the name on the menu is Hillstone, not Rude's Bar."

His lips tugged up on one side before he glanced between me and Esther. "What can I get you two?"

After we ordered a glass of Pinot Noir for me and a *very* dirty martini for Esther, Jude leaned his elbows on the bar. "Celebrating your new career?"

"It's not a new career. It's a new connection to put more pep in my existing one." I bit back a smile. "That said, Rosaria is away on a regional tour, but we set up a lunch date for when she gets back." It had been a week since I'd attended her seminar.

"*Rosaria*. First-name basis and everything." He winked. "I'll be right back with your drinks."

"He's quite cute," Esther said when he was a safe distance away.

I took a sip of water. "Who? Jude?"

"Yes."

"She thinks so too." I motioned with my chin at the blue-eyed brunette tracking Jude's every move.

"You mean your twin?"

"She's not . . ." I lowered my voice as Jude entered our earshot to serve the group of guys next to us. "We look nothing alike."

"Um hmmm." Esther angled her body toward mine. "How's *your* bartender?"

"My what? Oh, Timothy! I wouldn't say he's *mine*, although I do like him." We'd only seen each other once since our first "date" at Tuttles, but he was very easy to be with. "In fact . . ." I removed my phone from my purse. "He texted while I was on the hunt for barstools, but I was afraid to take my eye off the prize." Now that we were seated, it was safe to read what he'd written. I touched my fingers to my lips. "How cute is this picture of his dog?"

Esther enlarged the photo of Eli wearing a New York Giants jersey and cooed. "Precious." She looked up from the phone, over at Jude, and back at me. "Do you have a picture of Timothy?"

"I don't make a habit of taking pictures of guys I've been out with twice, so no. Why?"

"I only saw him that one time, but am I wrong or do they look alike?"

"Who? Timothy and Eli? They're both cute and cuddly but that's the extent of the resemblance." I laughed.

"Don't be daft. I meant Timothy and Jude."

I pursed my lips. "They look nothing alike. Timothy's taller."

"You and Nicole look like twins even though you're taller."

"What does that have to do with anything? We're sisters."

"I'm just saying, you have a type."

Along with the better part of the Manhattan population, Jude and Timothy both had dark hair and eyes and a penchant for scruff, which I supposed was my type. If there was a resemblance beyond that, I didn't see it. "Bored now," I said to Esther, before texting Timothy back.

> **Molly:** He just needs the right hair accessories, and he'll be ready for his photo shoot in Dogs Illustrated.

Esther clapped. "Drinks are here!"

Jude poured from a bottle of red wine into a glass he'd set in front of me, and we watched as he prepared a dirty gin martini for Esther—expertly pouring, stirring, and straining—the sleeves of his white shirt pushed up to his elbows to showcase tanned arms dusted with dark hair.

Suddenly hot, I removed the cardigan I'd worn in the event it was cold inside the restaurant. It was late August and places often over-compensated for the heat outside by blasting the air conditioning.

After garnishing the martini with three jumbo olives, Jude said, "Let me know if it's dirty enough."

Esther lifted the glass to her lips and looked at Jude from under her eyelashes. "It's perfectly sullied. Thank you."

"I aim to please."

Choosing not to comment on my closest friend's blatant flirtation with my known former enemy, I watched as Jude made his way over to his date. I didn't see a strong resemblance beyond our similar coloring. It was possible we had the same build, but I couldn't tell while she was sitting down. Was she his girlfriend—the lawyer or a new one—or just someone he was sleeping with? They were *definitely* getting it done. That much was obvious from her body language. She leaned in toward him and touched her lips, neck, and ears at regular intervals like she was imagining *his* hand caressing her and *his* fingers stroking her skin. As heat pooled down low, I wondered if I should add sex to the agenda for my next date with Timothy. Clearly, I needed to get laid if the idea of Jude having sex got me hot.

I crossed my legs and turned away from them, eager to hear about Esther's latest trip to her uncle's. "What's wrong?" The ruddiness I'd seen in her cheeks was gone, and all color had drained from her face.

She gripped the stem of her martini glass. "Killian is here."

"What?" I whipped my head around. "Here? Where?"

"Right behind you," she said between her teeth.

I saw him then—shaved head, deceptively pretty sea-green eyes, broad build—the epitome of smarmy—and he was making his way through the crowd toward us.

He reached our stools and smiled a too-broad grin. "This place is a madhouse."

"What are you doing here?" Esther's expression was pinched.

"I saw your post on Instagram, was in the area, and thought I'd join you." He spoke the words as if his behavior wasn't at all stalkery.

"I'm here with Molly."

"The more, the merrier." He gave me a half-assed wave before inching his way in between us and lifting her drink to his mouth.

I gasped. *The nerve.* She should have listened to me and blocked him.

He placed the glass back on the bar. "Not bad."

Esther slid the cocktail closer to her. "Do you mind?"

"Just a little try before I buy."

I gaped at her behind his back and mouthed, "What the fuck?"

"What are you *really* doing here, Killian?" She was the picture of cool, but I could tell from the quake in her voice she was more rattled than she was letting on.

"Between Connecticut and"—he gestured at me—"your friends, you've been too busy to make plans. I thought I'd make it easy for you." He struck an innocent pose. "Do you mind?"

She clucked her tongue. "I do, actually. I told you I wasn't comfortable hanging out."

"But we're so good together. Give me another chance." He rubbed her shoulder.

Esther visibly flinched under his touch.

This was bad. I tapped him on the back. "Maybe you should give her space," I said. *Keep it light and no one gets hurt.*

"Who asked for your opinion?" he spat.

"*She* did!" I said.

"Is that what you want, Star? You want me to leave?" He pushed out his lips, probably attempting to look angelic and pull on Esther's heartstrings . . . either that or draw her attention to his mouth. In better days, she'd bragged about his talent in the oral arts. His use of a nickname previously known to leave her weak in the knees also didn't go unnoticed.

I prayed it wouldn't work . . . that she wouldn't romanticize the dumpster fire that was their three-year on-and-off-again relationship and invite him to stick around.

"I don't want to make a scene, but yes. Please leave."

My shoulders relaxed, and I clapped my hands softly.

Killian was quiet for a moment as if contemplating.

I gritted my teeth. *Go!*

He crossed his arms over his broad chest and shook his head. "It's a public place, Star. I have as much a right to be here as you."

This was getting ugly. Out of the corner of my eye, I saw Jude approach, a neutral expression on his face.

Jude kept his stare on Killian even while pouring the remains of Esther's martini into a fresh glass. "Is there a problem here?"

"Not at all. Can I get one of these?" Killian pointed at Esther's drink.

Jude ignored him and jutted his chin at Esther. "Are you all right?"

She shook her head.

It took a lot to leave my outspoken and spirited bestie

speechless, and it pained me to watch this play out. I'd be her voice. "She's not okay," I said to Jude. "He's stalking her. She asked him to leave and he refused." I willed him with my eyes to make it go away. To make *him* go away.

He gave me a *look*. It said, "I've got this."

I nodded in silent acknowledgment and gave him my trust, maybe for the first time ever.

Jude turned back to Killian. "I'm not in the habit of kicking people out of my bar, but you're making the women uncomfortable and that's unacceptable. How about you leave voluntarily and come back on another night? The gin isn't going anywhere."

My natural instinct was to debate the accuracy of the phrase "my bar," but I was too grateful for his interference to argue semantics.

Killian didn't share my reluctance. He snarled. "Is this *your* bar?"

My breath hitched. *Oh no he didn't.*

Jude's eyes darkened. "As it pertains to your future entry into the premises, it might as well be." His face contorted into a picture of disdain far worse than anything he'd thrown my way over the course of two decades. "You have ten seconds to leave before I ban you permanently."

Killian's nostrils flared. "This place is basic anyway." He turned to leave, pausing to whisper something in Esther's ear. It sounded a lot like, "You're not worth it."

When he was finally gone, a round of applause followed. We'd caused a small scene and had the rapt attention of the patrons in the vicinity of our stools.

"Now we can get back to the business of drinking," Jude said matter-of-factly.

"Thank you so much for stepping in." Esther's voice was rich with emotion.

I wanted to echo her sentiment, but the words escaped me. As a bartender, Jude was probably used to pushy guys who refused to take no for an answer, but this was personal to me. I wondered if he'd have been more or less likely to interfere if Esther had been a stranger and not the companion of his rival ex-neighbor.

He gave a slow nod. "Glad I could help. But be careful. Guys like him don't give up that easily." His eyes met mine. "You're awfully quiet."

I felt myself flush under his scrutiny. "I just...um..." I ran a hand through my hair. "Thanks."

He cocked an eyebrow. "Anytime. Your next one's on me." He turned his attention to other customers as my phone pinged a text message.

Timothy: Does this count as a hair accessory?

Accompanying the message was another photo of Eli wearing a New York Giants dog collar along with the jersey. It was adorbs, but the context went over my head. Hair accessory? I scrolled to my previous message and my eyes widened in horror. Rather than explain myself, because I was a generous glass of wine past that ability, I kept it simple.

Molly: Totally counts.

I stared at the food the waiter was setting before us on the bar and contemplated how I'd confused Eli with Yogi before we'd even had our first drink. Being the same breed did not make them the same dog with the same fetishes. *For shame, Molly. For shame!* I would bring Eli a special toy the next time I saw him to make up for it. Just not a hair band.

Two drinks, three sushi rolls, and an order of spinach and artichoke dip later, I forgot all about the mix-up. The ugly incident with Killian behind us as well, we enjoyed the rest of the evening. We toasted the successful potty training of one of Esther's twin nieces. We contemplated the necessity of buying a new dress for the anniversary party and whether it was too early to ask Timothy as my date—the consensus was yes to both.

But try as I might to make it stop, I was hyperaware of Jude's every move. I watched when he leaned over the bar to kiss his date, girlfriend, *whatever* goodbye. I listened as he suggested drinks based on a woman's preferences for "sweet but not too sweet" cocktail. I observed how seamlessly he worked the busy bar and dealt with thirsty and increasingly inebriated customers without ever losing his cool. His competence as a bartender...*sommelier*...was evident. And he seemed happy. Nothing about his behavior or body language implied he mourned the baseball career that wasn't. Things had turned out okay for him in the end, like he'd said.

"What are you smiling about?" Esther said, breaking me out of my contemplation.

I touched a finger to my lips. "Nothing."

She raised an eyebrow. "If you say so." She stood. "Going to use the loo one more time."

With some restraint, I managed to refrain from asking her to repeat herself. It was just...the *loo*. The British lingo never got old.

I slipped my credit card back in my purse and hoped Jude wouldn't see our 50 percent tip until we'd already left. The crowd had emptied out, and he was currently wiping down the bar in a circular fashion. I walked over to him and sat down.

"Mole," he said without looking up.

"How'd you know it was me?"

He slowly raised his head. "Your smell."

I rolled my eyes. "Thanks again for stepping in tonight."

"Not a problem." He went back to his cleaning.

"You'll probably use these words against me, but you're a decent guy, Jude Stark."

His hands stopped moving. "I will definitely use those words against you, Molly Blum."

We locked eyes, neither of us blinking. And then he smiled.

My balance faltered, and I slipped halfway off the stool.

He steadied me with his hand.

I gulped. His smile was dazzling. "I think I'm drunk."

"Just don't puke until you get home."

I summoned the sobriety necessary to rise and spotted Esther by the exit. I gestured for her to wait up.

From behind me, I heard Jude say, "This was unnecessary."

I turned back to him.

He waved our bill. "I'll just use the extra cash to buy your parents a better anniversary present and make you look bad in comparison."

I shook my head. "Of course you will."

"Of course I will." His eyes twinkled. "Get home safe."

"Will do." I turned to go and stumbled. I was definitely drunk. It was the only explanation.

Chapter Fifteen

*L*ess than two weeks later, Rosaria and I met for lunch at Pershing Square, a bustling restaurant serving American food but disguised as a French bistro, across the street from Grand Central Terminal and conveniently located within walking distance of my office.

It was a perfect humidity-free day for New York City post Labor Day, and we opted to sit at an outdoor table and chat while surrounded by a mix of tourists and locals walking by.

Within the first few minutes, I was convinced we were kindred spirits. We both ordered lobster salad and an iced tea, and when the busboy came over with a basket of assorted rolls, we gushed, "I love the butter here!" at the same time before yelling, "Buy me a Coke!" But it was true; the butter was so soft and creamy, you never had to worry about the roll crumbling under your knife.

I gave her the SparkNotes summary of my transition from lawyer to legal recruiter, leaving out the part about Maxine. "Your origin story for Ceiling Crashers spoke to me."

Rosaria wrinkled her nose. "You're also the daughter of a single Puerto Rican woman who had to build her life from the ground up?"

I felt my face flush. "No. I was born draped in upper middle-class white privilege, but I *do* know how it feels to wake up each morning with a belly full of dread over the impending work day." I stabbed a cherry tomato with my fork and popped it into my mouth. "My first priority is, of course, filling open positions for the company's clients and helping candidates find new jobs," I said after chewing and swallowing. "But my mission...my *passion*...goes beyond sealing the deal and making a commission. *Cha-ching*, as my manager likes to say." I sighed, picturing Michael's pompous face. "But our mental state at work, where most of us spend so much time, has a huge impact on our quality of life, and that matters to me too." I swished around my salad for a remaining remnant of lobster meat among the baby greens, tomatoes, and cucumbers.

Rosaria dabbed her lips with a cloth napkin. "Agreed. My company's mission is to help the members of our community transition to a job or career that supports the life they *really* want, which is typically not the one they're currently living."

"It's so special. Truly," I said, shaking my head in wonder. "There's only so much a human resources manager is going to share about their company, besides the basics: job description and hours, benefits, et cetera. Although I do outside research, I can only find what's out there to be found." Like on the "forbidden" Vault and Above the Law sites. "But I have more leeway with the individual candidates. Some tell me, 'No more law firms' or 'Anything without billable hours.' Some say, 'Show me the money!' But I also try to sneak in questions that delve deeper. I'll ask if they like baseball if I know MLB is looking for someone..." My mind drifted to Jude before I quickly shoved his unwanted presence out of the way. "Or if they're clearly fashionistas, I might search for openings at a clothing or accessories company. I'd love to take it a step further...have this information all in one place as part of the pre-interviewing process, so by the time we have a face-to-face, I have a better understanding of the person's ideal position." Like her questionnaires.

Rosaria nodded. "Like my questionnaires."

"Exactly!" *Kindred spirits.* I smiled down at a little girl with striking red curls and pink glitter shoes toddling passed us holding a woman's hand, then turned back to Rosaria. "I think I need to focus on speeding up the process. As much as I hate to admit it, my manager has a point that sometimes I'm slow to set up interviews. I don't want to bite the hand that feeds me—I'm a recruiter, not a career coach. But it doesn't mean I can't try to make all parties involved as happy with the end result as possible and help connect people to jobs they won't want to leave in another year, right?"

"Right," Rosaria repeated, before smiling wryly. "You do realize what you just said probably goes against *your* employer's mission statement—without any turnover, they wouldn't have a business. You wouldn't have a job."

I squirmed in my metal chair. "Yikes."

"Sorry to bum you out." She chuckled. "But I get your preference for meeting face-to-face over telephone. A facial expression tells a lot about a person's true feelings. Video calls work just as well, though, and are much easier to schedule. People can be more flexible when they don't have to commute somewhere. Or wear pants."

"For sure," I said, giggling. "I will consider that." My body was light with joy. It was so nice to chat with someone who truly got it.

We paused our conversation when the waitress came over to ask about coffee and dessert. We both ordered a cappuccino.

When we were alone again, Rosaria leaned forward. "You said you had some thoughts about Ceiling Crashers?"

"Yes!" I pulled my phone from my purse, opened up the relevant note, and read the first item to refresh my memory. "I scrolled through your social media." If reading every post since the company was founded four years ago counted as *scrolling*. "I love the way your IG is curated—it's so soft and visually appealing. Quotes from inspiring women, short snippets of advice, a sprinkle of personal photos of you living your best life. It's really great. But most of the videos are of you speaking to your clients and prospective community members. Have you ever thought about inviting them to post their success stories with Ceiling Crashers on Instagram and even TikTok, where you're not currently as active? Even asking members to do take-overs or, if you want to retain control of the content, you can interview them instead. Video testimonials could be a huge factor in growing your community." I braced myself for her reaction.

Rosaria beamed as brightly as the warm sun shining down on us. "I love this idea, Molly!"

I grinned. "Really?"

She gave me a look that was equal parts reassuring and amused. "Yes! It's brilliant advertising. I wish I'd thought of it myself."

I nearly burst with pride. It had seemed a wasted opportunity to limit the company's social streams to only posts by Rosaria, and TikTok could help attract a younger audience.

"What else have you got?" She sipped the cappuccino the waitress had just placed in front of her.

I followed the path of my notes with my finger. "You have a newsletter, but other than quick links to subscribe, I didn't notice any incentives." I looked up. "Have you thought about offering free content to all subscribers as a way to build your list?"

"Hmmm. I like it. One of my decorative planners might work." She scribbled something illegible on a small notepad. Apparently neat handwriting was where our commonalities diverged.

"Also... I was thinking... have you done any targeted advertising to members from more low-income communities?" I asked.

Rosaria paused with her mug at the edge of her mouth. "I like where this is headed. Go on."

I took a sip of cappuccino. "For instance, a giveaway or contest offering deluxe memberships to women who might not be able to afford it otherwise... who might not see another way to pay the bills besides working minimum wage. There must be women who could use personalized guidance and encouragement. Law firms do pro-bono work. Can Ceiling Crashers offer something similar?" I held my breath, afraid I'd overstepped.

She placed her cup back on the table and widened her eyes. "This is gold, Molly. I appreciate all the thought you put into this. It must have taken hours!"

"Not really." The lie rolled off my tongue easily, but I'd enjoyed it so much, I hadn't even noticed how much time had passed until my eyes refused to stay open.

"My hand hurts from writing all this down, and I'm afraid I won't be able to read it later." She made a face. "My handwriting is atrocious."

I clamped my lips shut. I wasn't about to argue—one lie was enough—but agreeing outright was unnecessary and mean.

Her forehead crinkled in thought. "Would you mind emailing me this list? I can send you one of our questionnaires in exchange."

I blurted, "That would be amazing!" with a tad more enthusiasm than intended. I'd wanted to ask but feared it was proprietary.

"Fantastic." She glanced at her watch and grimaced. "I'm so sorry, but I need to get going."

So did I. On my agenda for the afternoon was reviewing résumés, following up with hiring managers and prospective candidates, posting ads on LinkedIn, scouring firm websites/ job boards for prospective candidates, and sending out cold-call messages. The squeaky wheel got the grease and all that. I insisted on footing the bill since lunch was my idea, and a few minutes later, we said our goodbyes on the corner of Vanderbilt Avenue and 42nd Street.

Rosaria extended her hand. "Thank you so much. This was a true pleasure. Next time is on me."

"I will hold you to it." Giddy there would be a *next time*, I was tempted to pull her into a hug, but kept it professional and accepted her hand, shaking with a firm grip as I'd been taught by my dad in high school to prepare for college interviews.

My phone rang as I floated back to the office. The man himself. "Hi, Dad!"

"How's my Squirrel?"

My heart warmed at the nickname. There was no rhyme or reason to the animal moniker—just my dad being weird. Nicole was "Goose" and Michelle was "Bear."

"Never better! I just had a really productive meeting." I was always quick to assure my parents of my well-being, especially since leaving the law and the steady paycheck that came with it, so they wouldn't worry about me alone in the big city.

"I'm looking forward to dinner with you girls next month. It will be nice to catch up, just the five of us."

"Totally!" I only felt a little guilty about the half-truth we'd told our parents regarding the anniversary party. We said it would just be our nuclear family—no spouses or grandkids, much less the Starks and *their* extended relatives. The end justified the means in this case.

"Like *My Three Sons* with daughters, *Little House on the Prairie* the early years, and *Full House* minus the dead mom."

"Dad!" I laugh-yelled. Growing up, my father had loved to compare our family to old television sitcoms. He said if he divorced Mom and married Mrs. Stark, we'd be a bizarro *Brady Bunch* because he was an architect, like Mike Brady, and Laura was a stay-at-home mother, like Carol, and they each had three children. The six of us found episodes of the show on TV Land and were forever traumatized. Not to mention, given my parents' real-life temporary separation, even joking about a permanent one—much less the idea of my dad and Mrs. Stark as a couple—didn't sit well. "I should get back to work," I said, still chuckling.

"Don't be a stranger, Squirrel."

"I won't. Love you." We ended the call.

Back in my office a few minutes later, I was too wired from caffeine and jubilant over my meeting with Rosaria to focus on work. Lucky for me, a text came in from Eddie confirming his parents had bought into his and his wife's invitation to spend the night of the party at their house to try out the newly installed hot tub. Jude's response came quickly.

Jude: Bathing suits optional?

I flipped the phone screen-down as if it could erase the cringe-worthy visual the words had summoned. Not that the Starks were unattractive people, but they were *the Starks*. Seeing them naked that one time in the basement was more than enough. Jude hadn't made up my crush on Eddie way back when, but I preferred *all* the Starks in clothing these days. Suddenly, the memory of Jude rubbing down the bar at Hillstone in a "wax on, wax off" motion came to me. He had nice arms, I'd give him that.

The whole situation at Hillstone had been weird. I'd almost felt...I shuddered inwardly...*attracted* to him. What was that about? It had to have been the abundance of wine and the whole alpha male thing. The way he'd taken charge and kicked Killian out had been sexy for a hot minute but...gross. Wanting to get it done with Jude was just...*gross*. The guy had once planted a dead caterpillar on my hamburger, for the love of God. Pursuing a friendship with him after all these years was strange enough given our history. Even contemplating more would force me to unload baggage better kept packed away forever...for everyone's sake.

Still, I was dying to tell him about my meeting with Rosaria. In his Jude way, he'd encouraged me to go for it. He probably wouldn't care or would claim to have no idea what I was talking about.

I buried my face in my hands. So why I was dying to tell him anyway?

Chapter Sixteen

That Saturday, I was on my third date with Timothy. We went to Tap Haus 33, a sports bar where you poured your own craft beer from forty different self-serving stainless-steel taps that lined the wall. Kind of like a Sixteen Handles but with beer and hard cider instead of ice cream or frozen yogurt, and twenty-four more flavors. I'd never been there before and was excited to check it out, watch some baseball, and get to know Timothy better. He already felt familiar to me, which was weird considering we'd practically just met.

Although there were spots available at the long communal table in the center of the venue, we chose a private table near the entrance. It was a warm day in September, and we enjoyed the soft autumn breeze coming in through the open door while watching the Yankees and hoping they'd sweep the Orioles at home.

I took a sip of my berry rosé cider as the television screen on the wall showed Yankees pitcher Gerrit Cole strike out the Orioles player currently at bat. I clapped softly. Like Jude so cleverly joked earlier in the summer, Gerrit had a much stronger arm than I did. "Do you play baseball or just watch?" I asked

Timothy, who was freshly shaved and wearing a lightweight gray sweater and black jeans.

Timothy turned away from the screen and focused on me. "I just watch, unless you count casual scrimmages with friends. I played football in high school."

I rested my elbows on the wood table and cupped my chin. "What position?"

"I was a running back for the Edison Eagles until I got injured."

Haunted by a different high-school athlete's career ending prematurely, I leaned slightly away before remembering the stools were backless. I sprang back up awkwardly. "What...what happened? Do you know?"

Timothy looked confused by the question. "It was hard to miss. I dislocated my shoulder when the cornerback from the opposing team blocked a pass." He finished the last of his beer. "I got lucky and didn't need surgery, but I couldn't move my arms...like not at all...and it hurt like hell. I was done. My mom was happy. Not about the injury, of course, but that I wasn't going to play in college. You know moms." He blushed.

"Do you miss it?" I plucked a sweet potato fry from my plate and broke it in half.

"It wasn't like I was going to go pro anyway." He moved the tea lamp on the table to the side to brush my hand with his. "But enough about me. You had that meeting with that woman last week, right? How'd it go?"

I'd told him about Ceiling Crashers via text and was impressed he remembered and cared enough to ask. "Yes. I had that meeting with that woman last week," I said teasingly.

Timothy dipped his head bashfully in a way that reminded me of something I couldn't place. Regardless, I found it charming.

"It went swimmingly. I've spent every night after work since devising plans inspired by her company's questionnaires." Not wanting Timothy to think I plagiarized, I added, "With her permission, of course." I planned to start sending my amended version out to candidates the following week.

Timothy's eyebrows drew closer. "Why *after* work?"

I squirmed. "I don't have a choice. My manager isn't thrilled with how much extra...shall we say, *creative* effort I put into my job, so I did it on my own time." I pushed the shredded lettuce that had fallen out of my now-demolished taco to the side of the plate. "Do you think it's reckless? Sometimes I feel like I'm on a slippery slope," I confessed. Challenging authority was way out of my comfort zone.

Timothy leaned back, not wobbling despite the lack of support behind him, and folded his nice arms across his equally lovely torso. "I guess it depends on how much you value your manager's opinion—"

"Not much." I giggled.

Timothy grinned and continued. "—how much power he truly has over you, and whether it's worth the risk. Based on the way your face lights up when you talk about your *creative* work, it seems like it's worth it. It's legal, right?"

"Naturally!" The idea of me doing something criminal was laughable. Jude would lose his shit over the mere possibility. I recalled his face when he saw my temporary tattoo and bit back a smile.

"Then screw your manager and do it! You regret the things you *don't* do."

I blinked. Those words. Where had I heard them before?

Jude. About my attending the Ceiling Crashers' seminar. It was good advice, but how strange that I'd sought it in the first place.

His suggestion to "yes" Michael while continuing my due diligence practices in secret was unsolicited, yet I had taken it. Which meant I could now count the times I felt grateful to Jude on two fingers. Make it three—he'd ousted Killian from *his* bar. Too bad the only thing I ever did for Jude was ruin his baseball career.

"Molly?"

Timothy's voice broke through my mind trip.

I forced a smile at him as guilt washed over me for entering a time warp in the middle of our date. "Sorry!" Jude was happy. Why couldn't I let it go? The last thing I wanted was to ruin a date with a sweet, hot guy by thinking about Jude.

"Clearly my performance as your companion tonight is lacking if your daydream is more scintillating." His eyes crinkled in the corners, demonstrating he was less concerned than his words suggested.

I squeezed his hand across the table. "It's not. I promise." *Truth.* "Where were we?"

"You were telling me about the illegal nature of your undercover work." He glanced over his shoulder. "Don't worry. You can trust me." He gave me his best "I'm so trustworthy" face.

"Haha. Let's talk about something else. How's culinary school? What was the last dish you made?"

"Pommes Dauphinoise."

"Poms Daphne..." I wiggled my nose. "Huh?"

He grinned. "In layperson's terms, potatoes au gratin."

"Now *that* I know. Not how to make it, obviously, but what it is and how to eat it."

Timothy laughed. "How about I make it and you can eat it? You can wash the dishes too."

"Sounds like a plan. Have you always wanted to be a chef?" I liked the direction this conversation was taking, particularly the absence of it having a connection to Jude. I took a sip of my cider.

"No. I actually started out with a sommelier certification, but culinary arts is a better fit."

I choked as the cider I'd just swallowed went down the wrong pipe, then blurted, "Do you know Jude Stark?"

Timothy rubbed his chin. "Who?"

"Never mind." I wiped the cider off my chin and took the opportunity to scrub the napkin over my forehead, now dotted with sweat. What was wrong with me? It wasn't like all certified sommeliers knew one another any more than lawyers did. And I had no idea where or even when Jude got his certification. Most importantly, I didn't care.

So why had I asked the question in the first place?

Chapter Seventeen

A few weekends later, I met Esther for brunch at Penelope, a popular neighborhood café. I had just told my best friend how my questionnaire had unlocked a candidate's fascination with the art world when the second-year litigation associate had said his favorite book in the last year was a thriller about an international art scandal. "It just so happens there are law firms that deal strictly with art. One in our system is seeking a junior attorney. I set up an interview for next week!"

Esther raised her mimosa. "Cheers to Molly living her best life."

I clinked my glass against hers. "L'chaim."

"So, besides taking the recruiting world by storm, what else is going on? How's Jude?" She waggled her full, nearly white eyebrows.

I hadn't even told Esther about my brief but *temporary* attraction to Jude at Hillstone, but she had fallen under his spell after he had ejected Killian from the premises. It *had* been kind of hot. I swallowed a bite of Nutella French toast and ordered myself to think about one of Jude's less heroic activities of late, like when he sent me on a wild goose chase to a tattoo parlor. "And, anyway, I wouldn't know. I haven't had a reason to see him and probably won't until the party next month. But I hung out with Timothy again."

Esther froze with her glass at her lips. "And how's that going?"

"Good. I like him." I told her about our date at Tap Haus 33. "He wants to cook for me." Hopefully something besides that Pom Daphne dish.

"How's the sex?"

The diners next to us stopped their conversation. The tables were packed close together, and any personal tea spilled was a free-for-all. I whispered, "I don't know yet. Been so busy with work. We haven't had a chance to have it." This was true. What I didn't admit was how confused I was. Sometimes Timothy would do or say something and I'd have all the feels...like, *take me now!* But just as often, as great as he was, my passion for him ebbed. Until the pendulum swung more to the take-me-now side, I was in no hurry to sleep with him.

Esther opened her mouth to respond at the same time my phone lit up with an incoming text from Rosaria. We hadn't talked since the emails after our lunch when we traded my list of ideas for Ceiling Crashers for her questionnaire. I took a swig of my mimosa and read the message.

> **Rosaria:** Hope all is well! Can you call me when you have a minute? I have something to run by you.

"Hold that thought," I said, pointing at my phone. "I just need to respond to this. It's Rosaria."

"No worries. You text. I'll drink." Esther held the carafe of orange juice and champagne close and shimmied her shoulders.

I snorted then turned to my phone.

Molly: Sure. When would be a good time?

I held out my glass to Esther for a refill. "Don't be a hog."
Ping.

Rosaria: I'll be around all day, but it can wait!

I was too intrigued to wait. "We're pretty much finished here, right?" Our food had been untouched for the last several minutes and we'd just emptied the carafe. All that remained was draining our glasses.

Esther yawned. "Yup. I need a nap. You can tell me why you haven't screwed Jude's twin on a bed, against the wall, or on the kitchen table yet later."

"What do you mean, Jude's twin?"

She stretched her arms over her head, the fabric of her black form-fitting dress moving with her. "They look alike, have the same dog, and are both bartenders. Actually, they're not twins. They're clones."

I growled. "Give it a rest." Although these coincidental similarities *could* explain why I'd been weirdly attracted to Jude. Maybe he reminded me of Timothy. Or maybe I wasn't ready to seal the deal with Timothy because he reminded me of Jude. Both possibilities left me cold.

More likely, Esther was mocking me for the pure joy of it. It wasn't as if Jude and Timothy were actually that similar. *Definitely the last one.* "I mean it," I said, wiggling a finger at her.

While Esther snickered, I texted Rosaria back that I was on the way to my apartment and would call her in twenty.

When I got home, I chugged a bottle of Dasani water before brushing my teeth and gargling with Listerine. Rosaria wouldn't be able to smell the eggs or champagne on my breath through the phone, but the exercise helped me transition from Sunday Funday with my best friend to professional business chat with a networking partner. Any buzz I had was soaked up by a combination of the food, twenty-minute walk home, and eagerness about what Rosaria wanted to "run by" me. After a quick text asking if she was ready, I stretched my legs the length of my couch and called her.

I insisted she hadn't interrupted my day (although Esther might have disputed that statement), and after a bit of small talk, she got to her point.

"I was thinking about what you said over lunch," she said.

I waited for her to elaborate. I'd said many, many things.

"You said you're a recruiter, not a career coach. And I wondered why that was. Why aren't you a career coach?"

I looked up at the ceiling. "Truthfully, I didn't even know what a career coach was until I saw Ceiling Crashers' sponsored ad on Instagram. Many non-practicing attorneys make the transition to legal recruiting, and it seemed the natural step for me too. I always enjoyed the people more than the practice." With one notable exception.

"Ceiling Crashers is still in early stages, but we're growing fast. Cone of silence, but I'm being interviewed by *Forbes* next month."

I squealed and kicked my legs in vicarious joy. "I'm so happy for you!" An article in *Forbes* could really put Ceiling Crashers on the map.

Rosaria laughed. "Maybe you can be happy for both of us." She paused. "Listen, Molly, I'm going to be straight with you. It's clear to me you're more passionate about what I do than what *you* do. So, I was thinking, how would you like to join my team?"

I shot up. "What?"

"I know this comes out of left field. I wasn't looking to hire. We're small by design, but your ideas were so well thought out and your enthusiasm fits right in. I think you'd make a great addition, and I know you'd be happy."

I tried to picture myself working for Ceiling Crashers. Would I meet with women every day, helping them turn their career dreams into reality? Provide input into the questionnaires? Give talks at the Y?

Rosaria continued. "I don't have a specific position in mind, but we could discuss. The thing is...I can't pay you much. In fact it's probably a lot less than you're making on commission now." She gave me a number. "But if you stick with me for a couple of years, the number will go up. Possibly significantly."

She kept speaking, but my mind was spinning. What she was offering amounted to $30,000 less than I had made so far this year on commission thanks to placement of high-salaried attorneys. It would mean a huge step backward. Molly Blum didn't go backward. She steadily climbed. Not to mention Rosaria didn't have a position to fill. She wanted to make one for me. Flattering for sure, but risky. What if it didn't work out and she let me go? Even with the uncertainty of a commission-based salary, my current position offered more security. And Michael had mentioned an early promotion. I was making so much progress!

"What do you say?"

Chapter Eighteen

As flattered as I was by Rosaria's offer, I couldn't accept. Of course I couldn't. Leaving my job? *Already?* Switching careers? *Again?* Not to mention the pay cut. I had student loans and a mortgage to pay off. It was an offer I had to refuse. Rosaria had understood, and with a promise to keep in touch, we'd ended the call.

Over the next two weeks, I put in extra hours in the office—*home* office, in my case—trying to set up enough interviews *my* way to avoid alerting Michael I was still doing research. I was exhausted. At least today was Friday. I lowered my head onto my desk at the day job with the promise it would only be for a minute. I closed my eyes. *Just a minute.* I could go home early, but I lacked the energy at present for even the short commute to my apartment. What I really needed was a dress for the party. With my eyes closed, I pictured Jude with the girl from Hillstone on his arm. I hadn't decided if it was too soon to bring Timothy around my family. *What does one thing have to do with the other, Molly?*

When my phone rang, I reluctantly lifted my head and pressed the green call icon. "Hi, Mom."

"What's wrong?"

"Nothing." I sat up straight and wiped the drool from my mouth. "What makes you think something's wrong?"

"You sound drowsy, like you've just come out of anesthesia."

I chuckled. "I'm tired, but it's not post-surgery related. I think I'm coming down with something." I regretted the words the moment they came out. Unlike Nicole, who coveted the extra attention the three of us got while sick, growing up I tended to keep my colds under wraps, not wanting my parents to fight over who should stay home with me. I made no false assumptions Mom would drive into the city to make her famous orangeaid (diluted orange juice, a dash of vanilla, and a maraschino cherry), but I didn't want her to worry. "It's just a cold. It will pass."

"Take it easy tonight. I know it's the weekend, but use it to rest. Not drink."

I chuckled. "No worries. I'm going straight home tonight to relax." Tonight was for curling on the couch and catching up on my Netflix shows. I'd wake up on Saturday morning refreshed and prepared to enjoy the weekend like the twentysomething I was as opposed to the haggard old lady who'd taken over my body of late. I could go out with Timothy without falling asleep like I had the week before during our movie date. Maybe I'd even buy a dress for the party.

"Okay, good." After a mutual exchange of "I love you," we said goodbye.

When I woke up on the couch Saturday morning, I had a splitting headache. I straightened my legs, wincing when they cramped from the sudden movement. After wiping the sleep from my eyes, I used my palms to ease myself to a standing position and slipped on the plastic lid of a Swiffer Wet box, falling on my ass in the process. *Fuck you, lid.* I limped to the bathroom, rubbing my butt cheek. There would be a bruise by lunchtime.

Except when I woke up next, it was four a.m. Monday morning. My Saturday plan to rest my mind and catch up on sleep had morphed into a thirty-six-hour nap during which whatever I'd been coming down with arrived like an uninvited guest to a party. I hadn't literally slept the entire time—my currently throbbing head held a fuzzy recollection of taking multiple woozy trips to the bathroom, my eyes opened to slits just wide enough to see where I was going—but I might as well have.

Now on my bed, I ran my tongue along my teeth. A teeth brushing was in order, but blowing my nose was all the exercise I could handle at the moment. I sat up and the room spun. I lay back down. *Monday. Shit.* I sat back up again. I rarely took any sick days. By the time I finished asking myself if I was *really* too sick to go in, I was usually showered and out the door. Not happening today. I was physically incapable of going more than a hundred feet from this bed.

I reached for the phone on my nightstand to call reception, knowing I'd get voice mail at this hour. While leaving the brief message I was calling out sick, each word out of my mouth felt like a monologue. I ended the call and passed out.

My eyes opened again at 9:42. Upon hearing about my sick day from the receptionist, Cindy had texted to see how I was feeling. I answered with the cold face, dizzy face, and masked face emojis, since spelling actual words required more energy than I had.

I woke up again two hours later with cold sweats and the frantic realization I hadn't checked on Esther's cat since Friday evening. *Fuck.* What if Poppy's automatic feeder malfunctioned like Esther's assistant's best friend's cousin's had? What if she'd died of starvation? *Fuck squared.*

Pushing off my comforter, I flipped my legs over the side of the bed and swooned as my blood sugar dropped. I gripped the bottom of my mattress and closed my eyes for a beat until I regained my equilibrium. *You've got this, Molly. One foot in front of the other.* My body just had to acclimate to being vertical. *Do it for Poppy.* I tried again. Tears built behind my eyelids, and I flopped back onto the bed with a whimper. Esther's apartment was only two blocks away, but the journey felt as monumental as Neil Armstrong's trip to the moon. But...Poppy! Someone had to check on her...and fast... *Think, Molly.* Unfortunately, thinking while chills permeated my body and my head was stuffed with phlegm was an uphill battle.

There was Timothy, but asking him would require handing over Esther's house keys. *I* trusted him with her belongings, but *my* level of trust wasn't the point. She'd take the risk to save her feline child, though, right?

My breath hitched as it occurred to me she might not have to. What if there was someone else I could ask—someone who'd already earned her trust and admiration? Jude lived in the neighborhood and didn't work regular nine-to-five hours, which meant he was probably home. I didn't *want* to ask him, but I had no choice. It was life or death. Which meant I didn't have time to second-guess myself or worry about how he would respond to my asking him for a favor.

I found Jude's number in my call history, pressed the green button, and put the phone on speaker. It rang twice. *Pick up!* Jude might not save *my* cat, but my instincts said he'd do his best to save Esther's. I propped my back against my two pillows, rested the phone screen up on my chest, and closed my eyes. Whatever energy I had on reserve for emergencies was depleting by the second.

"Are you there, Mole?"

My eyes flew open. "Ju...Jude?" His name came out froggy, like I hadn't spoken out loud in a long time.

"Who else were you expecting to answer my phone?"

"Sssh." *So loud.*

"You called me!"

I covered my aching eardrums. "Please help."

"What's wrong?"

The alarm in his voice bolted through me. With every bit of stamina I could arouse, I sat up and projected my voice as if my life depended on it. "S'posed to feed Esther's cat. I'm sick...too weak. Please come?" I shut my eyes again.

"I'll be right over."

I let out a relieved whoosh of (bad) breath and ended the call. Resisting the powerful temptation to sleep, I lifted my dead weight off the bed with a loud groan and inched my way to the front door to unlock it for Jude in case I passed out before he arrived. I covered my matted and knotted hair with the lavender knitted beanie my grandmother had made me. Then I plucked an Altoid from the tin on my coffee table and popped it in my mouth. Even on my deathbed, my vanity was loud and clear in its instructions. No sooner had I set my germ-infested body on the couch when the doorman alerted me to Jude's arrival. A few minutes after that, there was a knock on my door.

"It's open." My voice came out as quiet as Tinker Bell's. I was about to try again when I heard him enter.

"You called about a cat." Jude, wearing a black hoodie with worn jeans, stopped short at the sight of me. "You look terrible."

"As far as insults go, that's a pretty tame one coming from

you." I whipped my head back in a surprise burst of energy. "Ouch," I said, rubbing my neck.

Jude skimmed the room. "At least you'll perish in a clean apartment."

"Her keys are over there," I said, pointing aimlessly.

Jude chuckled. "Over *there*, huh?" He took a few steps to the right.

I craned my still-achy neck to watch his path. "You're getting warmer. Keep going. Warmer. Hot. There!"

"Over there equals kitchen table. Got it." He scooped the keys off the Formica surface and rejoined me in the living room. "Now where am I going?"

"One sec." I blew my nose, making a loud trumpet-like sound, and tossed the dirty tissue on the floor. Ignoring Jude's shudder, I recited Esther's address and told him where she kept the cat food. It wasn't a doorman building, which meant all he needed for entry were the keys. I fiddled with my beanie. "I'm scared. What if I killed her?" My stomach lurched in a way that felt unrelated to whatever ailment I had.

Jude's eyes softened. "She'll be fine. Get some sleep." He turned to leave.

"Thanks, Jude," I said to his back, hoping my delayed gratitude didn't go unheard.

He waved without turning around.

When the door closed behind him, I blew my nose again before granting my doorman permission to let Jude back up automatically—in case I perished in his absence. Then I turned on the television to *The Young and the Restless*.

Sleep? No way. Not until I knew Poppy was okay.

Chapter Nineteen

I woke up to a wet tongue on my toes.

"Stop it, Yogi," I heard someone say.

I sat up and blinked. "Wha...what's happening?" Then I remembered. "Poppy!"

Jude stood in the center of my living room holding a plastic bag. "She's fine. It took me a second to coax her from her hiding spot behind the couch, but she's hydrated and fed."

"Thank God!" A wave of relief crashed through me.

"I wasn't sure when Esther would be back, so I brought the cat to my apartment in case you're still not okay tomorrow. You're allergic, right?"

"Y-yes." I was surprised he remembered. But since he'd just done me a massive favor, I refrained from pointing out the time he strategically left clumps of his childhood cat Gizmo's hair on my toys in our basement and laughed when my eyes swelled shut.

He gestured to Yogi, who was curled at my feet. "I hope you don't mind."

I smiled down at the dog. "Not if you don't. I'm probably contagious."

"I don't think dogs can catch human colds." He scratched at the layer of stubble on his jaw. "When was the last time you ate?"

Until he asked, I hadn't noticed the hollow pit in my stomach, both desperate to be filled and repulsed by it. "I don't remember."

"I figured as much." He walked away, leaving me alone with Yogi, who'd jumped onto the couch and promptly fallen asleep.

I followed Yogi's example until the sound of clanking pots woke me up. "What are you doing?"

Jude returned to the living room carrying two bowls. He placed the dishes on the coffee table.

"What's this?"

"Matzo ball soup. My nana sent me home with two gallons of it the last time I saw her."

My breath hitched, which had the unfortunate effect of making me cough...and cough. I covered my mouth until the spell ended and drank from the water Jude had brought me from the kitchen. "That was really kind and...um...unnecessary of you." Even in my weakened condition, "nice" Jude was unnerving.

"It was nothing." He blew on a spoonful of soup. "We needed room in the freezer for vodka."

I stared into the yellowish broth filled with carrots, noodles, and two large matzo balls. "Too bad my appetite is MIA." I sniffled.

"Doesn't matter. You need liquids." He twisted his face. "I sound like our moms."

"Are you comfortable kneeling on the floor like that? I can make room for you on the couch. Chair?"

He waved off the suggestion. "Remember when we had the

chicken pox at the same time and they made us quarantine together?"

I frowned. "I recall you tossing cotton balls soaked with calamine lotion at me in rapid succession."

"Yeah, sorry about that."

"No, you're not."

He grinned. "You're right."

My belly fluttered. His smile was so...so...

He waved his spoon at me. "Eat."

I nodded. "Okay." My stomach was so empty, I could actually feel the soup travel down my esophagus.

"How do you think you caught this bug?"

I took another spoonful of soup and curled back under the blanket. "I'm using that rebellious streak you know so well and working overtime behind my manager's back. Like you suggested." Ordinarily, admitting I'd taken advice from Jude was at the bottom of my to-do list (more like off the page) but I was too weary to take it back now.

Jude froze with his spoon an inch from his lips. "I don't recall telling you to work yourself sick...not exactly my style." He stood and stretched, his shirt riding up to expose a sliver of his flat belly and a trail of dark hair leading into his jeans.

I gulped, then looked away as he brought his empty bowl to the kitchen. My lightheadedness ticked up a notch, and I didn't want to think about why.

Over the sound of running water, I said, "I want to do work *my* way without getting in trouble with management. I'd hate to disappoint my parents again."

The water was turned off, and he returned to the living room. "I get that."

"You do?"

"I crushed my dad's dream of his son playing major league baseball."

It was like someone plunged a needle into my heart. "I'm sorry." I was tempted to ask if it was *his* dream too—still—or if he'd move on, but I couldn't get the words out. Whether it was due to my fever or a desire to hold on to his earlier answer, that he had no regrets about the way things had worked out, I was too weak to contemplate.

"The only thing you should apologize for is the way you smell. Please take a shower. I'll stick around in case you faint."

"If you have to rescue me, just cover your eyes!" My already clammy skin heated up like my fever had caught a fever, and I poured my concentration into standing up to avoid looking at him.

"You need help?" He extended his hand.

I took it and let him pull me up. We stood too close for comfort, but I didn't drop his hand. It was soft but not wimpy. *Stop analyzing his fingers, weirdo!* "Your eyes are blue."

"They're actually hazel with blue flecks."

"All this time, I thought they were brown," I whispered.

"You never looked hard enough." He scratched his neck.

I followed the path of his fingers with my eyes and was hit with an impulse to nibble on the trail of skin between his ear and collarbone. The flu had turned me into a vampire. *Lovely.*

He dropped my hand and pushed me toward the bathroom. "Shower time."

Taking a shower was some hard work. My legs were unsteady from lack of use, and my stomach heaved. After washing and conditioning my hair, I bent down in the tub and closed my eyes, letting the water rush down on me. *Just for a second.* This was nice.

"You all right in there?" Jude knocked on the door. "Mole?"

"Fine!" I spat the water from my mouth and slowly stood, using the wall for balance. Then I turned off the shower and sat on the edge of the tub. I needed time to regain my bearings...like seven hours or so.

"If you don't come out in five seconds, I'm coming in."

"No...no...I got this." My legs wobbled like the bones had been removed.

The doorknob turned. "You decent?"

"No!" The thought of Jude seeing me naked was terrifying, but if I were being honest, it was a different kind of scary than years past. I was in no condition to process it. *Blessedly.*

"I'm covering my eyes."

I hid behind the shower curtain. "Toss me the towel hanging on the hook. Please."

The door opened, followed by the thump of terrycloth hitting me over the head. I wrapped the white towel around my body and slid open the shower curtain. Then I looked up at Jude. "Is this what we have to look forward to when we're old?"

He gave me a wry smile and lifted me up.

I held on to him with one hand, using the other to secure my towel, and he led me to my bedroom. "I'll wait out here. Put some clothes on and get back into bed."

My impulse was to make a joke about sleeping naked but that would be flirting. Jude and I didn't flirt. So I put on clean underwear and an oversize t-shirt and slipped under the covers instead. "You can come in now."

Jude entered carrying a glass of water. "Dehydration is bad." He handed it to me.

I took a few gulps and placed the glass on the nightstand.

"I think you'll feel better next time you wake up."

"What will you do now?" Was it weird that I wanted him to stay? It was totally weird. *Don't say it out loud.*

"I have to walk Yogi who, by the way, dug up some weird hairband that looks like it has cherries on it. Sorry."

"It was my mom's. They called it a 'bunch' in the seventies. Very retro." I closed my eyes.

"Shit."

I mumbled, "Don't worry about it," and fell asleep.

When I woke up next, the plague had ended, and Jude was gone.

Chapter Twenty

After three months of planning, the party was the coming weekend. The six "siblings" had a Zoom call the Thursday before to discuss the final details. By some miracle, seven p.m. worked for everyone, although it was clear from the view out the window behind Alison that she was still at her office in Manhattan. And, from the noise coming from Jude's computer, he was at Hillstone.

"Mute your computer, little brother," Eddie said.

"Sorry. Sorry." Jude shrugged apologetically.

My cheeks heated up. Why was I blushing? And imagining him straight out of the shower in a towel? I doubted he was flashing back to seeing *me* in a towel. Why was my mind even connecting Jude with either of us in towels? *Snap out of it!*

This was Jude—the guy who'd cut the hair off my favorite Barbie doll and drawn a dick between Ken's legs. I'd pulled equally, if not more, immature stunts on him— acts I could justify when Jude was my enemy, but not the object of my fantasies. Not to mention the whole shattered-his-baseball-career abomination. Yes, it was safer to see him as my rival—my not-at-all-sexy rival—than wrapped in a towel with water glistening from his lean but muscular bare chest.

"We won't keep you long," Nicole said, bringing the meeting to order. "I just want to make sure everyone understands the plan for Saturday."

"You Blums have it easier, since your parents already know they're going into the city for dinner. So, all you need to worry about is timing," Eddie said.

"They're planning to arrive in my neighborhood around six, park in the area, then the four of us will take an Uber to the restaurant," Nicole said.

"Patrick and I will be at the venue by five-thirty to greet early guests. You know someone will show up early." Michelle's scrunched-up face expressed annoyance at the prospect.

"Great-Aunt Arlene!" Nicole and I said at the same time. Our nani's younger sister was a passive-aggressive nightmare.

"And she'll wonder why the food isn't out yet even though the invitation said six," Michelle said with an eye roll.

"That Aunt Arlene." Jude shook his head. "Always causing problems."

"Dana and I will be there early too," Alison said.

"We'll tell Mom and Pop Stark we're going out for dinner, although they'll know something's up when we drive through the Lincoln Tunnel. But they'll never guess what's waiting for them." Eddie grinned and rubbed his palms together like an evil scientist.

"Which leaves the juniors. What's your plan?" Nicole said.

While Jude scowled, probably in response to the "juniors" remark, I replied. "We'll be at the restaurant by six like everyone else."

"Us too," Jude said.

"Who are you guys bringing?" Nicole waggled her eyebrows, looking ridiculous.

I answered first. "His name is Timothy." Initially, I was afraid inviting him to a family party would give him the wrong idea about my feelings for him...or spook him. We hadn't even slept together yet, and things between us were still too casual to warrant an introduction to the parents. But I'd slickly gotten confirmation from Nicole that Jude was taking someone and didn't want to be the only one going stag.

"The baseball player?" Eddie asked.

My eyes flickered to Jude in the video screen below mine. He'd changed his screen name to Junior. "No. He's a bartender and a culinary student. He works at the bar across the street from my apartment. We're not serious, but—"

"We don't need his date of birth and social security number, Mole."

I rubbed the dampness from the back of my neck. "Sorry." *Sorry?* Apparently, the days of my instant snappy retort were so last summer.

Jude smiled. "I'm fucking with you. I'm bringing Charley. She's a matchmaker."

"We'll have both Molly and Charley at the party. Too bad we're not drug dealers." Eddie winked.

"Speak for yourself."

The gallery collectively rolled their eyes at Jude.

When he smiled shyly and ducked his chin, my belly flipped. *Not good.*

"Two bartenders. Jude and Timothy can talk shop," Eddie said.

"Same with Molly and Charley. Molly's a matchmaker of sorts, as well!" Alison grinned. "Matching people to jobs!"

Michelle took a swig from a bottle of Magic Hat #9. "Jude and Molly's current flames have something in common. How unanticipated."

"What's that supposed to mean?"

My intention to echo Jude's question disappeared when I dropped my gaze to his screen again. He stared into the monitor with his not brown but "hazel" eyes, and I *knew* he was looking right at me. I shivered.

I was fucked.

Chapter Twenty-One

At half past five the night of the party, Timothy and I entered the Walker Hotel and headed toward Society Cafe. I wore a sleeveless blue, white, and orange printed dress that gathered at the waist and flowed to my knees, paired with nude peep-toe pumps and a cropped denim jacket. Shivering with the cold heat of anxiety, I told myself there was nothing to fear—Nicole and Eddie were on track to get both sets of parents to the venue when they needed to be there and not a second sooner—but my stomach felt like an overused trampoline. I ignored the voice in my head theorizing the true cause of my nerves had less to do with the party and more to do with my confusing feelings for Jude. Since when did I get so bashful and flushed around him?

Oblivious to the workings of my mind, Timothy, clean-shaven and wearing black dress pants and a matching button-down shirt, spent the Uber ride to the restaurant sharing humorous stories from culinary school. His nonchalance in contrast to my nerves was a blessing.

I told the hostess we were with the Blum-Stark party and led Timothy to the room George had showed us at our second meeting. At the entrance, I looked up at him. "Ready?"

He grinned. "Whenever you are."

I mumbled, "Here goes nothing" under my breath, opened the door, and gasped in delight. The dining room was perfect. The fireplace was lit, the cascading flower bouquets to mimic both couples' eighties weddings were vibrant and gorgeous, and the chandeliers were set to the optimal meeting place between so-dark-the-senior-citizens-would-complain and so-bright-the-senior-citizens-would-complain. "Happy Anniversary" Mylar balloons hung from the high ceiling, and photos of both couples and their children and grandchildren had been set up around the periphery. There were even two decorative boards—one for each family—for guests to sign. It was very "Sweet Sixteen."

"Molly!"

"Nani!" A moment later I was swept up in my grandma's plump but strong arms, inhaling her signature perfume, and squeezing her tight.

When toddler Michelle had first called our maternal grandmother "Nana Nina," Dad said it sounded too much like "Nanu nanu" from the seventies television sitcom *Mork & Mindy*. Instead, they'd combined the grandmother nickname, Nana, with her first name, Nina, to form "Nani."

She disengaged from our embrace and grabbed onto my hands. "Such a shayna punim."

I did a twirl, then turned to Timothy. "My grandmother said I had a pretty face in Yiddish."

His dark eyes did a circle of my face. "I have to agree with her."

"Thank you," I said, patting his arm. "Nani, meet Timothy."

She dropped my hands to shake his before appraising him without a hint of subtlety, the way only grandparents could get away with. "Handsome boy."

I beamed. "Agreed!"

"Thank you," Timothy said.

"Looks just like Jude."

My breath hitched. "W-what?"

Just then her sister, Great-Aunt Arlene, came over and whisper-yelled, "There's more pictures of the Stark couple than Stacey and David!"

As a bellow of laughter filled the room, I located the source—Jude. Of course he'd heard. We locked eyes and he mouthed "Aunt Arlene" with a shrug.

I raised my palms in apology before appraising him and his date in a way I hoped was less obvious than Nani's. Jude had shaved for the occasion—I guess he'd received the same memo as Timothy—and was wearing black dress pants and a dark purple button-down shirt. His date was the same brunette and blue-eyed woman from Hillstone. Now that she was standing, I could see she was about my height with a similar slender build. Like me, she wore a sleeveless knee-length patterned dress.

I turned back to Nani. "I'm sorry I haven't called in a while." Between work and getting sick, I'd been a negligent grand-daughter. It was unacceptable. She was the only grandparent I had left.

"That's okay, my sweet. I'm sure you have your hands full." She glanced between me and Timothy and winked. "I remember it well." Even as her blue eyes twinkled, a shadow crossed her lined but still beautiful face.

My heart slowed. She'd been married for sixty years. How did one go on after such a significant loss? "How about I come visit you in Riverdale next week? We can watch reruns of *Mary Tyler Moore* and *Rhoda* on Hulu." I doubted my company would fill the hole left by Papi's death last year, but it was the least I could do.

"I would love that." She planted a kiss on my cheek, surely leaving a pink lip-shaped mark behind, and whispered, "Enjoy your date."

As she joined her sister, I spotted one of mine, Michelle, making her way toward me, her husband, Patrick, at her side.

"I just molested a strange woman thinking it was you from behind," Michelle said.

"Because molesting *me* would have been normal?" I asked.

She scoffed. "I swiped her ass. BFD. But it was Jude's date. She could be your twin."

I clenched my jaw. "She looks nothing like me. Why do people keep saying that?" I realized I was whining and flicked an invisible piece of lint off my dress.

Patrick said, "She resembles all three of you. All five of you, actually." He turned to Timothy, whom he hadn't technically met yet. "The entire family looks perversely similar, like they were cloned over and over again. And then there's me. Like a Black polka dot among a sea of white blue-eyed wonder quintuplets."

Patrick was right. While growing up, we elicited looks whenever we went out as a family, all of us with fair skin, dark brown hair, and blue eyes. My dad said it was because we were head-turningly attractive. I suspected it was because we looked like freakish multigenerational replicas.

"I only married you to end the cycle." Michelle jutted her hip against his, then threw her hand against her mouth. "Maybe Charley's our secret bastard sister from another mother. Remind me to ask Dad later."

"Because asking him about an illegitimate daughter at his

thirty-fifth wedding anniversary party wouldn't be weird at all."
I shrugged her off, wishing I could unhear her comments about
my alleged resemblance to Charley as easily, and snuck in be-
lated introductions to Timothy just in time to be attacked by
my niece.

"Aunt Molly!" Four-year-old Eris, wearing a darling pink
pleated dress and matching Mary Janes, ran circles around me.
She stopped to catch her breath, allowing me to kiss the top of
her head and drink in the floral scent of the Frozen by Disney
spray I'd bought for her last birthday. "Aunt Molly," she repeated
through puffs of breath. "There's 'nother lady here who looks
just like you!"

I sighed in defeat. *Fine.* Charley and I were arguably the
same "type" appearance-wise—dark-haired, light-eyed, medium
height. Maybe being a child, Eris's depth of observation was still
so underdeveloped, she saw us all the same.

But wait. If Charley was Jude's type, did this mean I was his
type too?

I did a slight shake of my head. Who cared what Jude's type
was? I was here with Timothy, who was…who was…I chewed
my lip. Timothy was *great.* He was easy on the eyes, sweet,
and funny. There was nothing *not* to like about him. From
the first time we'd met, he'd been a safe and weirdly familiar
presence.

But his compliment about me being pretty earlier hadn't
turned my insides to mush. I didn't *pine* for him. And I definitely
didn't see us celebrating sixty years of marriage someday like
Nani and Papi.

I glanced at Jude across the room and quickly back to Timothy. Where was I going with this and why right now? It was my

parents' party. I could figure out my love life tomorrow. I turned to Timothy and smiled away the angst swirling around my gut. "I need a drink."

"I hoped you'd say that."

I chuckled and gave him a comforting pat on his lower back. This was probably as awkward for him as it was for me. At least I was related to these people.

I had taken one sip of my Pinot Noir when my phone pinged a text message from Nicole that they were on their way.

> **Nicole:** We'll let you know when the eagle has landed.

I snorted. To anyone listening, I said, "The Blums will be here soon."

"The Starks too."

My eyes met Jude's. "H-hi," I stammered. All our co-planning had led to this moment. I had no idea where we even were in terms of our dynamic, only that it had changed drastically since the first planning dinner in Hoboken.

"Mole," he said in acknowledgment while scraping his phantom scruff. "Nice hair thingie."

I touched the side of my head where I'd worn one of the butterfly barrettes he'd bought me and cleared my throat. "This is—"

"Timothy?"

"Charley!"

I glanced at my date, who was beaming at Jude's. "You guys know each other?"

"We...um...went out." Charley blushed and tucked a long

strand of dark hair behind her ear before looking up at Jude. "Just once."

"Only because you never texted me back."

"You texted?" Her blue eyes widened to the size of quarters.

"Yes!" Timothy fiddled with the top button of his black dress shirt.

"I never got it." She dabbed at her neck. "I assumed...I would have..." She glanced at Jude and back to Timothy. "Never mind."

Jude coughed. "Wow, this is...what a small world."

"Totally," I agreed, nodding at Jude.

"Listen up, everyone," Michelle called out.

Happy for a legitimate reason to end the current conversation, I turned around to face my sister, who stood at the front of the room with Alison.

"We have it on good authority that both couples are about ten minutes away," Michelle said.

"If you need to leave this room for any reason, do it *now* and be quick." Alison jutted her head in the direction of where her family sat at a round table. "I'm talking to you, Benjamin."

As her son buried his curly head into the crook of his other mom's neck, the gallery oohed and aahed at the little boy's adorableness.

In the final minutes before the guests of honor arrived, I took stock of the room. It was now filled with both couples' children, grandchildren, parents, aunts, uncles, and closest friends and colleagues. Warmth filled my heart. I couldn't wait to see Mom's and Dad's faces when they discovered they'd been played. My phone pinged in my hand. "They're here!"

The room grew quiet. My pulse raced. "This is it." I smiled

up at Timothy, but he was gawking at Charley. Did he wish he was here with her instead of me? Did I care? To my relief, the door opened before I had a chance to answer my own question. Tonight was about my folks and Mr. and Mrs. Stark.

Nicole entered first and stood to the side so that the two couples, who I assumed had met up in the lobby, could enter the room at the same time.

The rest of us erupted into a collective shout of: "Surprise!"

The Starks squealed. Laura slapped a hand to her mouth. Randy, looking healthy if not a tad thinner since the heart attack, burst into laughter and gave Eddie a bear hug. In contrast, my parents were silent. Their jaws dropped, and they shared an expression of shock.

Giddiness rushed through me. We'd fooled them but good! I dashed over to them and pulled Dad into a hug. "Happy anniversary!"

When he released me, there were tears in his light-blue eyes. "I can't believe you guys did this," he said, his voice choked with emotion.

"Are you surprised?"

He scratched at his salt-and pepper-haired head. "That's one way to describe it, Squirrel."

Mom joined us, looking stylish in a gray V-neck cashmere sweater, black corduroy skirt, and tall black leather boots. "Thank you, sweetheart."

She was oddly subdued, which I attributed to shock. "We wanted to do something nice after the difficult year both families had."

Her chin-length bob, now dyed chocolate brown to match her daughters', swayed as she took stock of the room. "This is certainly...nice." She smiled, but it didn't quite reach her blue eyes.

I twirled my hair and frowned. Compared to the Starks—whose collective shrieks of unadulterated delight were still going strong—my parents' joy seemed muted. Before I could give it another thought, Nicole pulled me into a side hug.

"We did it." She beamed at me and clapped her hands together. "The venue is perfect. Who would have thought you and Jude would make such a great team?"

"Not me," I muttered, ignoring the squidgy feeling in my belly.

"Where's your date?" she asked, scouring the room.

"Over there," I said, pointing in his direction. He was at the bar...with Charley.

"Where?" She squinted. "*Oh!* He looks so much like Jude from far away!"

I balled my hands into fists and gritted my teeth. *Do not engage.* "Cute dress!"

She lowered her chin like she'd forgotten her outfit for the night—a sleeveless mini dress the color of a Granny Smith apple.

Her husband, Dean, joined us. "Don't you just want to take a bite out of her?" He opened and shut his jaw in a biting motion.

"Can't say I do." I laughed and kissed his cheek in greeting.

After Eddie made a short toast wishing the Starks and Blums a collective seventy-five more years of wedded bliss and thanking everyone for coming, dinner service got started.

Between the salad and main courses, Michelle and I went up to the bar to refresh our drinks.

In front of us, Great-Aunt Arlene waggled her finger at the

bartender. "Not too much ice. If I wanted ice water with a splash of vodka, I'd ask for it." As she walked away sipping out of a cocktail straw, she muttered, "Too much ice."

Michelle and I looked at each other and burst out laughing.

Dad came up behind us and did a double take. "How did you get here so fast?"

I pointed at myself. "Me? What do you mean?"

He blinked. "Didn't I just pass you on your way to the bathroom?"

"That was Charley, Dad. Jude's date," Michelle said with a snort.

My mouth fell open. "Are you for real? Did you seriously confuse a total stranger for your daughter?"

Michelle hooked her arm through Dad's and leaned against him. "I did the same thing."

I groaned. "Methinks you both drank some funky Kool-Aid."

Even though my initial plan at the party, before our unspoken truce, had been to stay as far away from Jude as possible, I found myself sharing a table with him and Charley at some point. With guests moving around between courses and mingling, it was unavoidable. Timothy was also exceedingly interested in the kitchen management at Hillstone, except that, even while directing his questions to Jude, his eyes were on Charley.

"Everyone raves about the sushi," Timothy said, staring at her. "But I can't get enough of the ribs."

Eddie and his wife, a gorgeous catalogue model who was a dead ringer for Zoë Kravitz, joined us. "What do you think?"

Sienna shook her head in wonder. "You're right. I stand corrected. You were not exaggerating."

Jude scowled at his brother and sister-in-law over the rim of his whisky tumbler. "You must have been at math club the day Mom and Dad lectured us on the rudeness of having cryptic conversations in front of others."

Eddie laughed before downing the rest of his drink. "Enjoy your bizarro world." He kissed his wife on the cheek. "C'mon, babe. Let's make out in the coat closet."

"Your brother is weird," I said to Jude. *Please don't bring up my former crush.*

"No argument there, Mole."

To Charley, he said, "My brother is usually cooler than..." He let his voice drop off. Charley was deep in conversation with Timothy about the magic of ground chipotle pepper. "I prefer nutmeg, actually," Jude told me, straight-faced.

"Cinnamon." I sipped my wine and pretended this wasn't awkward. Just making small talk with Jude about condiments while our respective dates hit it off. Nope. Not awkward at all.

Later, in the bathroom, I was reapplying my lipstick when I locked eyes with Mrs. Stark's reflection in the mirror. I smiled. "Having fun?" It was our first opportunity to interact aside from a quick "Happy anniversary" hug when they'd arrived at the party.

"It's one of the most special nights of my life. Thank you for your part in planning it."

"It was my pleasure!" *Mostly.*

Laura brushed her shoulder-length auburn hair. "None of us can get over how much your date resembles Jude. Only not as handsome." She waved her hand. "See you out there."

I forced a smile and waved back even while my dinner sat uncomfortably in the pit of my stomach.

I left the bathroom but froze at the entrance to the party

room to observe Jude, Charley, and Timothy talking in a small circle about twenty feet away. Nani wasn't imagining it. Hell, even Jude's own mother saw it. Three months earlier, seeing Jude within an inch of the guy I was dating would have left me paranoid...and certain...that my most embarrassing moments were about to be leaked. It would have been uncomfortable for sure. But *this*...the realization that the guy I was dating bore an *uncanny* resemblance to the boy I'd hated since before I learned long division...well, uncomfortable didn't even begin to describe it.

I stole a closer look at Charley. First Esther had confused us at Hillstone, then Michelle tonight...even my own father couldn't tell the difference. I didn't think the resemblance was *that* strong, but I was done denying the affinity. We looked alike. With a little Photoshop and creative filters, she could play me in a movie. She could lock me in a basement and, with some hypnotism of my family members, probably eat my plate of turkey and stuffing at Thanksgiving with nary a blue eye blinking.

I broke out in a cold sweat.

Nicole approached. "You don't look so good, little sis. What's wrong?"

"Bathroom. Now."

Chapter Twenty-Two

Michelle sat on the bronze-colored loveseat in the bathroom. Nicole had texted her to join us here immediately. "Did you honestly never notice before?"

I hovered over the sink where I'd just splashed cold water on my face. I hadn't puked yet, but the night was still young. "No. I swear." It was the truth. I'd been seriously oblivious. Or had I been in denial? Esther had pointed out the resemblance from the very beginning. But Jude was my enemy. Or at least he had been when I first met Timothy. Why would I want to date someone who looked like my enemy?

"Timothy isn't the first either."

A shiver ran through me. I turned to face Nicole, who was standing next to me in front of the mirror. "The first *what*?"

My middle sister glanced between me and Michelle while chewing on her peach lipstick. "Have you ever even dated a guy with blond hair?"

I harrumphed. "It's called a type. I like dark-haired men—"

"Who look like Jude," Michelle interrupted.

My head spun. It was like the early aughts all over again—being ganged up on by my bossy older sisters. Although, to be fair, they were way meaner to each other than they ever were to me. "I'll give you Timothy. But claiming *every* guy I've dated looks like Jude is grasping at straws." Wasn't it? I leaned my back against the edge of the sink and crossed my arms over my chest.

"It's not just looks," Nicole whispered before ducking her head.

My heart thudded in my chest. "What?"

She lifted her chin slightly. "Amal was also the youngest of three kids."

I blew a raspberry. "Fluke. Lots of people have two older siblings, including me. It proves nothing." I worked to sound assured on the outside, but inside I was losing ground—fast. Fearing my legs wouldn't hold out, I joined Michelle on the couch.

"What about Isaac from law school? Didn't you say his mechanism to relieve tense moments was to break into dance? Sounds a lot like Jude back in the day. And let's not forget the minor league baseball player you dated before Timothy." Nicole squeezed into the small space on my other side. Three grown sisters on a couch built for two.

"Jude hasn't played baseball since high school!" *Wait.* Was that the root of all of this? I felt awful about Jude's accident in high school and therefore sought guys who reminded me of him in order to . . . to *what*?

Michelle snickered. "Don't get your G-string in a bunch, *Mole.*" She stood.

I scowled up at her. "Easy for you to say."

Nicole rubbed my arm affectionately. "If it makes you feel better, Jude does it too."

"Right. I mean . . . c'mon . . . look at Charley!" Michelle froze as the bathroom door opened.

We all turned around.

Charley.

"Hi!" She waved cheerily. Unaware she'd been the topic of our conversation mere seconds earlier, she entered a stall while the three of us spent the next half minute gaping toward the space she'd just abandoned.

A noise escaped Nicole's mouth right before she clamped her mouth tightly closed.

Michelle pressed her hand to her stomach and hinged at her hips.

"Pull yourselves together," I hissed. This was not funny. Wouldn't Charley find it odd that the three of us were in the bathroom in total silence, aside from the squeaks Nicole made every few seconds when the temptation to laugh got to be too much? We had to say something. "So...did you try the prosecco? Do you guys know the difference between prosecco, Champagne, and cava?"

My sisters stared at me with matching wrinkled brows.

I mouthed, "Act normal" and pointed at Charley's bathroom stall.

"Uh. Oh yes. Cava's from Spain, and Champagne's from France," Nicole said.

Was I the only one who hadn't known this?

The toilet flushed. Charley exited the stall with surprising force, the door banging against the hinge. While washing her hands, she said, "I never knew the difference!"

For some reason, this made me feel worse.

"See you out there," she said.

When it was just the three of us again, Michelle said, "Where were we?" Her chin quivered.

"All of Jude's girlfriends are weirdly similar to Molly too," Nicole said before cracking up.

I let them have fun at my expense before tapping my feet impatiently.

When they finally stopped laughing, Nicole said, "Sorry."

Michelle's expression softened. "It's true, though. At the table earlier, the four of you were like weird mirror images. Everyone was talking about it."

I rolled my eyes. "I feel so much better now."

"And Charley is a matchmaker, which is essentially a recruiter for love." Nicole clapped her hands to her face à la Macaulay Culkin in *Home Alone*. "Didn't he also date a lawyer? You were a lawyer!"

"Still a lawyer," I mumbled.

Michelle turned to Nicole. "Am I imagining this, but did the girl Jude took to the prom remind you of Molly?"

I gawped at her. "Haley? How do you even remember who Jude took to the prom?"

Nicole's face was now the Pink Lady apple to her Granny Smith dress. "Yes! They all took limo pictures together, and Haley and Molly were yapping away between photos about law school versus medical school." She looked at me fondly. "It was adorably studious."

Michelle nodded energetically. "Haley was the first of the clones!"

Nicole chuckled. "That we know of."

My heart skipped a beat. "You all knew about this? Even Eddie and Alison?" Everyone except me and Jude. All the snickering behind our backs finally made sense. "So we both have a track record of dating each other's doppelgänger. What does it mean?"

"Personally, I always thought your hate for him was a little 'the lady doth protest too much,'" Michelle said.

Nicole nodded. "Same. I always suspected you had a little crush. Both of you. All the traits you claimed to hate about each other secretly turned you on."

"No way!" This was where I drew the line. Even if my physical reactions to Jude of late had been less "repulsed" and more...I didn't want to say "aroused," but fine...our antipathy toward each other growing up was as real as the hair on my head. It had to be. Otherwise, a huge chunk of our adolescence had been based on a lie.

"I can't deal with this right now." I stormed out of the bathroom in search of Timothy. It was rude to leave him unaccompanied for so long, especially to vent about another guy—one who could be his twin. Oh, God. They even had the same breed of dog. And they both named their dog after a famous athlete! They both drummed their fingers, quoted Beatles songs...the list went on. *We're all Groot.* My stomach lurched again.

I didn't get far. Standing outside the door of the men's room with their backs to me were Jude and his parents.

"It's time to consider what you want to do with your life. You can't be a bartender forever." Laura reached out her arm to comfort him, but he dodged her touch.

"Your mom is right, son. Once you're my age, bartending won't have the same draw. Women won't be handing you their phone numbers when you have a dad bod. Trust me." Randy rubbed his slightly protruding paunch.

A flush of heat swept up my neck. Why were they saying this to him now...in the middle of a party he threw for them?

Jude shook his head in disbelief. "Are we really having this conversation at your fortieth anniversary party? I'm not *just* a bartender. Did you know I chose this place? My expertise in the restaurant industry helped us find it."

Way to steal all the credit, Rude.

"Molly and I actually," he amended.

I touched my fingers to my lips in surprise and unexpected pleasure.

"Your father was just saying his company was looking for assistant merchandisers. They have a great training program. Right, Randy?" his mom said.

Merchandising? Jude? No way.

"I have less than zero interest in the garment industry," Jude said.

Enough.

Interrupting their squabble, I said, "Just the person I was looking for."

All three turned to me.

"I can give credit where it's due. The wine selections were perfect." I beamed at Jude's parents. "Your son is quite the sommelier. He really knows his grapes."

Jude widened his eyes. *Hazel with blue flecks.*

"Also, Esther wanted me to thank you again for what you did that night." I stepped closer to them as if confiding a secret. "I don't know what would have happened if you hadn't stepped in." Again, I turned to the Starks. "My best friend is having some trouble with an ex. He stalked her location on social media and followed us to Jude's restaurant, then refused to leave. But Jude took charge and got him out of there peacefully. He's so much more than a bartender. He practically runs the place. You must be so proud of him!" I swung my head from left to right. "I should really go find my date. I'll see you guys later!"

I could feel their eyes boring into my back as I marched away with my heart slamming against my chest. Someone had to stand up for Jude, but did it have to be me? What if I'd made things worse?

I joined Timothy in the party room. Charley was at his side. "I'm sorry I've been gone so long. Family drama and all that." I raised my palms in apology.

Jude came up behind me. "Same." He darted his eyes to me and quickly back to his date's.

"No worries," Timothy said. "I'm actually not feeling so hot. Would you mind if I cut out early?"

I frowned. "Not at all. I'm sorry you're not feeling well." He'd been all smiles and laughter when I approached, but I wasn't going to accuse him of lying.

Charley gave Jude a contrite smile. "To be honest, I'm not feeling so great either. I think I'm going to leave."

"Want to share a cab?" Timothy asked.

"Great idea!"

Beaming at each other, they said, "Bye!" in harmony before shuffling off with a renewed burst of energy. I stared after them, waiting for the tears to spring, to feel like my heart had been ripped from my chest. Having a date leave with someone else was the stuff senior prom nightmares were made of, but I felt nothing... for Timothy, anyway.

"That went well," Jude said.

I resisted the urge to smooth down his hair where it was standing up from his frequent self-tussling.

We stared at each other unblinking. *How long have you been dating my doppelgängers? Are you secretly attracted to me too?* "So."

"So."

"Charley's pretty." I cringed, as one did when they essentially flattered themselves. Maybe he wouldn't notice. For all I knew, no one had alerted Jude to the whole lookalike situation.

"Timothy's hotter."

My breath caught. Not what I was expecting. But then I laughed. "You never fail to surprise—"

"Sorry to interrupt you two. Molly, can I steal you for a moment?"

I cocked my head at my mom. "Is everything all right?" I was torn between annoyance and relief at the interruption.

"Your father and I need to speak with you and your sisters." She turned to Jude. "You don't mind, do you?"

He waved a hand. "Of course not."

I followed Mom out of the party room into the hotel lobby where Dad, Michelle, and Nicole sat on two suede couches. The working fireplace and dim lighting gave it a cozy feel—perfect for a family powwow. I assumed they wanted to shower us with thanks in a more private setting.

Michelle patted the space next to her on the burgundy couch and studied me. "You recovered from your epiphany yet?"

"No comment," I mumbled, sitting down. Jude had, in not so many words, acknowledged the peculiarity in our choice of party companions, but I wasn't sure either of us was prepared to interpret the deeper meaning behind it.

Dad stood from the gray couch to join Mom. "Thanks for humoring us. Your mother and I have something to tell you and wanted to do it face-to-face, while we're all together." He passed the invisible baton to Mom.

She nodded. "First of all, thank you all for throwing such

a wonderful anniversary celebration. The planning it must have taken. We know the Starks were thrilled...forty years! Can you imagine?" She laid a hand to her collarbone. "Wow."

I glanced at Michelle from the side of my face. The *Starks* were thrilled? What about the Blums? And also, last I checked there was only a five-year difference between thirty-five and forty.

Dad continued. "We'd planned to have this conversation at dinner with just the five of us, but since that was just part of the hoax to get us here, the lobby is the best we can do, and we wanted to catch you before you left. We've put it off long enough." He dropped his gaze down to his black Oxford shoes and back up again, then cleared his throat. "The thing is...well...there's no easy way to say it, so I'm just going to—"

"Rip off the Band-Aid, David." Mom eyed us one at a time and released a sigh. "Your father and I are separated."

Chapter Twenty-Three

You could have heard a cotton ball drop to the carpet.

"Did you say...separated?" Nicole asked, while Michelle and I froze with our mouths wide open.

Dad paced in front of us as Mom scooched her way between Michelle and me on the burgundy couch. "We wanted to tell you at dinner, but not to an audience of fifty," she said.

Dad returned to his spot next to Nicole. He patted her thigh. "We're so sorry. The timing is awful, but who knows when we'd get another chance to have you all together and without your partners?"

On the verge of tears, I stared across the glass table at my dad. After thirty-five years of marriage, my parents were separating again. I pinched myself, but the accompanying sting erased any hope I had of this being a dream/nightmare. I asked the trillion-dollar question. "Why?"

They exchanged a look.

Oh no. I tensed from head to toe.

Nicole's eyebrows formed a triangle. "Is there another woman?"

I gulped and slid an inch away from Mom. "Or man?" Dad was the goofball. Mom was the flirt.

"No!" they shouted in unison.

In a much softer voice, Mom said, "We grew apart. We got married so young. I was barely your age when I had Michelle," she said, looking at me, her blue eyes pleading.

I blinked back a tear and squeezed her hand while trying to comprehend what was happening.

"We still love each other," Dad assured us.

"You just don't *love* each other," Nicole whispered.

"Sixty is the new forty," Mom said. "We both have too much life in us to stay in a marriage that's become more of a friendship."

"You're not getting it done," Michelle said absently.

I wanted to laugh. I *needed* to laugh. But I couldn't. "So what now?" *Please don't say divorce.* A separation could be reversed more easily than a legal divorce.

The word "divorce" was never used, but Dad had moved into a two-bedroom apartment in an over-fifty-five community not too far from their house. "There's a pool and gym if spending time with your dad isn't incentive enough." He smiled wryly, though it was clear this was killing him.

My heart pinched. In an instant, we'd rewound almost twenty years. I was seven years old again, in my childhood house, eavesdropping while my parents complained about how hard it was to raise three girls. I was staring at Dad's empty chair at the dinner table wondering what I could have done to make their job easier. He'd tried to paint a prettier picture of reality by homing in on there being a pool then, too. But he'd come back and stayed! They'd already had their separation and worked things out. Why was this happening again now, when the hard part—taking care of us and making sure we were fed, clothed, and didn't end up in prison—was over?

"Do Randy and Laura know?" Michelle asked.

There was a slight hesitation before Mom answered. "They're our best friends. It would have been impossible to keep it from them even if we wanted to."

"How awkward sharing an anniversary party with a couple who's no longer together," Michelle said.

"When did you move out?" Nicole asked our dad.

"It's been a month," he said. "We only waited because we thought an intimate dinner would be the right setting to tell you all at the same time. We had no idea what you'd planned."

Nicole pushed out her lower lip. "Sorry for throwing you an anniversary party. We won't do it again!"

Dad chuckled. "There's my favorite middle child for you. Pouting, throwing tantrums, kicking her feet. Too bad there's no door to slam." He gave her a side hug and kissed her cheek. "My Goose."

We all huffed out a collective humorless laugh before staring at one another in silence. What else was there to say?

A hard lump settled in my gut. Was this the last time we'd sit together, just the five of us? The separation explained the sub-dued reaction my parents had compared to the Starks when the surprise was revealed, but the explanation sucked big-time.

When we were kids, my dad moving out had fueled the flame of my bitterness toward Jude. His recent rejection of our friend-ship had meant he wasn't there for me when I needed a friend. Driving the knife deeper was the reality that *my* parents split up while their best friends, *his* parents, were still together. I had been bitter, angry, and jealous.

Tonight, though, I was none of those things. Timothy had been my date for the evening, but I had no interest in seeking his comfort. Chances were, he was balls deep in Charley right now anyway. In a comical twist, the only person whose company I could stomach in this moment, even more than Esther's, was Jude's. The strange, exciting, and wildly uncomfortable buzz of electricity between us could no longer be ignored or dismissed as being one-sided. I craved his particular brand of "straight talking" comfort and then some.

It was the "then some" that frightened me the most.

Chapter Twenty-Four

By the time we returned to the dining room, it was empty aside from Laura and Randy, Alison and Dana, and Eddie and Sienna. Jude had left, which I took as a sign that my weird thirst for his comfort should go unquenched, at least for now. I hugged Laura and Randy goodbye. Ignoring the sympathy, doubling as pity, now worn freely on their faces, I said, "Here's to another forty years."

Randy began counting on his fingers. "That would make us—"

"Please don't do the math," Laura joked, but then her eyes narrowed at me. "Are you okay?"

My lips quivered. The answer was no, but I wasn't about to rain on their love parade. Notwithstanding my sadness over my own parents' separation—a status my optimistic spirit refused to accept as permanent yet—the enduring passion between Mr. and Mrs. Stark filled me with joy. Randy's heart had already been literally broken and sewn back up the year before. He should at least be spared a figurative heartbreak.

I said goodbye to my parents last, doing my best to maintain a stiff upper lip. I was a grown woman, after all, and didn't want to add to their stress. But when they smoothed down my hair and assured me everything would be all right—like they did when I was little and had a booboo—the tears fell...like they had when I was little.

"Are you okay to leave? Timothy will make sure you get home safely, yes?" Mom asked.

The tears came faster, not because Timothy had already left with Charley, but because Mom's concern was another throwback to all the times she and Dad had stood on the porch to defend against an attempted abduction or bear attack when I took out the garbage at night.

"Sure," I said, wiping my eyes. There'd been enough relationship drama for one night. I didn't need to throw the weird doppelgänger quartet into the mix. Mom had been the only family member not to comment on the double resemblances.

"I can't get over how much he looks like Jude," she said, ending her exception status with one sentence.

I grumbled, "You don't say," kissed them both one last time, and headed out.

The temperature had dropped about ten degrees since I'd left for the party, so when I got home a half hour later, I switched out my denim jacket for a pale blue hooded windbreaker and sat on my balcony with a glass of wine. The private outdoor space was the best part of my apartment, and yet I didn't take nearly enough advantage of it as I should. It was Saturday night in New York City, in a residential area crammed with bars and restaurants, and the noise coming from the cars and people driving and walking along Second Avenue made me feel less alone.

I stared into the distance. Although too many other buildings blocked Jude's apartment only six blocks away, I was well aware of its proximity. Was he home? Was he upset about Charley? Did he already know about the separation? Had he known before I did? I sipped my wine. Why was I asking myself these questions and not him?

I balanced my phone on my palm. I could text him. Mom, Dad, Randy, and Laura practically raised all six "siblings" as a unit—soliciting hugs and doling out life lessons, and even the occasional punishment, freely. Besides me and my sisters, Jude was one of the only people who might remember my parents' first separation. Maybe he could help make sense of their second one. And seeking his opinion and advice had become a habit of late. Venting to him now would simply continue the ongoing trend and shouldn't come as a surprise. Maybe he was even awaiting my call.

Let's not go crazy, Molly.

I slumped against my clear hoop-shaped porch chair. It was safe to say Jude wasn't staring at his phone willing me to reach out. Still, my doing so wouldn't be that strange or unexpected in our new normal as *friends*, unlike in our old normal as enemies, and it wouldn't have to *mean* anything. Jude was my first-ever play date. He knew my parents...was emotionally attached to them. His picture was prominently displayed in their—make that *her*—house, for heaven's sake. It was possible he wasn't taking their separation well either. We could comfort each other. I groaned. I was ridiculous and pathetic, and he'd be the first one to tell me so.

I imagined him staring at me, his unusual shade of hazel eyes dilating with desire and his full lips parting as he leaned in to kiss me. I tried to shake the vision out of my head like an Etch A Sketch, but it was no use. Once you fantasized about the buildup to a first kiss, it couldn't be unseen. I touched a finger to my lips remembering the feel of his finger there the first time he'd come over to my apartment to discuss the party. Did he use his hands to cup a woman's face when he kissed her? I squirmed in my seat. *This has to stop.*

I stood and went back inside, locking the balcony door behind me. After placing my dirty wineglass in the kitchen sink, I grabbed my purse, turned off the lights, and stepped into the hallway.

My logical side whispered warnings to abort the mission. It wanted to protect me from opening a Pandora's box filled with destructive matter. But its opposition had the louder voice.

One way or another, this had to stop.

Chapter Twenty-Five

When the elevator door opened to the lobby, I pulled my jacket tight to my chest, and waved goodbye to the doorman on duty. I stepped out of the revolving doors leading outside and gazed upward at the dark starless sky, not quite black thanks to cars driving by and lights on in the surrounding buildings. Then I remembered I didn't know what floor Jude lived on or his apartment number.

Maybe I'd overhear one of the many twentysomething tenants, who were always loitering at the entrance this late on their way in or out of the building, talking about him and casually mentioning his apartment number. *Did you hear about Jude Stark, in 14B? He's secretly lusting after his ex-nemesis while dating her lookalike.*

Because *that* happened all the time.

It also dawned on me I had zero clue what to say once I found him. And it was late. Booty-call late. These were all signs our talk should wait. It made sense to prepare my opening statement before I told him I was coming over . . . in case I changed my mind.

Then I saw him. My heart leaped into my throat, and I stopped short, causing a traffic jam on the pavement. I muttered awkward apologies and cleared the path. He was standing on the sidewalk with his hands jammed into the pockets of his olive green bomber jacket and looking up at my building.

"Jude?" I said his name like a question—as if it might not be him—like maybe it was his double, Timothy, coming to apologize for ditching me at the party.

Jude jolted and dropped his gaze to my face. "Oh, hey."

"What are you doing here?" I smoothed down my hair, like my appearance suddenly mattered, and I hadn't already been on my way to see him.

"I was just walking Yogi."

I glanced from left to right but didn't see the dog. "Where is he?"

"Right." He scratched his cheek. "I walked him before coming here to check on you." He wet his lips. "First you got dumped. Then the whole thing with your parents. Rough night?" He moonwalked a few steps.

My throat tickled. "You really need to work on your bed-side manner." I cocked my head. "Do you...um...want to come up?"

His cheeks pinked. "Sure."

My knees wobbled. Bashful Jude, a version I hadn't known existed until recently, rendered me boneless. I turned my back to lead the way inside in case my complexion matched his.

Our words were scarce in the elevator. To an outside observer, we could have been two strangers heading to separate destinations. Outside my door, my hand shook as I fiddled with the key.

"Wherever you were going before, was it important? I don't want to keep you," Jude said from behind me.

I closed my eyes for a beat as his breath teased the back of my neck. "I was on my way to see you," I admitted.

"Yeah?"

"Yeah." *Yeah?* Cursing my lame response, I pushed open the door, dropped my purse and keys on the storage bench in the entryway, and slipped off my jacket. "Want me to hang up your..." I whipped around to ask for his coat, but the words hovered in the air because he'd stepped into my personal space. I didn't feel threatened, but his face...his *mouth*...was so close to mine. The nearness stole my breath. "Jude." My voice cracked.

He stepped back.

I inhaled, both welcoming the distance and pining for him to close it again.

"I just came over to tell you I don't hate you anymore," he said.

"Me too." I cleared my throat. "I was coming to tell you the same thing."

He narrowed his eyes. "You only hated me because I hated you first."

"Is that what you think?"

His lips formed an almost-but-not-quite smile. We both knew he was right.

Neither of us made a move to stray from my twelve-foot foyer. "Well, thanks for telling me. I was going to ask for your jacket, but I guess you can leave now."

He removed his coat and handed it to me. "How are you handling things?"

I brought it to my nose and then, realizing I was about to sniff his outerwear, dropped it an inch. "You mean my parents or Timothy?"

"Both."

"If I talk about my parents, I'm going to lose it, and you'll mock my ugly cry."

"I already saw your ugly sick and sniffed your ugly smell and there was no mocking."

I wrinkled my nose. "There was a little mocking."

He ignored this. "What about Timothy?"

"Would you think I was mean if I said I didn't care about Timothy?"

"I already know you're mean."

"Only to you." Sometimes it had been fun. Oftentimes it had been out of pure reflex to defend myself. One occasion still kept me up at night a decade later.

He nodded. "Only to me." He took a step forward, lessening the distance between us to almost nonexistent.

We stared at each other. *Kiss me. Don't kiss me. Kiss me.* "What about Charley?"

"We're done." Without taking his eyes off me, he removed his jacket from my arms and flung it onto the bench. "Molly."

Molly. Not Mole, but Molly. "Yes?" My voice was a whisper. His lips were like a magnet, pulling me to him. I grabbed onto his shirt collar and tugged him toward me. Then I froze. Could I do this...kiss Jude? Life as I knew it would never be the same. Two versions of Jude Stark flashed before me. The one who had worn his distaste for me like a security blanket for most of my life. And the one I'd met recently, who made me laugh like no one's business and nursed me back to health. Soft Jude. Which one was I getting?

Jude's gaze traveled from my eyes to my lips and back again. "Molly." He drew out my name like he was in pain.

I clenched my thighs to relieve the building pressure down there. If his desire was an act, a prelude to some sort of cruel joke, he deserved an Academy Award. It didn't matter because I was a goner. *You regret the things you don't do.* I pulled him all the way to me, closed my eyes, and braced myself for impact.

The first touch of his lips to mine was soft and tentative. We lingered in that sweet spot for a while—touching, savoring, sampling—neither of us rushing to deepen the kiss too soon. His mouth tasted like vanilla and citrus, and his eleven o'clock shadow scratched against my chin. When he finally probed my mouth open with his tongue, I welcomed it with mine and sighed contentedly. Jude Stark was a fantastic kisser. I was unreasonably envious of all the girls who knew before me just how amazing he was.

Quickly, what began as just lip-on-lip action became a free-for-all. Jude's hands pulled and twisted my hair. I slid mine under his dress shirt and rubbed down the sinewy muscles of his back. "Jude," I moaned into his mouth. We were still in the foyer. "Bedroom," I whispered into his ear. I took his hand and guided him in the dark.

Once in my room, the frenzy abated. We removed our clothes slowly and with deliberation, allowing the other to notice all the small things...and the big things. Jude was no longer the little boy in bathing trunks with race cars all over them, kicking sand into my face. I made private observations about him in a way I never did with other men I hooked up with. When he sucked on my lower lip, my mind went all, *I'm kissing Jude Stark.*

Jude Stark had the softest earlobes, and he grunted appreciatively when I lightly tugged on them with my teeth. Jude Stark had a beauty mark right above his belly button. (I'd be sure to tease his "mole" at a later date.) Jude Stark had more than a smattering of dark chest hair, but wasn't too hairy. *Jude Stark. Jude Stark. Jude Stark.*

He lowered me onto the bed and slid his hands slowly from my neck, circling my breasts, which hardened against his palm, across my belly, making me shiver, and stopped at the seam of my panties before sliding them down my hips.

I ached for him and spread to give him full access.

His fingers worked me so hard and so well.

I bucked against his hand. "Jude Stark is making me come!"

He paused his work and hovered over me. "Did you just call me by my full name?"

"Argh! I wasn't supposed to say that out loud!" I hid my face with the pillow.

He barked out a laugh. "You can't hide from me, Mole."

I peeked over the pillow. "Are you really going to call me Mole while fucking me?"

"Hard habit to break."

"Noted." I wiggled my bottom half, anxious to get back to it.

"Molly Girl?"

"Yes, Jude." What would Jude Stark look like post-coital and sated?

"I like your face."

It took me a moment to get the Beatles reference, but then I grinned. "Are we really going to do this?"

"Fuck yeah." His brow furrowed. "With your consent, of course."

Jude Stark is asking for my consent. I tapped the wrinkle between his eyes with my finger. "Consent provided. Do you have a condom?"

"Never leave home without one."

I snorted. *Jude Stark is so cocky.*

After grabbing it from his wallet, he flopped back onto the

bed and slid back under the covers. "Molly and Jude, getting it done!"

I giggled. "Our siblings would be so proud."

And then the joking ceased because Jude Stark was moving inside me, and it was serious business. I lifted my legs on either side of him and we rocked together over and over again. The sounds we made blended with the squeaking mattress to create a blissful melody. Jude Stark, the boy who cried when I stole all the candles from his eighth birthday cake, was moaning, "So good. So fucking good" in my ear while beads of sweat formed on his hairline. Jude Stark, who'd avenged my thievery by smooshing a handful of chocolate buttercream against the back of my tiny True Religion jeans to look like I'd crapped myself, was hitting all the right spots and about to make me come harder than I ever had before.

Was this fated? When our mothers set our bassinets side-by-side while they drooled over George Clooney in *ER*, did they predict their two youngest children would *get it done* someday? As for me, I never saw it coming. Yet in the moments before I shattered around him, crying out his name, I wished on every errant eyelash, all my future 11:11s, and the elusive shooting star that this would be the first time of many.

Chapter Twenty-Six

After Jude rolled off me, we both lay on our backs, staring up at the ceiling and breathing hard. "Not bad, Molly Blum," he said, rubbing the side of my leg.

"I'll take that as a compliment, Jude Stark." I curled on my side and studied him. His face was flushed, and a damp strand of hair clung to his forehead. I'd just had sex with Jude. *Jude!* It hadn't quite sunk in yet. How had we gone from barely tolerating the other's presence to literally connecting as one? Was he as blown away by this development as I was? "So... when exactly did you stop hating me and start..." I placed a hand on his belly. "Lusting me?"

He lifted an arm over his head. "I didn't *hate* you, Mole."

"Um hmm." He *so* hated me.

He tickled my arm. "Hate is a strong word. I didn't like you."

"But why?" I cringed for a second, fearing I sounded desperate and not wanting Jude to think I cared. But I did care. We were naked and in bed together. I was allowed to care what he thought of me. "We were friends and then we weren't. What changed?"

He turned on his side to face me. "Honestly, I don't remember much except how perfect you became...like the world might end if you messed up or underperformed."

I ducked my head. He wasn't wrong.

"Your general sweetness gave me cavities. 'Let *me* clear the table! No, *I'll* take out the garbage!'" he said in a slightly higher-than-normal voice and with exaggerated enthusiasm. "Everyone would whisper about what a good little helper you were and then side-eye me."

I pouted. "No one stopped you from helping too."

"I didn't want to help. I wanted to play!" He laughed. "And you were so put together and in control. You always knew the right things to say to the grown-ups, whereas I was always mixing up words and putting my foot in my mouth."

My throat tickled. One time, Jude *complimented* his great grandmother's new hairstyle by saying the color reminded him of a "Brillo pad!" I snorted and threw my hand against my mouth. Or when he said Derek Jeter was the *impotence* of awesome instead of epitome. "Haha."

He gave me fake evil eye. "There's the mean flag I was talking about. But I knew how to take your confidence down a notch. Watching perfect Mollyanna get rattled and frustrated was the sweetest revenge."

"Perfect? Who, me? You were the charming one." I pointed at him. "Always stealing the show—at home and in school. People loved being around you. You were so easygoing and friendly to everyone. Except me. I had to meet you at your level."

"And you did. You still do. But then you started asking my advice—"

"I never—"

"In not so many words," he said, raising his voice. "And taking it. I don't know." His eyes softened. "I realized I preferred being nice to you over being mean."

"Wow. That's almost romantic." I took him in again—the boy from across the street, now the man in my bed. Jude Stark was mad cute.

"And then I saw you naked through the shower curtain, and it sealed it for me."

I shot up. "The shower curtain was see-through?"

He smiled devilishly and pushed me back on the bed. "What about you? When did you start lusting me?"

I thought back over the last three months. "I knew something was off when we searched my bedroom for Yogi and I started sweating. It got worse from there." Mesmerized by his hands making drinks at Hillstone. The desire to nibble on his collarbone even through my fever. I bit my lip. "My sisters suspect my hate was a mask for a secret crush."

"I always thought so."

I shoved him.

He grinned goofily. "I mean…you kept dating guys who were poor substitutes for me."

"You're one to talk! *My* sweetness gave you cavities, but you dated a *lawyer* who was too nice for her own good?"

His response was a blank expression.

"I overheard you talking to her on the phone outside my apartment the day we went to Sakagura."

"*Pfft*. Coincidence."

"My *dad* mistook Charley for me."

Jude laughed and climbed out of bed to toss the used condom in the trash.

My mouth watered at his backside. Jude Stark's bare ass could win trophies.

He turned to face me, unfortunately blocking my view of his full frontal with his dress pants. "Do you know my middle name?"

Considering how long we'd known each other, my answer should have been a resounding yes, but I couldn't recall any instance when Jude's parents had referred to him by his full name. "Only that your middle name starts with a D. Jude D. Stark. *Judy* Stark." I giggled, then got up to pee.

"You're such a pain in the ass." He pulled his driver's license from his wallet. "Read."

"Jude Desmond Stark." I gasped. "Desmond?"

"After my great-grandfather. Desmond and Molly." He slipped back into the bed while humming the tune of "Ob-La-Di, Ob-La-Da."

After using the bathroom, I joined him in bed and snuggled into his side. "My parents are separated." Mind-blowing sex had made me forget, but the amnesia was temporary.

"I'm sorry."

"Me too." I didn't want to ruin the moment by talking about it. I didn't want to talk at all. I straddled him. "I know just how you can make me feel better."

I woke up covered with goose bumps. My first thought was: I slept with Jude last night…*twice.* But the shock had mostly worn off after round one, unlike the anguish caused by the knowledge of my parents' separation.

Next to me, Jude was hogging the blanket. I tugged the floral comforter to my side.

Jude stirred, then muttered, "Blanket stealer" with his eyes still closed.

"Good. You're up."

He played dead.

"Jude." I poked him. "You up?"

He opened one eye. "Are you always this annoying in the morning?"

I sat up. "I was thinking about my parents' separation."

He stretched. "Understandable."

"You want to know why I was such a goody-goody when we were little?"

This got his attention. He stopped moving, his arms at a diagonal. "Because you're a nerd?" He caught the pillow I tossed at him and laughed. "Kidding. Tell me."

"Remember when my dad moved out when we were kids?"

"I'd forgotten about it, but yeah, I do," he said through a yawn.

I told him about the fight I'd overheard and my resolution to make raising three girls as easy as possible by being the perfect little lady. "I wish being on my best behavior was enough to keep them together now." I held my breath for Jude's reaction. Despite the change in our status, he was still Jude. Was it too soon to go all-out Molly on him? With a rush of pleasure, I realized it was precisely *because* he was Jude that I was incapable of being anyone other than authentic Molly.

"Poor Molly girl." He squeezed my hand. "I doubt anything you did or didn't do made the difference then or would now. Sometimes other people's happiness is out of our control."

"Rosaria offered me a job."

Jude's smile split wide open. "Interesting segue, but congratulations!"

The raw happiness on his face jarred me. "I didn't take it! The timing is really bad to switch careers, not to mention the pay cut. It would be a huge step backward."

Jude scratched his head. "Is the timing ever good to make big changes? You just make them when they feel right. And money isn't the only measure of success." He shrugged. "Your life, your decision. But I'm missing the connection to your parents' separation."

I scraped my fingers along the fabric of the comforter. "Nothing really. I just... I was always the solid one, and then I burst that balloon quitting the law. What if it caused stress in their marriage that grew and grew until—"

"Molly!" Jude flipped his legs over the side of the bed and stood. "I know we're trying out this 'being nice to each other' thing, but I've gotta say, you're giving yourself way too much credit here. You had nothing do with your parents' decision. They grew apart and chose to seek a different happiness for their golden years."

"You're probably right, but—"

"No buts. You can't spend your life taking responsibility for everyone else's choices."

I shrugged, not convinced, but I'd let it go for now, choosing to focus on the positive. *We're being nice to each other.*

Jude was gathering his things.

"Are you leaving?" I asked.

"I need to walk Yogi." He slipped his arms through his shirt. "Do you want to come?"

"Please don't feel pressured into spending time with me the 'morning after.' We don't even know what this is yet."

He sat on the edge of the bed and began buttoning his shirt. "What do you want it to be?"

I pushed away his hands and took over. He was doing it crooked. And it was easier to answer him without looking at his face. "I can't believe I'm saying this, but I like you." My cheeks burned.

"I like you too. We fit."

I stopped buttoning, my fingers seeking out the warm skin and soft hair on his chest. "Yeah?" I braved eye contact.

He smiled down at me and tucked a lock of my hair behind my ear. "Sure. We're still Molly and Jude. Except now instead of being at war, we get to bone."

I resumed my buttoning. "While we're on the subject...sort of...remember when you got in trouble for breaking my mom's antique dresser?" Mom had won it in an auction and left it on the driveway for Dad to bring inside through the garage. Before he got the chance, Jude and his friends, in a drunk trespassing adventure, horsed around and accidentally knocked it over, cracking the mirror and chipping the wood.

"Because you ratted me out? No, I have no recollection of not being able to go on the school ski trip as punishment," he deadpanned.

At the time, Jude was so angry, he threatened to climb my roof, sneak through my bedroom window, and leave feces on my bed. He never clarified whose feces. It didn't help that his friends had met Derek Jeter and Minka Kelly on the slopes and talked about it for weeks.

I dropped my hands from his shirt. "I know you think I did

it to get you in trouble, but you taking the fall was really just a casualty of me trying to break up a nasty fight between my parents. My father kept the dresser on the driveway all night after promising Mom he'd bring it inside. She accused him of being careless and inconsiderate as usual. He called her a shrew and said if it was that important she should have brought it in herself." Even my music on the highest volume hadn't been enough to drown them out.

"If he'd kept his promise, the trespasser—you—wouldn't have had the opportunity to knock it over and crack the mirror. Anyway, I swear it wasn't intentional. The next morning, you were in your yard, sneaking guilty glances at my parents fighting, and shifting the blame to you was all I could think of in the moment. I'm sorry you missed the ski trip and meeting Jeter."

"I was more upset about missing Minka Kelly."

I rolled my eyes. I was sure Jude wasn't blind to the actress's beauty, but Derek Jeter was one of the best baseball players of his generation.

Jude raised and lowered his hands. "Fine. As an aspiring baseball legend at the time, I hated not being there. And I blamed it on you, even though I was the one who broke the dresser in the first place." He rubbed his neck. "I used to think not meeting Jeter was the beginning of the end for me in some sort of weird cosmic way."

Shame settled in my soul over truths still not spoken. I'd been trying to talk myself out of feeling guilty. *Jude is happy! Jude likes his job!* But it was no longer only about how Jude felt in the present. It was about what I had done in the past. I grasped the comforter like a life jacket as a tsunami of nerves brewed in my stomach. "There's something else I should—"

"I really need to get home to Yogi," Jude said, glancing at his phone. "With my roommates away, he's been alone all night. Call you later?"

My shoulders relaxed. "Sounds good," I said, giving a silent thanks to Yogi for granting me more time to come clean with Jude that it wasn't the cosmos that had ruined his baseball career. It was me.

Chapter Twenty-Seven

From my high-top table at Hillstone a few weeks later, I watched Jude shake a cocktail for a customer at the large circular bar.

Losing my neighborhood watering hole of Tuttles, at least temporarily, was a small price to pay to avoid the awkwardness of Timothy serving me beer while Charley sat at the bar playing jacks with peanuts. He had texted me the day after the party to formally end things and apologize. He claimed Charley was "the one who got away." Even though he'd worn his lust for her like a facial tattoo and neither of them could act their way out of an open room—*not feeling well, my ass*—his written confirmation alleviated whatever guilt I had for sleeping with Jude that very same night. Instead, I upgraded to Hillstone. The venue wasn't as easy on my wallet and the freebies were limited, but seeing Jude in action was a worthy consolation prize.

Esther snorted, pulling me out of my rapture.

"What?" I asked.

"You're making goo-goo eyes like he's a Chris," she said, tapping the rim of her martini glass. "You have zero finesse."

I sucked my teeth. "Oh stop it! He's *Jude*. We might be dating now, but we're not like that." I sipped my wine and gazed at him over my glass.

He caught my eye and winked.

A buzz of electricity zipped through me. We'd been together almost a month now and known each other forever, yet our intimacy still felt very much new.

"You're not like *that*, huh?" She gave me side-eye. "Deny. Deny. Deny."

I lowered my chin to my chest. Who was I kidding? "Fine, but *shhh*. Not in front of…" I motioned to Jude's roommates, who completed our party of four at the table. Thankfully, they were too fixated on their phones to pay us any attention at the moment.

"We heard everything," Alex said, not looking up.

"He's right." Jerry placed his iPhone face-up on the bar. "We can see without watching and hear without listening."

Esther pushed out her lips and squinted at him. "What does that even *mean*?"

"Come closer and I'll explain it to you," Jerry said, his voice husky. Then, as if startled by his own attempt at flirtation, his blue-gray eyes widened and a film of red crept up his neck. "I didn't mean to… I'm sorry… never mind." He dropped his gaze to his feet.

Esther and I shared an amused look.

"I agree with Esther." Alex straightened the black tie tucked under his red, black, and white argyle sweater. "You're both very much like *that*. I even heard Jude talking to Yogi about picking up new hairbands… I think he called them bunches… for his sweetie pie." He pulled a face.

"That's because Yogi slobbered over all of mine." I smiled into my drink. Jude called me his sweetie pie. Not that he'd admit it. *Talk about deny, deny, deny.*

Alex and Jerry were Jude's friends from college, but the two had been almost like brothers since grammar school where they grew up in Los Angeles. They were also business partners who designed mobile apps for fitness centers.

Alex, a slight guy who wore black-rimmed glasses and owned a collection of argyle sweaters in multiple color combinations, was nerdy cute and only slightly smoother than Jerry, who was attractive and on the cusp of chubby with eyes the color of a Siberian husky's and a thick head of prematurely graying hair.

Their lack of game made the pair's crush on Esther immensely entertaining. Until they were sidetracked by an email from a potential new client, a popular topic of conversation that night had been what it was like living in New York as a British expat.

Continuing where he'd left off, Jerry asked, "Do you miss Jaffa cakes? What exactly *are* Jaffa cakes?"

"What's dating like across the pond?" Alex asked.

Esther's eyes wandered around the restaurant. "Honestly, I wouldn't know. I moved to the states in college." Her voice was flat as her interest in the conversation appeared to wind down.

"Does that mean you didn't date in high school? Because I didn't." Jerry frowned.

"Are you dating anyone now?" Alex asked.

"Smooth," I muttered under my breath.

Esther stood. "If you'll excuse me, I need to use the loo."

Jerry made moon eyes. "I'll go with you. Not to the ladies'. To the men's."

"I'll come too," Alex said, nearly tripping on his tassel loafers.

I observed the two of them shuffle off after her with a smile in my heart. This was the Esther I knew and loved—the sarcastic, strong, and sexy woman who turned dorks to dust, but with humor and kindness, not by cruel dismissal. In all the years I'd known her, only Killian, who'd finally taken the hint and left her alone, had been able to steal her sparkle. Alex and Jerry were way better catches than her ex, but I doubted she'd go for either of them. I was just glad to have my best friend back. With her twin nieces firmly potty trained, she'd cut her Mary Poppins duties down drastically and was no longer commuting back and forth between the city and Connecticut several times a month to help her uncle. Poppy was grateful too, even if her typically aloof cat personality refused to show it.

I turned my attention to Jude, who was flanked by customers. His booming laugh reached our table. I'd always resented Jude for his easygoing and open personality because it suggested a confidence I didn't share. But now that he was *my* guy, I could admit it was sexy as all get-out. He was no doubt in his element working the bar, but was bartending his passion or was it simply what he did to pay the rent?

I squirmed on my stool and ordered myself not to go there. I still hadn't confessed to letting the air out of Jude's tire all those years ago, unintentionally ending his aspiring baseball career when he was thrown off the defective bike. We were having so much fun together, both in and out of bed, and I didn't want to ruin it. Besides, who would gain from the truth coming out? Sure, it might alleviate my own guilt, but would it change anything as far as Jude's career in baseball? No. And would he hate me all over again? Most definitely. Why risk our future by bringing up the past? This way of thinking worked wonders.

As if affirming my decision to let the past go, at least for now, my phone pinged a text message from Nicole to me and Michelle.

> **Nicole:** What's the deal with Thanksgiving?

A pit formed in my stomach. What *was* the deal with Thanksgiving? We were only a week from the holiday and no solid plans had been made. Every other year we'd celebrated as a family at our parents' house. Thanksgiving dinner was the only holiday we always reserved just for us. Now that my parents were separated, would Dad even be invited?

> **Molly:** No idea. Have either of you talked to Mom? She's dodged my last few calls.

Admittedly, I was okay with this since Jude and I hadn't decided when to come clean to our families that we were an item. Not telling her about Jude was a fib by omission, and I hated lying to my mom.

The dancing bubbles appeared on my screen followed by a text.

> **Michelle:** Calling her now.

I placed the phone back on the table as Esther, Jerry, and Alex returned from the bathroom. "That was fast."

Esther straightened her maxi skirt and sat down. "I told them not to wait for me, but..."

I beamed at the guys, who were suddenly very busy examining

the menu. Their crush was seriously adorable. I was still kvelling when Jude appeared with plates of food for the table. "Hiramasa roll, salmon mango roll, spicy tuna roll, and an order of Hillstone's famous ribs." His lips quirked up. "Timothy's favorite."

I giggled. "Can you join us?"

"This is technically my pee break, so not unless I want to risk pissing my pants." He looked at me fondly. "It's worth the risk." As he grabbed another chair, I moved mine over a few inches to make room.

Once seated, he turned to his roommates. "I'm sorry I left you alone with Molly for so long. She's annoying, but she'll grow on you eventually."

To Esther, I said, "Same with Jude. In about twenty-seven years, you won't want to strangle him anymore."

While our three companions exchanged exasperated eye rolls, Jude placed a hand on my thigh and squeezed. I leaned forward and placed a soft kiss on his lips. It was comforting how little had changed in the way we interacted. We still ribbed each other as much as ever, except now, as Jude so eloquently put it, we got to bone. I rubbed a hand along his lower arm, loving the feel of the soft hairs where his sleeves were rolled up. Then my phone alerted me of a new text.

> **Michelle:** Thanksgiving is at the Starks' this year—buffet style.

I sighed. So much for a Blum family holiday.

> **Molly:** What about Dad?

"You okay, Mole?"

My heart tugged at the nickname that just a few months ago had me seeing red. "We're having Thanksgiving at your parents' house this year." Did he already know?

His eyes widened, and I had my answer. "Is that a bad thing?"

I plucked the mango out of a piece of sushi. "It just breaks tradition. Everything is changing so fast." My chin trembled. As a grown woman, the status of my parents' marriage had no bearing on my daily life, so why did it hurt so much?

Jude inched closer to me and rubbed a hand up and down my back. "Not all the changes have been bad, though, right?"

I bit back a smile. "No. One change in particular doesn't suck."

"We can break the news over turkey and mashed potatoes."

"You mean sweet potatoes with marshmallows."

He stopped rubbing and grimaced. "Just when I think you aren't half bad, Molly Blum, you say something like that. Next you'll say you like canned cranberry sauce."

"It's my favorite!"

"We're so doomed."

My phone lit up. "Hold that thought."

> **Michelle:** Dad will be at Thanksgiving.

I beamed at Jude. "My dad is coming too."

"Nice. He can have my sweet potatoes and cranberry sauce."

My hopes soared. "Maybe all isn't lost."

Jude raised an eyebrow. "Meaning?"

I elbowed him. "Separated and divorced are not the same thing."

Chapter Twenty-Eight

According to Jude, homemade sauce made from boiled cranberries and sugar was only marginally less disgusting than jellied cranberry sauce from a can. I wildly disagreed—both were delicious and perfectly tart. This was why, when I handed my contribution to the Stark Thanksgiving dinner to his mother—homemade cranberry sauce—I grinned evilly over my shoulder at him. From a few feet away where he stood in his childhood kitchen, he saw my snark and raised it with a sneer of his own, mouthing, "Foul."

To anyone observing, it was the same hateful exchange we'd been having for years, but major eye screwing was in play beneath the antagonistic masks we wore. No one would think to look beyond the surface, since no one knew about us yet. With both of my parents in attendance, and their separation now common knowledge, we hoped the announcement of our coupling would replace any tension or awkwardness with joy—or at least shock and stupefaction. Only Nani, who had opted to spend the holiday with Aunt Arlene this year, would have to wait a little longer for the news.

A few minutes later, after we'd both greeted our families, we waited for the right moment in the Starks' open-concept kitchen–living room–dining room. Guests milled about, either standing or sitting on the white leather sectional couch, armchair, or charcoal-and-white counter stools. The grandchildren from both families played together on an oversize "Grandchildren Spoiled Here" floormat set off to the side.

I noted with dread that my parents were on opposite sides of the room. Dad was on the couch watching football while Mom hovered over the buffet that had been set up on the dining room table. But I had a plan, and it was time to execute it.

When I caught Dad's eye, I gestured for him to come over. Then I foolishly called out, "Mom," earning the attention of five-plus mothers in the room except, of course, my own. *Let's try this again.* "Stacey!"

Mom turned from the food table and joined us. With narrowed eyes, she said, "We're on a first-name basis now, are we?" She glanced between me and Dad. "What's up?"

I gauged their body language, searching for any sign to suggest their flame hadn't burned out completely. I couldn't find one.

"Did you want something, Squirrel?"

I snapped to attention and removed the folded check from the pocket of my high-waisted gray pleated skirt and held it out. "This is for you guys." Venmo would have worked fine, but I wanted to witness the stress leave their faces when I gave them the tangible money. "It's essentially my most recent commission check. A thank-you for continuing to pay most of my law school loans even though I'm not practicing anymore." I lifted my chin proudly.

Mom wrinkled her brow. "We appreciate the gesture, but it's unnecessary."

"Can you even spare it?" Dad asked.

"Yes!" I clapped my hands. "I've closed a few deals lately, and this would otherwise go into my savings." I pushed it toward Mom. "I thought it might help you guys." I swallowed hard. "You know...ease your burden." My heart did a nervous flutter.

My parents exchanged bemused looks, neither touching the check. "Help us how?" Dad asked.

"What burden?" Mom said.

I frowned. "In case you're having any financial problems of your own." *For example, the marriage-ending kind.*

They wore matching faces of amusement mixed with concern. "Are you okay, Molly?"

I held back a tut-tut. The entire point of the gift was to *lessen* their worries, not cause more. "What part of excess funds makes you think something's wrong?" My cheeks stretched into the most genuine smile I could fake.

"We're not having financial problems. *Ptu, ptu, ptu.*" The spitting sounds were Mom's attempt to ward off the evil eye.

"Your mother's right." Dad curled my fingers over the check in my palm. "Why don't you send this directly to Sallie Mae yourself? Make a dent on your portion of those loans. Sound good, Squirrel?" He squeezed my shoulder and returned to the couch. Conversation over.

Mom's cheeks brightened as she glanced over my shoulder. "Mini quiches!" With a tap on my head, she returned to the buffet.

Before I could bemoan the epic failure of my plan, Nicole and her husband, Dean, waved me over to where they stood by the Starks' wooden bar cabinet.

Nicole handed me a glass of red wine. "How did you get here?"

It was a reasonable question given I usually caught a ride with them when commuting from Manhattan to our childhood home in the suburban town of New City, New York.

"Thanks," I said, taking a sip of wine. "Jude drove me."

Her mouth opened and closed.

While she recovered from the shock, I carefully stepped backward toward the buffet. I closely examined the crudité platter until I overheard Laura ask Jude when his date was expected to arrive.

Turning to the rest of us, Laura raised her voice. "Jude's dating someone...someone 'special,'" she said, using air quotes. "I'm not sure how special she can be considering he was dating someone else a month ago, but that's my Jude." She pinched his cheek. "The ladies' man."

My eyes prickled. I was *special*. I pressed a finger to my lips and waited with bated breath. Our families' minds were about to be blown.

"Actually, Mom, she is special...and she's already here."

Eddie barked out a laugh. "Welcome to the Stark family, where harsh judgments come before introductions."

Laura sucked in a breath as a flush crawled up her neck. "Oh! I didn't mean to suggest she wasn't special. I'm sure she's *exceptional*." She scanned the room with a furrowed brow, then turned to her youngest child. "Where is she? You didn't make her hide in a closet, did you?"

"That was me in middle school, remember?" Alison joked.

Laura waggled a finger in Jude's face while pressing her other hand against her jutted hip. "We're a crowd of lambs, not lions."

"Speak for yourself," Patrick mumbled into his vodka tonic.

Jude laughed. "Relax, Mom. It's fine. My girlfriend has had years... *decades*... to acclimate herself to this crowd."

Girlfriend. I was Jude Stark's girlfriend. I imagined hearts floating above my head.

He crossed the room in my direction.

My heart went *pow pow pow.* This was it.

He winked at me. "Everyone, meet my new girlfriend." He took my hand. "Her name is Molly. She's a singer in a—"

I jabbed him with my hip, giggling even as a droplet of sweat trickled down my back. But we were in this together.

"Ta da!" I said, doing jazz hands for the crowd.

Clink. A glass (thankfully plastic) crashed to the floor. Twenty-plus jaws hung low while eyes bugged out like tree frogs.

Say something. Someone.

Finally, after a moment of silence too long to be called a *moment*, Laura slapped a hand to her heart. "Oh, my God!"

My dad stood and raised his fist. *"Woot!"*

Eddie blinked. "No fucking way."

His wife repeated, "No. Fucking. Way."

The toddlers and small children abandoned their toys and chanted, "Fucky way! Fucky way! Fucky way!"

My mom ran over to Laura. "Yippee!"

"We called it!" The two high-fived, then hugged while jumping up and down.

"You sly fox," Michelle whispered in my ear.

As the wolf-whistles and clinking of glasses continued, Jude and I stood back and observed our families' transition from shock to euphoria and finally to acceptance. In the hour following, conversation expanded beyond the news of our coupling to the football scores, replenishment of drinks, status of the turkey, and other small talk, but before long, it always veered back to us.

My mom stood in front of the armchair where Jude and I were squished together and shook her head in awe. "I can't get over how well things worked out with your dates getting together too."

Patrick pointed a stalk of celery at us. "And the two can play your stunt doubles when they make the movie."

From behind us, Nicole patted my head. "Who would have thought all those times we forced you to play together we were making a love match?"

"We did," both moms said in harmony.

Alison entered the living room clutching something against her chest. "I have one word for you." Revealing the topless photo of the two of us in the baby pool, she said, "*Precious!*"

"I'm happy to report Molly has developed since then," Jude said, squeezing my thigh.

My dad cleared his throat while I buried my head in my hands. Everyone else laughed.

Jude's dad set the platter of hot hors d'oeuvres on the coffee table. Plucking a pig in a blanket from the top, he said, "I'll never forget Jude's first day of first grade. He came home and said Molly wasn't his friend anymore because she dropped his hand in front of the girl classmates and agreed when they said boys were gross. He insisted he'd hate her forever. We tried to talk him down, but the boy can hold a grudge."

I gasped, then turned to Jude. "Really?" Was it possible our twenty-year rivalry stemmed from me shunning him in front of a gaggle of six-year-old girls? I didn't remember the incident, but it rang true given the many other times I had succumbed to peer pressure as a kid.

Jude shrank against the seat cushions and averted his eyes. "I barely remember."

I held a hand to my heart. "Aw. It was so traumatic, you blocked it out?"

"Don't make light of dissociative amnesia. It's a real thing," said Dean, a physician assistant.

"And I don't have it. It's fuzzy, but it's there. You really hurt my feelings, but there was no way I'd give you the satisfaction of knowing it. Revenge was more my style."

Jude's smile was cocky as he said the words, but he'd shown me the sensitive soul behind it. I visualized a six-year-old Jude, his hair in disarray, with a scraped knee and perpetual dirt on his cheek, bruised by the callous and disloyal actions of his best pal. My eyes filled with tears.

Jude smacked his forehead. "Don't *you* cry! *I'm* the victim!"

I pushed out my lips. "What's the accepted timeline for apologies? Because I'm truly sorry."

Jude glanced at his watch. "Twenty-one years. You just made it."

I snuggled closer to him and ruffled his hair. "I promise to kiss you in public all the time. I'm here for *all* the PDA."

"Apology accepted." He wiggled out of my hold and stood.

As I watched him dance his way to the buffet table, something pulled in my chest. I was falling for this man. *Hard.* When not too long ago I could still summon the bad blood between us like it was happening in real time, I was now detached from it. I recalled the dirty tricks he'd played through a haze of newly discovered lust, which I suspected was rapidly becoming so much more... not so astonishing considering we'd been in each other's lives forever. I'd absolved him of all his infractions, but had he truly forgiven mine? Was it even possible to forgive a transgression you didn't know about? The closer we became, the harder it was to keep my secret. So far, he'd been quick to chalk everything up to ancient history, but how many crimes could one person absolve before reaching their threshold?

About two hours later, my mom rubbed her tummy. "Another Blum and Stark Thanksgiving dinner in the books."

Her statement stung. With the big reveal about Jude and me over and the tryptophan setting in, my parents' separation was again at the forefront of my mind. "We've never had a collective Thanksgiving before. It's always been our holiday!"

Mom rubbed my back. "You know what I meant."

I studied her. How was she handling the separation *really*? She'd married Dad in her mid-twenties and was now sixty. Did she want to stay single indefinitely or seek a replacement for Dad? And if the latter, was she afraid of re-entering the dating jungle, or had she already joined the number one dating site for singles over fifty? Bias aside, she was way prettier than most women her age, and without the aid of plastic surgery. Coupled with her intelligence and dry wit, her profile would definitely stand out from the others. Something about her appearance was different today. Haircut? Her makeup! "I like the purple shadow."

She beamed. "You do?"

"Totally. It brings out the blue in your eyes. Dad thinks so too." *Wait. What?*

Her brows drew closer. "Really. Your dad said it 'brought out the blue in my eyes'?"

"Not in those exact words," I said, chewing on a nail. "But he definitely said your eyes looked pretty." I lifted my wine to my mouth and gauged her reaction through the glass.

Nicole joined us. "What are you guys talking about?"

"Your baby sister is trying to parent-trap me and your father." She waved her coffee mug in my face. "I need a refill."

Nicole cocked her head. "You're not taking this well, are you?"

I shrugged. "I'm sad. Aren't you?"

"Of course, but it's not going to affect our lives on a daily basis."

"It's not *our* lives I'm worried about. It's theirs."

"And it was *their* choice to split." She jutted her chin toward the bar. "I'm going to have one more glass of wine. Want one?"

"No, thanks."

Nicole walked away, and I went in search of my mother, who had wandered off. Had she gone to find Dad to thank him for complimenting her eye makeup? Probably not, since she knew I'd made it up, but at least they would converse directly with each other and maybe bond over their precocious twenty-seven-year-old daughter's attempt to "parent-trap" them.

Laura and Randy were hugging by the refrigerator. I smiled wistfully at the happy couple, despite the hollow feeling in my chest. I turned away from the private moment just as Laura said, "I sent Stacey to the basement for your beta blockers. Thanksgiving is not the time to stop taking your heart medication."

Mystery solved. Mom was in the basement. An idea whirred in my brain. If I could get Dad . . . I scanned the room. *There he is!*

I marched over to where he was talking to Jude. "Dad! Would you mind grabbing another bottle or two of wine from the basement? Laura asked. I'd do it, but I really need to use the bathroom." I shifted my feet for emphasis.

"I'll go—"

"No!" I cut Jude off and looked up at my dad with soft eyes. "Please?"

"I'll do it right now." He patted Jude's shoulder. "Good luck saying no to this one."

I counted to two-Mississippi before following him to the basement, quiet as a mouse. When my father started down the stairs, I locked the door and shut it behind him. Then I leaned against the closed door with a satisfied smile.

Jude stood before me. "I thought you had to use the bathroom."

"The feeling passed."

He crossed his arms over his chest. "What are you up to, Mole?"

I chewed my lip. "I'm trapping my parents in your basement, so they're forced to talk."

His mouth quirked. "Seriously?"

"Yes! Remember all the times we were locked in there?"

He raised his eyebrows. "Sure do. And somehow we still hated each other when they let us out." He sighed. "Are you trying to fix things again, like you did when you were little?"

"So what if I am? They're my parents. How would you feel if *your* folks separated after forty years of marriage?" I poked a finger at his chest. "I want them to be happy." *Happy and together.* I slumped against the door.

"I'm sorry." Jude stepped closer and put his hands on the door behind me.

I lifted my head to meet him for a kiss when the basement door crashed open and banged into me from behind. "Ouch!"

My parents pushed past us, uttering *excuse me*s.

When the pain eased, the surprise set in. "But . . . *how*? The lock!"

Jude laughed quietly beside me. "I forgot to mention, the lock broke ages ago."

"I couldn't find any wine down there. Sorry, Squirrel," Dad said with an apologetic shrug.

I rubbed my back. "S'okay." Once he was gone and I was alone again with Jude, I lifted my arms and let them fall. "Best-laid plans."

Jude's eyes twinkled. "I have a better idea."

"To reunite my parents?"

"No, to reboot our old basement episodes to an X-rated version." He took my hand and led me down the stairs.

"I can't believe...*pant*...we're fucking...*moan*...in your... *grunt*...basement." It was a few minutes later and I was against another door one floor down with my skirt hitched up, panties off, and legs wrapped around his hips.

Jude, his jeans down to his ankles, gripped my butt cheeks and drove into me again and again. "Fantasies do come true," he grunted.

Later, I might ask if he'd really fantasized about this moment. I had not, but only because I'd already despised Jude by the time I *had* sexual fantasies. The pressure building, I grasped his shoulders and wrapped my legs tighter around him as he increased his tempo. "Fuck, Jude. Oh, God!"

A door slammed, followed by the *clomp clomp* sound of footsteps growing nearer.

Jude stopped rolling his hips.

"It's the best news ever."

My mom. I stared at Jude wide-eyed. We were in the basement's small office—Alison's bedroom during her college breaks and when she lived at home temporarily after graduation—and thankfully not in clear sight. If my mom caught me in flagrante, I'd die. *Die.*

"Can you imagine if they got married?" someone (Laura?) said.

"We wouldn't have to worry about nightmare in-laws."

Laughter abounded.

"Maybe Molly will be a good influence on Jude and get him thinking about his future more. I worry he's never recovered from not being the next Derek Jeter."

I stifled a moan at Jude's sudden movement. He was still hard and inside me.

"I didn't play shortstop," he whispered.

I frowned. How tired he must be of hearing this. But was there truth to it?

"As long as she's not too busy trying to reunite me and David. It's sweet. My Molly always wants people to be happy. Ever since she was little. It's like her mission or something."

I lowered my gaze to the empty condom wrapper at our feet.

"I found it."

"Great. Let's go."

The *clomp clomp*s resumed then ebbed.

"They're gone," Jude said. He slipped out of me, no longer hard. *Game over.*

Chapter Twenty-Nine

*I*t was the week following Thanksgiving, and I was in the office catching up on emails after back-to-back video calls with candidates. I clicked an unread message from Michael from a few hours earlier.

> Great work these past few weeks. This position with Bluetronics has been in the system for a while. The company is very motivated to get it filled. It's a high-commission position. Read: closing this deal will look good when I talk you up for a promotion later this year.

My body tensed. I didn't need to click the attachment as I'd seen the listing in our internal database already and had passed it right by.

The global gaming company Bluetronics had a Glassdoor rating of only 1.9 out of 5 in employee satisfaction and was included in countless lists of worst companies to work for due to unhealthy office politics, chaotic management, and little room for internal growth. Prospective employees were lured in by the cool gaming aspect only to quit within six months.

I slumped against my chair. I didn't want to touch this one with rubber gloves *and* a grabber tool. I typed a response.

I'll see what I can do.

I didn't mean it, but hoped the six-word sentence would get Michael off my back while I came up with an escape plan.

Needing a pleasant distraction, I reached into my royal blue leather tote bag and pulled out the most recent issue of *Forbes,* which I'd bought at Hudson News in Grand Central before work. According to the latest Ceiling Crashers newsletter, Rosaria's interview had been published, but I hadn't had a chance to read it yet. After scanning the table of contents, I flipped straight to Rosaria's interview. Her passion for helping women in career transition jumped off the two-page spread sending a zing of vicarious pride and joy through my body. By the time I got to the end, my cheeks were sore from smiling. I set a calendar reminder to send Rosaria a congratulatory text later.

My phone pinged.

Jude: Baby Bo's. 7?

Dinner at our favorite neighborhood Mexican café? Yes, please. I responded without hesitation.

Molly: Sopapilla!

I waited for the inevitable gag and puke emojis. Jude lacked a sweet tooth and didn't share my appreciation for fried flour tortillas covered with cinnamon and honey. I probably wouldn't

order dessert after dinner, but I lived to rile Jude up. I was starting to live for Jude *period*—joking with him, texting him, eating
with him, watching TV with him, kissing him, *fucking* him—he
was the time of my life. I was fully vested in this relationship like
never before.

But we were like a house of cards: one blow from caving in. If
I continued to hold on to my secret, I feared it would infect me
from the inside out like poison. On the flip side, if I came clean,
I could lose everything. Either way, I was screwed.

After dinner that night, Jude and I stepped off the elevator of
his building and, like clockwork, rambunctious barking sounded
from inside apartment 7C.

"How does he know?"

Jude's face screamed *Duh*. "Shrewd Jude has a shrewd dog."

I snorted. Jude Stark had become no less cocky since we'd
started dating.

The door hadn't even closed behind us before Yogi lost his
mind. Jude kneeled on the floor, and the puppy placed his paws
on his shoulders and licked his face all over. "Hiya, big guy,"
Jude said between licks and hugs. "I know. I missed you too."
He laughed as Yogi practically jumped over his head. "I know,
buddy. I know."

I observed from the side, moved by this display of emotion
between man and his best friend.

Yogi tired out and Jude stood. "You need to go out, buddy?"

"I just took him." Alex wiped his glasses with the bottom of
his green-and-red argyle sweater.

"Isn't it early for an ugly Christmas sweater party?" Jude asked
his roommate.

Alex swiped his middle finger from the bridge of his glasses down his nose while I exclaimed, "*Rude!*"

Jude raised his palms. "Kidding."

Five minutes later, Jude, his two roommates, and I sat around the guys' brown leather sectional couch watching *Glee* on Netflix. Jude insisted Alex and Jerry *forced* him to watch the old show, but he was full of shit. He couldn't stop himself from singing along and drumming his fingers to the music. It wouldn't surprise me if the guys broke into dance. *Dorks.*

"What's Esther up to tonight?" Jerry yawned, his eyes on Quinn and Puck singing "Just Give Me a Reason" on the flat-screen.

I pretended I bought his yawn, even though it was obviously fake to throw me off the scent of his massive crush on my best friend. "I'm not entirely sure. Should we invite her over?"

Jerry shot up. "Oh, I don't know. The apartment's a mess and..." He darted his eyes around the room and scratched his arms.

Jude laughed. "Dude, are you breaking out in hives over a girl coming over?"

"I just remembered. She's on a da...dinner. A working dinner." She was on a date with a guy she met on Tinder, but there was no reason to break the guys' hearts.

Jerry sat back down. "Too bad. Maybe another time," he said, clearly relieved.

"What kind of dinner?" Alex asked.

"Does she eat meat?" Jerry tapped his chin. "I don't think she had any ribs at Hillstone."

Jude squeezed my knee. "See what you started?"

"She had at least one rib. She's a carnivore." Alex lifted his chin at me. "Right, Molly?"

"Look!" Jude pointed out the window. "A solar eclipse!"

When the guys turned around, Jude dragged me off the sofa and we raced to his room and closed the door, laughing. Then he pushed me gently against the wall and pressed his lips to my forehead, nose, chin, and finally mouth.

The kiss was so soft, it rendered me weightless, like my feet had lifted off the ground and I was floating.

He pulled away. "Hold that thought. I need to use the bathroom." Wiggling his finger, he said, "Whatever you do, don't leave this room because I'm not sure I can rescue you from Leonard and Sheldon again."

"I won't move a muscle," I said, breaking the promise a second later when I relocated to his bed. Something told me he wouldn't mind.

I let my eyes wander the expanse of his room. After the way he'd teased my level of tidiness, I had expected Jude's living space to be a sty. But aside from his perpetually unmade double-size bed and clothes spilling out of his closet and unfinished wood cubby shelves, it wasn't *that* bad—two steps above a college dorm and three steps below a sophisticated, mature man's abode. I agreed with Jude's assumption his mom would undoubtedly compare it unfavorably to mine. I chuckled but stopped laughing when he re-entered the room with an obvious limp. "Did you hurt yourself?"

He joined me on the bed. "Only about ten years ago when I fell off a moving bike. My knee pain flares up occasionally. Especially during a solar eclipse." He grinned.

My throat swelled. My parents had mentioned his osteo-arthritis, and even though I'd witnessed Jude clutch his knee on occasion, this was the first time I'd heard about it straight from him. I dropped my gaze to his gray-and-black comforter.

"What's wrong?"

I took a deep, pained breath and closed my eyes.

"Is this about your parents?"

I touched a finger to my quivering lips. I couldn't carry the weight of what I'd done any longer. It was time. "It's my fault." My voice was one level above a whisper.

"No, it's not." Jude rubbed my back soothingly. "You need to let them make their own choices, whether you like them or not."

I hugged myself to stop shaking. "I'm not talking about my parents."

"Then what?"

I opened my eyes and pointed at his knee. "That."

Jude blinked. "What?" He stopped rubbing my back.

"Your knee. It's my fault you got hurt, lost your baseball scholarship, and still limp during a solar eclipse!" I wiped my nose.

Two deep furrows nestled between his eyebrows. "I don't understand. How is it your fault?"

"I let the air out of your bike tire."

Jude gave a confused shake of his head. "What? When?"

I swallowed hard. "The night of your accident. I...I was home—grounded because of that fucking video of me drunk and puking...that you took! I had no idea you planned to ride the bike to the school. I thought you were already there!" A shower of guilt rained down on me for trying to justify my actions in the midst of my confession.

"Still doesn't answer my question. Why did you..." He paused as if bracing for the next words out of his mouth. "...let the air out of my tires?"

"*Tire.* Just one. I was so mad at you for"—I waved my arms toward him—"being you! I'd just gotten rejected from two Ivy

League schools, despite studying my ass off for years. On top of that I was stuck at home after my first and *only* offense as a *typical* teenager while you were at a game about to be lauded by our classmates for a talent you barely worked at. It wasn't fair, and I lost it."

Jude stared at me, not saying anything, prompting me to babble to break the silence.

"That composure you say I have? My inability to do anything without a plan?" I scoffed. "Well, now you know what happens when Mollyanna doesn't think before she acts."

Still stoic, he asked, "What was your end game?"

I raised and lowered my arms. "I didn't have one! That's the point. I didn't plan any of it. I just grabbed the closest 'weapon' I could find—a wire hanger—ran across the street, and plunged it into your back tire in a rage. I regretted it immediately."

I reached out to touch him, but he stood and backed away from me.

"I never ever imagined you'd ride the bike that way," I said. "Worst-case scenario, I figured you'd discover it the next day and be inconvenienced for a few hours before it was fixed. I planned to anonymously pay for a spare tire."

Jude narrowed his eyes. "How? With a GoFundMe campaign?" He crossed his arms over his chest.

I ignored the rhetorical question. "When I found out what happened—that you tried to ride the bike anyway and it blew— I was so ashamed. I hated you in the moment, but I never ever wanted you to get hurt. I certainly didn't expect or want you to lose your baseball scholarship…your future," I said, the last two words whispered for my ears only.

"You sure about that? You said yourself you resented how

easily baseball came to me when you worked so hard for everything. Somewhere deep inside were you happy?" His eyes pierced mine accusingly.

I vaulted off the bed, genuinely surprised and hurt by the accusation. "No! Absolutely not. You have to believe me. Seriously, Jude. I'm not cruel!"

His eyes refused to meet mine this time.

"Not that it excuses me, but why did you ride it anyway? Why didn't you call a friend to drive you to the school when you realized it was flat?" Neither of us had our own cars in high school.

"I didn't notice it until I was on my way, and I was already late for the game. Scouts from Northwestern and Florida State were coming to see me. I had to get there. Besides, it was only one tire and it wasn't completely deflated. I thought I'd be fine. I'm always fine."

"Exactly why I was so mad." I winced.

"But I wasn't fine." His voice was so resigned, it killed me.

"I'm so sorry. I'm *so* sorry." I pleaded with him to see inside my soul...to know how deep my remorse ran. "I felt horribly guilty, but I was so afraid to tell you the truth. Then we graduated and...my God, Jude, I never thought we'd be here." I pointed between us. "Like this."

"So it was okay that you crushed my dream as long as we weren't fucking?" His tone was even, but his fists were clenched.

My breath hitched. "Of course not! I've carried the guilt with me always. I've tried so hard to stay out of your way since then. It's not easy, because you're relentless. But I took comfort in how mean you always were to me...even years later...I told myself you asked for it. You're the one who started up the pranks this time."

I paused to catch my breath. "And then everything changed. We stopped fighting and became friends. You brought me soup! I fought catching feelings for you. How could I share your bed—touch you intimately—after what I'd done? But you're kind of irresistible." I attempted a smile and walked closer to him. "You never complain about your job or talk about your baseball glory days. You said yourself you had no regrets. I convinced myself you were happy and telling you would only open an old wound. I didn't want to risk losing you over something we couldn't change."

Jude ran his tongue along his lower lip. "Why are you coming clean now?"

"Because you deserve to know, and honestly, keeping the secret is killing me."

He walked to the window with his back to me.

What was he thinking? "Jude. Say something. *Please.*" *Please let us be good.*

Finally, he turned around, and I knew immediately we weren't good in any way, shape, or form.

"I hope you feel better now that you've gotten it off your chest."

"I don't. I'm so sorry—"

He put his arms up as a shield...a shield against me. "Please just go, Molly. I need to be alone." Then he opened the door of his bedroom to show me the way. When I didn't leave soon enough to suit him, he walked out first, leaving me behind with my unwanted apologies.

Chapter Thirty

He couldn't avoid me forever.

Could he?

Perhaps two days was too premature to think about *forever;* yet, here I was, approximately forty-eight hours since my confession, unable to focus on anything but Jude: how he was feeling about the truth of his injury and about me. About *us.*

After leaving his apartment, I'd gone straight home, undressed, and slipped immediately under the covers for a pity party of one. I wanted to honor Jude's request for space, but I still needed him to know how remorseful I was. I sent one last bordering-on-groveling text, then stared at the screen waiting for the dancing ellipses that never came. I woke up the next morning with an indentation from the phone on my chin and no response from Jude. He had to know I hadn't purposely caused his accident. And there wasn't a grain of truth in his accusation that I was subconsciously happy he got hurt and lost everything. He'd said it in anger. But eventually he would understand and forgive me.

Eventually wasn't soon enough for me. I was unable to take the silence another day. After work that night, I jumped on the

6 train two stops to 28th Street and walked the one block south to Hillstone. I wasn't even certain he'd be working, but based on his response rate lately (0 percent), asking first was unlikely to provoke an answer. Best-case scenario, his eyes would light up at the sight of me, and he'd jump over the bar and dip me in a Hollywood-style kiss. Worst-case scenario, he'd dump me on the spot. But at least I'd know.

With my pulse in my throat, I approached the revolving doors of the restaurant. It was an ever-popular venue; several others were doing the same. "After you," I said to two smiling women who appeared significantly less anxious about entering than I was.

Breathe in. Breathe out. The hard part—the confession—was over. The ball was in his court now.

I raised my palms to push the door for my turn only to step back again to allow another group to go ahead of me as my last thoughts reverberated back at me. Not knowing if Jude's need for space was temporary or permanent was killing me, but it wasn't fair to confront him at his place of business and force him to talk before *he* was ready. He'd reach out in his own time, the operative word being *his*. I turned on my heel. *He's probably not even in there.*

Was he? I tapped my shoe. What was the harm in taking a peek through the window?

A moment later I had my answer when the sight of Jude behind the bar sent a burning pain through my heart. He was pouring a glass of wine, his hand wrapped around the bottle. Oh, how I'd missed those hands. What were the thoughts behind the easy smile he shared with his customers? Were they of us? Of me? He'd shaved and combed his hair. *Whatever that means.* A fresh wave of sadness crashed through me. I didn't want us to be over. I wasn't ready...not by a long shot.

Jude stilled.

I sucked in a breath. Did he sense someone watching him?

In what felt like slow motion, he turned his head toward the window. Our eyes met.

I pleaded with mine. *I'm sorry. Forgive me.*

He didn't answer.

An eternity passed until his head snapped back to a waiting customer.

I left before he looked over again, mostly because I was afraid he wouldn't.

Chapter Thirty-One

The first night of Hanukkah was the following weekend, and I headed to my childhood home to celebrate with my family. I still hadn't spoken to Jude.

Nani placed a paper towel in front of me on the kitchen table. On it was a sizzling latke straight from the frying pan. She kissed the top of my head. "I love this *keppe*."

I beamed up at her. "I love your head too, Nani."

The scent of potatoes and onions frying in oil had been wafting through the kitchen for the last twenty minutes, and I was finally able to sample the merchandise. Nani was the queen of the potato pancake and had assumed command of the kitchen. Mom was in the four-bedroom house somewhere, and my dad? Well, I had no idea where he was today. If I could forget my own romantic troubles for more than five minutes, I'd probably be consumed with theirs. *Hashtag: bright side.* I blew on the hot latke before taking a bite.

"Is Jude across the street? I'm sorry I missed the big announcement at Thanksgiving," Nani said.

To keep my mouth occupied, I finished the potato pancake and resumed staring at my open and long-dormant text exchange with

Jude. In what had become a relentless nasty habit, I crossed my fingers, hoping I'd catch him in the process of writing me back.

Our entire senior year of high school had been fraught with misunderstandings. Jude's running for the election had nothing to do with me, yet beating me was an unavoidable side effect. My justification for tattling on him for accidentally breaking Mom's dresser was to distract my parents from fighting. Yet Jude missed the ski trip as a result. It was like one big game of dominoes, but neither of those incidents changed our lives in any meaningful long-standing way. Unpremeditated or not, I couldn't say the same about beating the shit out of his bike tire with a wire hanger.

He was never going to forgive me.

The front door swung open. Little-girl footsteps and squeals saved me from further questioning as Eris ran into the kitchen and straight into her bubbe Nina's arms. My niece knew the family hierarchy at Hanukkah. She'd already chomped her way through one pancake when Michelle and Patrick, holding a sleeping Henry, entered the kitchen. A few minutes later, Nicole and Dean returned from the mall, and we lit the menorah and said the Hanukkah blessings.

For the next hour and a half, each time someone mentioned Jude, I had to "use the bathroom," "make an urgent phone call," or "check something in the oven."

I stood and stacked a couple of dirty dishes. Clearing the table was another excuse to leave the dining room before anyone brought up the "J" word.

"The Starks will be here soon for coffee and Bubbe's famous jelly donuts."

Crash.

"Molly!" Mom yelled.

"It *had* to happen." Nicole chuckled.

"Aren't you glad you didn't use the fancy plates?" Michelle asked.

"Sorry!" I bent to collect the shards of what used to be two Disney Princess ceramic dinner plates. My family continued to speak around me, but I could only focus on one thing—the Starks were coming over. Jude wouldn't be with them…no way…but I'd still have to face the wrath of Laura, who'd want my ass on a platter for hurting her youngest son, and Randy, who'd blame me, rightfully, for ruining his son's chances of making it into the National Baseball Hall of Fame.

The doorbell rang. I finished sweeping the broken plates into the trash and wiped my clammy hands on my blue jeans. Did I have time to slip out the back door and take a long walk (or two) around the block? Would anyone notice my absence?

Noises sounded from the hallway.

"Happy Hanukkah!"

Mwah, Mwah.

"Good to see you."

Smooch, smooch.

"Molly's in the kitchen, Jude."

My heart lurched upward. Did she say Jude?

"She broke a plate."

Laughter.

"Your aunt's got greasy fingers."

I stared at my hands, relieved there was nothing breakable in my grasp. *Jude is here.* A feeling of dread overcame me. Was I ready to face him without a glass wall between us? Did it mean anything that he'd referred to me as Eris's aunt rather than his girlfriend?

As footsteps approached, I was resigned to pulling myself together. I turned away from the sink as Jude entered the kitchen in a dark blue Henley and black jeans. Birds took flight in my belly. I'd missed his face—his hazel-blue eyes and dazzling smile. The scent of fried oil lingered in the air.

He walked toward me. I opened my mouth, realized I had no idea what to say, and shut it. He was coming closer. I could smell his laundry detergent. *He's right in front of me.*

"Hi," he said, leaning down to kiss my cheek.

I touched a hand to my face, already missing the feel of his lips on my skin, and blinked at him. *What the fuck?*

The room was now filled with Blums and Starks. They were watching the newest set of lovebirds with interest. Jude took my hand and swung it.

I dug my fingers into his palm and whispered, "Am I missing something?" My heart flip-flopped. Laura and Randy beamed at us. They didn't appear to hate me.

"Just go with it," Jude said out of the side of his mouth before confirming to my mom he preferred decaf coffee and would love a sufganiyot, one of the aforementioned jelly donuts.

"Since when do you like sweets?" Laura asked.

"My thoughts exactly," I mumbled. "Among others."

"You've foiled my plan. It was for Molly. She begged me to give her mine, so she'd have two."

"What?" I tried to pull myself from his grip, but he held firm. "Come with me, Jude. I...uh...need to show you something in my room...that thing I mentioned." I dragged him out of the hallway and up the stairs.

"Keep the door open, young lady!" Mom yelled after me.

"I'm twenty-seven!"

"Doesn't matter. My house. My rules."

"Fine!" We entered my room, unchanged since I was sixteen with a white-and-gold four-poster canopy bed and matching dressers. I turned on the light, leaving the door open as promised. I had zero plans to get it done with Jude in my childhood bedroom while my family was downstairs anyway. Thanksgiving in the Starks' basement was different. Hanukkah was a *religious* holiday, entirely inappropriate for secret sex; Nani was here...gross...; and most importantly, Jude and I were on a break that I prayed wasn't permanent.

Jude casually touched the spines of the books lining my shelves. I owned a wide selection of young adult dystopian novels and contemporaries like the *Pretty Little Liars* series popular in my teens.

It was odd...him being here. He'd snuck his way into my childhood bedroom more than once to carry out his nefarious schemes, but this was the first time he had my permission.

He turned around and held up a book. "*The Naughty List?* Living vicariously?"

I ignored this. He could tease me *after* he explained himself. "What was that downstairs? I haven't heard from you in over a week, and you're pretending nothing is wrong. I don't get it."

He slid the book back into its place and brushed his hand through his hair. "I didn't tell anyone we were in a fight."

I sat on the edge of my bed. "Why are you keeping it a secret?"

"I didn't want to say anything negative they could use against you if we made up."

"You were protecting me?" My heart palpitated. I was too afraid to ask the question dangling off the tip of my tongue: Did this mean we were going to make up?

"I figured I drove my bike over a nail or something," Jude

said, skipping over my question. "I was shocked when you told me it was you. There was no gloating. We always gloated after a prank." He visibly deflated, not unlike his tire.

I pressed my lips together. "An *American Idol* folder is gloat-worthy. Knee surgery, not so much. And it wasn't a prank."

He scrubbed a hand down his face. "The point is I was mad, Mole. That accident changed the trajectory of my life."

Shame burned through me, and I stared down at my toes. "I've never been more sorry about anything in my entire life."

He joined me on the edge of the bed. "I know, but I needed a minute. Then I saw you at Hillstone, and my first instinct was to run after you to kiss and make up."

I looked up. "It was? I couldn't read you."

"Poker face," he said, pointing at his own face. "The more I thought about it, the more I realized it was bound to happen. Our history of pulling pranks...it's a wonder no one ever got physically hurt before."

"It wasn't even a prank," I said for what felt like the trillionth time despite a strong sense of relief he didn't seem to hate me. "My gags were always meticulously planned. This? This was me losing my freaking mind and just going to town."

Jude let out a stifled laugh. "So not like you."

"*So* not like me!"

We laughed again, this time freely. And it felt like a Swedish massage of my soul.

His eyes roamed my face. "The bottom line is I know you never meant to hurt me...physically, at least."

"What does this mean for us?" I held my breath.

"It means I'm following my heart."

"What does your heart say?" My voice was a whisper.

"It says I'm over *it*, but I'm not over *you*." He drank me in. "I didn't know for sure what I was going to do, but then Eris ratted you out for breaking a plate and you looked so..." He chuckled. "Beautifully pathetic in the kitchen. I figured this was killing you, and Molly Girl, for better or worse, I like your face too much to see you hurt, especially when I have the power to ease your pain."

I sucked in a breath. "Let me get this straight. You forgive me *and* you still like my face?" His use of *pathetic* threw me, but I could work with beautiful.

His eyes twinkled. "I'm *way* better at streamlining than you and can answer your two questions with one word. Yes."

"Thank God." I grabbed on to his shirt collar and smashed my lips against his, deepening the kiss immediately. I wanted to swallow him whole. Then I wrapped my arms tight around him before he changed his mind.

Eventually, he wrestled out of my grasp and motioned at my bedroom door. "As much as I'd like to do grown-up things in your twin-size bed, we'd better go downstairs before your mom sends spies on us." He stood and pulled me up with him.

I pressed my palms against his chest, enjoying the physical closeness after what felt like forever. "Can I ask you something first?"

He stepped back and leaned against my bookshelf. "How to replace a flat tire in minutes in case you ever fly off the handle again?"

"Jude!"

"I couldn't resist," he said, chuckling. "What?"

"Are you happy?" I bit down on my lip. "Professionally?" *In other words, did I ruin your life when I indirectly ended your baseball career?*

He sighed. "Yes, Molly. I'm happy. You did *not* ruin my life by letting the air out of my tires. *Tire.* My knee is a different story." His lips spread into a slow smile. "But it's a built-in excuse to get out of running the Corporate Challenge with the rest of the restaurant staff. So...thank you?" He laughed.

I snorted. "Be serious for a minute." I peered into his eyes, wondering how it had taken me so long to notice the rare shade of hazel. "You sure?"

"No regrets. I swear. But if you must know, I do have bigger dreams."

"Do tell!"

He blushed as if sharing his dream was outside his comfort zone. Yet he was choosing to share it with me. "I want to open my own pub, where upscale food meshes with a laid-back atmosphere and reasonable cost. Michelin star for the working class."

"That sounds amazing, Jude!" My brain raced with questions. "When do you want to do this? Where? Here...in Manhattan?"

"Whoa!" Jude held up his palms. "Take it easy there, Molly*plana*. I haven't worked it all out yet."

I laughed. "Sorry."

He reached for my hand again. "Let's go downstairs."

This time I let him lead me into the hallway. Jude's forgiveness and assurance of his happiness was the best Hanukkah present ever. There was only one more gift I could ask for on this year's Festival of Lights, and when Jude and I reached the bottom of the stairs, I realized it was within my reach.

"Dad!"

As if reading my mind, Jude whispered, "One reconciliation at a time."

Chapter Thirty-Two

While I was at work a few days after Hanukkah, my office phone rang. "Molly Blum."

"Hi, Molly. It's Kevin from Pro City Sportswear."

I returned his greeting, disguising my surprise at his call. I'd sent several résumés to him months earlier and never heard back.

"Sorry for going dark on you. For internal reasons, we had to pause hiring new legal counsel, but the search is on again, and I wondered if any of those résumés you sent previously were still available by any chance. They were great."

I found the listing in our internal database. "I'll follow up and see if they're still interested." I, personally, hadn't placed them anywhere else, but that didn't necessarily mean anything.

"We'd love to start interviewing as soon as possible. This week or next preferably."

"Let me know the available dates and time slots and I'll reach out right away."

After he gave me the information, I called the original candidates. Two were still in the market and excited for the opportunity, including Romero Vasquez. He'd been in my first-year class at Fitzpatrick & Green.

"Yes! I'm definitely still interested," he said. "Big Law is a hamster wheel and I've been too busy to jump off and follow up with you. This is the push I needed."

"Fingers crossed!" I hated to play favorites, but I too would love if Romero got the position. During an associates' retreat when I was still practicing, we'd taken a lawyer personality assessment test. Romero and I were the only two in our class who had fallen under the "Advocate" umbrella, known for their idealist temperament. Back then, I'd never confided in him about Maxine, my abusive and gaslighting client, despite being tempted. Maybe he wouldn't have looked down on me for allowing a "mean" client to be the driving force for leaving the legal profession when many, I suspected, would judge me for being what they considered "soft."

We ended the call, and I sent the details for both interviews to Kevin just as my phone rang.

"Hi, Mom."

"Have you been avoiding me? I wanted to make sure you're okay."

"Okay about what?" And then I remembered. Ignoring Jude's advice to focus on one reconciliation at a time at Hanukkah, I'd made my parents open my present in front of everyone. Apparently, a couples massage wasn't an appropriate gift for a separated couple.

Without even bothering to pull me to the side, Mom had said, "You need to stop, Molly. This is not a cute look for you."

Dad was more sensitive. "I always think you're cute, Squirrel." His eyes had creased with a combination of love and exasperation. "But your mom's right. It's time to accept reality and grow up."

The public lecture had made me cry even while I was still celebrating Jude's forgiveness.

"I'm over it. I promise to keep my Hallie Parker and Annie James personas in the drawer moving forward, but can I ask you something?" I chewed a fingernail.

"Your father and I hate that you're hurting about this. The least I can do is answer a question."

"What really went wrong with you and Dad?" I waved at Cindy passing in the hallway, then stood to close my office door to sidestep any unwanted interruptions. "Was it something we did?" I sat down and braced myself.

"Who's we?"

"Your children!"

She tutted. "Of course not. Is that what you think?"

"No. Maybe? I don't know."

"You're all out of the house living your own lives."

"Exactly. Isn't the hard part over? I would have thought once you guys were empty nesters, the passion would reignite...like another newlywed period...not burn out. Can't you make it about you now?"

"You'd think so, wouldn't you? Raising you girls bonded us, and when you weren't there, our detachment became harder to ignore."

"I thought you were happy. We all did."

She sighed. "We changed over the years. Sometimes change brings you closer, and other times it drives you apart."

I didn't have to ask under which category they fell. "Changed how?" I held my breath in case I'd pushed her too far or, worse, she cited *performance issues* or something equally gross as their downfall.

"We stopped...I don't know...doing little things to make each other happy." Before I had a chance to request elaboration, she continued. "I remember when I would scour restaurant menus because your dad loved roasted chicken, and oddly enough, not many restaurants prepare it that way—chicken breast, chicken cutlet, fried chicken, yes, but not roasted. I had fun hunting down restaurants where your dad could order his favorite dish. Making him happy made *me* happy. And it wasn't just me. When I went back to work part-time after you started kindergarten, I felt lost. Everyone was either a stay-at-home mom, like Laura, or worked full-time. Your dad learned about Meetup. It was new at the time. He found me a group for mothers in the county who worked part-time. It meant the world to me that he cared so much."

I could hear her smile through the phone, and it was contagious. "That's romantic! So, what happened? You both stopped doing sweet things for each other? Did you ever talk about it?"

"I think when it doesn't come naturally...when it's not an instinct...it means the magic is gone."

I slouched in my chair. "If you're sure there's nothing we—I can do to make things better between you guys, I promise to stop meddling." I meant it. None of my plans had worked, and even though their separation gutted me, it was time to move on.

"You're my sweetest girl. The only thing you can do..."

My ears perked up.

"Is enjoy Jude and not worry about us."

"Fine," I said, my heart quickening at his name.

When we said goodbye a few minutes later, I was still smiling at the thought of my mom scouring restaurant menus for roasted chicken to make my dad happy. Those days were over, but Mom was right: it was time to focus on my own romantic relationship and leave theirs to them. I remembered what Jude had said about opening his own restaurant someday. Where had I read something recently about launching a restaurant? I squished my face as if it would help my recollection. Oh yes, it was in *Forbes*— the same issue as Rosaria's interview. I still had the magazine somewhere in my... I opened my desk drawer, where a photo of the US veep smiled up at me. *There you are!* I thumbed through the table of contents until I saw it: "Key Tips for Launching a Restaurant." Guessing there were more articles where this came from, I searched the internet for tips for opening a restaurant. *Only 167 million results.*

Even though my parents weren't together anymore, I could still learn from what Mom had said about the joy of making your partner happy. The most useful articles were probably in the first three pages of results. I'd print and hole-punch them into a binder for Jude. It would take hours, but what was time when you were helping someone you loved make his dream come true?

I sucked in a breath. *I love Jude Stark.*

Chapter Thirty-Three

After work that day, I circled the crowded bar at Hillstone until I found an available stool. It didn't take long for Jude to see me—or *smell* me, as he'd so charmingly once teased. He turned away from the patron whose order he was taking and cocked his head at me. The confusion on his face was expected since I hadn't told him I was coming. I smiled and waved. *I love him.*

His eyes lit up, and he gave me the "one second" sign before turning his attention back to his customer.

He finished what he was doing and walked toward me. "I'm happy to see you, but was I supposed to know you were coming? Did I forget?"

I shook my head. "Nope. I made something for you and couldn't wait to share it."

"You have me intrigued, but it's not a great time." He motioned around the crowded bar. "I can pour you a glass of wine if you want to wait until it slows down. Are you hungry?"

My panties semi-melted at his instinct to care for me. "Yes please, on the wine. Not hungry."

A minute later, Jude returned to his work, and I nursed a

generous pour of red and daydreamed about the launch of his restaurant. Much of the advice I'd read included hosting a "soft opening" with friends and family to sample the menu and work out kinks. I could already picture the Starks and the Blums, along with Alex, Jerry, and Esther, seated around a long table toasting Jude and his staff on a job well done.

"Lucky stem."

I turned my head to face my neighbor. "Excuse me?"

The guy, a thirtysomething "suit" with blond hair and a stocky build, motioned at my finger absently stroking the leg of my wineglass and blushed. "Bad pickup line?"

I laughed. "Cringeworthy."

Jude appeared before us. "I can talk now." He turned to my new friend as if first noticing him. "Unless you're otherwise occupied."

But for the twitch of his lips, I would think he was jealous. For better or worse, I doubted Jude Stark was capable of jealousy except, perhaps, when it came to my superior tidiness. "Now is good," I said, rolling my eyes.

Jude called over the other bartender to get cringy-guy a drink. Then he kissed me, marking his territory. *Maybe he does get jealous.*

"Odd for you to flirt with a blond."

"I wasn't flirting! *He* was."

His eyes danced. "Where's my present?"

With a rush of affection for my boyfriend's little-boy enthusiasm, I pulled the black binder I'd taken from work from my tote bag and set it on the dark wood bar. "I scoured the internet for everything I could find on opening a restaurant and gathered it all in one place." I opened the flap of the binder. "Here!"

Jude looked from the binder to me and then back to the binder. "Wow. This is...wow. You did this yourself?"

I blinked away the onset of mushy tears. "Yes. I wanted to help you. I also needed an excuse to avoid recruiting for one of Michael's pet projects, but I mostly did it to help you. It takes a village to make a dream come true!"

Jude leaned his elbows on the bar. "This was really sweet. Thank you."

"Inside are articles I printed from *Forbes*, *Nerdwallet*, um...*Restaurants Are Us*..."

Jude raised an eyebrow.

My lips twitched. "Okay. I made up the last one. I can't remember the sources, but they're all in here." I tapped the binder. "I even found a list from way back in the Ceiling Crashers archives. You're not a woman, but it doesn't mean you can't take the advice."

Jude offered an amused smile. "I'm relieved you're aware I'm not a woman."

"I'd do you anyway."

"Good to know." He laughed. "I'll put this in the back with my other stuff." His eyebrows furrowed. "You didn't expect me to read it right now, did you?" He glanced around the restaurant. "I'm working."

"Of course not. Read it later. Do you want me to drop it off at your apartment? You shouldn't have to lug it home."

"It's fine." He raised and lowered the binder in slow motion while making a face like a body builder lifting a heavy weight. "Me Jude. You Mole. I strong!"

"You sexy!" I leaned over the stool and kissed him—marking *my* territory.

Chapter Thirty-Four

Three nights later, Esther and I were taking advantage of the two-for-one happy hour drink special at Sachi, an Asian bistro and one of the more upscale and less frat-boy venues in the very post-college neighborhood. It was a predate cocktail for both of us—Esther had a Tinder date later, and Jude was meeting me for dinner after his early shift at Hillstone. I took a sip of rosé and placed the glass back on the long granite-top bar. "So, tell me about the guy you're meeting."

Esther looked at me over the sugar rim of her lemon drop cocktail. "I'm *positive* it will be my last first date. We'll lock eyes and just *know*."

I snickered. My best friend did sarcasm like she was up for an award. "It could happen."

She curled her lips in a dubious snarl.

I wiggled my finger at her. "Jude and I are proof that anything is possible, even meeting 'The One' on Tinder."

"If I recognize him from his profile pictures, it will already be an improvement on my last date." She wiped a crystal of sugar from her lip.

I gave her other hand a sympathetic squeeze. The last guy

she'd met had been in his sixties, but had used his son's pictures, claiming he looked *just* like him twenty-five years earlier. "Twenty-five-years earlier" being the key phrase.

"And the guy before Grandpa suggested we save the drink for *wink wink* dessert and invited me to his apartment over the bar for the main course." She blew her white bangs from her forehead. "I'm not opposed to sex on a first date if the chemistry is there, but can we at least *have* the date first? These guys make Killian look good."

"I high-key dispute that statement!"

Esther tapped her grape-painted nails on the bar. "Tell me, Little Miss Molly. Why do I attract losers?"

I frowned. "You attract *everyone*. You just need a better system for skimming the baddies." I sucked on an edamame and tossed the empty shell in a dish. "You can always give Alex or Jerry a shot." I raised my eyebrows.

"Hmmm." She took another sip of her cocktail. "What's the latest with Jude?"

I bit back a smile. "Please don't hate me, but he's great. *We're* great. Now that we've settled our past, we can focus on the future."

"I hate you a little bit, but I'm more happy for you. I knew he'd come around."

I'd finally told Esther what I'd done to Jude's bike. She was way more understanding and forgiving of teenage Molly than I'd been. "By now he's had a chance to look through the articles, and I can't wait to talk about them tonight." I'd made notes in the margins of a duplicate binder, the existence of which I'd kept from Jude, knowing he'd call me a nerd.

"How's the job? Michael behaving himself?"

"It's fine. He's fine. He's *Michael*." I gulped my wine to wash the rotten taste of his name out of my mouth. I'd wound up sending him one candidate for the Bluetronics position, a second-year associate who saw the job opportunity as a way to pursue his lifelong dream of combining his two greatest loves—games and the law—and insisted he didn't care about the company's questionable work environment.

Esther chuckled. "You don't sound too enthused. Maybe you shouldn't have turned down Rosaria's job offer."

I swirled my glass. "I probably couldn't afford these drinks if I took it!"

She jutted her chin over my shoulder. "Hey, Jude."

Without even turning around, I sang the next line of the song.

He kissed my cheek. "I can't believe you gave your panties to a geek."

"Said Samantha Baker, not Molly Ringwald," I replied dryly.

Esther's eyes slid back and forth between us, her expression a mix of confusion and amusement. Unlike me and Jude, whose parents had organized a John Hughes movie marathon for both families when we were younger, it was possible she'd never even seen the iconic, if problematic, eighties movie *Sixteen Candles*.

"I stand corrected. You're so much smarter than me," Jude said.

"And wouldn't you be the geek in this scenario?" I teased.

"You've never actually given me your panties. They just melt at my touch."

"TMI." Esther gasped. "Feck! I'm late." She moved for her wallet.

I put my hand up. "Your drinks are on me this time. Have fun!"

"Not likely, but thanks." She hugged me and waved goodbye

to Jude before racing toward the exit with only one arm through her coat.

I made a silent wish whoever she was meeting would be worth the rush.

I tugged Jude down onto the seat Esther had vacated. "You look yummy." He'd either gone home after his shift or changed at Hillstone, because instead of his uniform, he was semi-dressed-up in dark black jeans and a midnight-blue sweater that brought out the blue flecks in his eyes. And he was clean-shaven.

"We can skip dinner if you want."

"I'm starving."

He waggled his eyebrows.

"For real food!"

I closed out the bar bill, and we relocated to one of the more intimate red leather booths in the dimly lit main dining room, where Jude entertained me with anecdotes from his day at the restaurant. The latest—a woman who'd brought her own fresh vegetables from home—boggled my mind. "I don't get it. Was she trying to save money?"

"We charged her more! She just wanted a professionally prepared salad with veggies she grew on her own balcony." He dipped a piece of Philadelphia roll into low-sodium soy sauce and popped it into his mouth.

"People are weird." This wasn't new intel per se, but Jude's restaurant stories removed any doubt.

Jude's Adam's apple bobbed as he swallowed. "I thought it was charming."

"You would."

"You of all people should be grateful I like offbeat and quirky."

"Meaning?"

"Do I really need to..." He glanced over my shoulder, and whatever caught his attention stole his next words.

I turned around, gawking as the hostess led Timothy and Charley to the table next to ours. A clean-shaven Timothy wore black jeans and a dark purple sweater. I took in Charley's black-and-white polka dot dress, glanced down at my blue-and-white vintage stars-and-stripes dress, and gulped. They were...*us*...bizarro world Jude and Molly. I drained a shot of sake as the four of us waved awkwardly and called out various versions of "Hey."

"I have no idea what you saw in him."

I laugh-choked and covered my mouth. When I could speak again, I said, "Back at you."

Jude glanced at Charley, then back to me, and grinned sheepishly. "She's pretty and she reminded me of someone. I just didn't know who at the time." His cheeks pinked.

My knees wobbled. "Samesies." We eye-screwed for another ten seconds, then turned back to our food and tried to pretend our doppelgängers weren't twenty feet away.

I dug my chopsticks into a piece of salmon avocado roll. "Will you let customers in *your* restaurant bring their own vegetables?"

"The vegetables in *my* restaurant will be so sublime, no one will want to." He flashed a cocky smile.

"No doubt. Have you read any of the articles I printed out for you?"

Jude leaned against the foam padding of the booth. "Not yet. It's only been a few days."

I swallowed down my disappointment. "Have you thought about the menu aside from upscale but affordable?"

"I have some ideas." He swirled more wasabi into his soy sauce.

"For example?"

"Can we talk about this later?"

"According to one article, the menu should be the next step in the creative process after deciding concept and brand, which you already have, and before the business plan."

"I got it, Molly."

"And—"

"Molly!"

I hitched a breath at the aggression in his voice. The room had gone silent. Jude's face was scarlet. I looked to my left. Timothy and Charley had stopped talking to gawp at us, their hands connected across the table. *Are they sharing one set of chopsticks?* I shook my head. *Not important.* I turned back to Jude.

A muscle twitched in his jaw. "Give it a break."

My scalp prickled. "Why are you so upset?"

"I'm not..." He rubbed the back of his neck. "Can we just talk about something else? Anything?" He tilted his head at Timothy and Charley's table. "Like how our clones are eating sushi with one set of chopsticks?"

"I'm just excited for you. Sorry." I dropped my gaze to the enormous assortment of sushi we'd ordered, my favorite dynamite roll not nearly as tempting as it had been a minute earlier.

"I know and I love your enthusiasm," he said, squeezing my finger across the table. "But tonight I just want to eat out with my girlfriend and later, if she behaves herself, I'll eat *her* out." He looked at me with smoldering eyes.

"Oh my," I said, fanning myself as my brain redirected thoughts from business to pleasure. "Count me in. In the meantime..." I looked at him seductively from under my lashes and slowly slid my chopsticks off the table.

Jude's lips twitched.

I threw my hand against my mouth. "Oops. I guess we have to share."

Chapter Thirty-Five

A few days later, while waiting for Michael to finish his call, my eyes skimmed the wall behind his desk. Behind him hung his diplomas from Tufts University, where he'd earned his bachelor's degree, and Boston College, where he'd graduated law school. Also framed was the quote: *Arguing with a lawyer is like wrestling a pig in mud. Sooner or later, you realize that they like it.* If you asked me, Michael wished he was still a practicing attorney. But no one asked me.

He rolled his eyes and pointed at the phone, seemingly to demonstrate exasperation over the person on the other end. I didn't buy it. Making me wait was a power trip, as was his insistence on holding weekly meetings with all the recruiters instead of quarterly, like Jill had done, leaving me to ponder, once again, why he'd chosen to leave his law firm, where junior associates, paralegals, and legal secretaries were at his constant mercy.

What special kind of hell did Michael have in store for me today? Would he praise me on a job well done or ask me to recruit for a cult or drug trafficking operation? I fidgeted in my chair and darted a glance at him as he gesticulated silently for whoever he was speaking with to get on with it. I wasn't being fair. Michael wasn't a criminal. He just had tunnel vision in a forest I preferred to scope for thorny trees and bushes.

"Will do. Bye." Michael ended his call. "Thanks for your patience, Molly."

"Of course." *It's not like I had a choice.*

"Let's get right to business. What's the status with Pro City Sportswear?"

"After a long pause for internal reasons, they're looking to hire again. Two of the three candidates I'd sent to them originally were still looking and have now been asked back for second interviews." Professionally, I was impartial. Personally, I was rooting for Romero.

"Nice. Good going on the Bluetronics position as well." He pushed his chair back and kicked one leg onto the desk. "I'm glad you stopped being so picky with your candidates…you know…searching for the one perfect match. Just like one true loves, they don't exist. There's more than one pot for every kettle. It's about who gets there first." He gave a self-amused smile.

Who gets there first? I clenched my fists. This was quickly crossing the line to inappropriate, but telling him what I *really* thought about him wouldn't get me out of this meeting any faster. "Right."

"I brought up your name in my meeting with the board. They seemed favorable to an early promotion. Fingers crossed."

This was where I was supposed to express gratitude for his support. And I *did* appreciate what seemed like his authentic desire for my success even if I disagreed with his style. "Yes. Fingers crossed. Thank you."

He lowered his leg back to the floor and waved me off. "Just pay forward the lessons I've taught you to new recruiters and we'll consider it payment rendered."

The idea of passing on his *lessons* left me feeling like the nauseated emoji, and I hustled out the door before it shifted to its face-vomiting companion.

I returned to my office in a foul mood. Why wasn't I more excited about a possible promotion? Succeeding as a recruiter validated my choice to leave the law. I should have been thrilled.

I stared at my computer screen but lacked the focus to work. It occurred to me Esther hadn't filled me in on her Tinder date from after our happy hour at Sachi. I opened our text message exchange and clicked the video call icon on the top. The phone had barely rung before the call was declined. I slumped against my seat. *How rude.* Adding to my last unanswered text, I wrote: Still waiting.

My phone rang—Esther. "I was about to text you," I said.

"I'm just out of the shower. You can't just FaceTime me without warning."

"Since when? How was the date? Why are you avoiding me?"

"There's nothing to tell. We had one drink and called it. I didn't mean to leave you on read…just forgot to respond. I'm sorry."

I stood and paced the floor. "No funny stories?"

"Not this time. It was a case of mutual lack of chemistry, so we cut it short."

"Still an improvement over your last two." I had no intention of waxing optimistic about her finding the one when she wasn't looking. Like me before Jude, Esther wasn't desperate for her forever guy, but at the very least, she was due a decent regular shag.

"Agreed."

"By the way, why are you just showering now? Are you sick?"

"I'm fine. No need to send Jude over with a quart of soup. I took a lie-in from work."

"You don't know what you're missing. Grandma Jean's soup is sublime..." *Unless you have the flu.* "When your taste buds aren't on strike, that is." I heard a male voice in the background. "Is someone there?"

"Where? Here? No. It's...I have the TV on."

"What show is it?" The only words I could make out were "sweet peach."

"It's...um...*Hart of Dixie* on Prime. Lavon asked Zoe if she wanted sweet peach tea."

"Aha. Got it."

"Are you all right? It's not like you to FaceTime me in the middle of the day."

The guy on the television yelled something about naughty Santa. "Which episode are you watching? Is Wade wearing a shirt?"

"No idea. It's background noise. Listen, I'm shivering in my towel. Can we talk later?" Esther giggled and then...nothing.

"Hello? Are you there?" The call dropped. I tried to recollect the last time Esther had *giggled*—never. It must have been a *really* funny episode.

I sat back down and clicked my Outlook calendar to check the status of my open requisitions, but the words blended together on the page. I reached for the phone again.

"How are things in the new place?" I worried about my dad living alone for the first time in thirty-seven years.

"I've been using the gym every day. Have you ever ridden a Peloton bike?"

"I've taken spin classes, but never Peloton. I'll try yours when I visit." I used to cycle regularly until my favorite instructor, Adina, stopped teaching. I twirled a hair around my finger. "How's your eating?"

"Mom? Is that you calling from heaven? Will you ask about my bowel movements next?"

"*Ew*," I said, scrunching up my face. "I don't want you getting bad habits and having a heart attack like Randy is all."

"Don't worry about me. I have dinner plans tonight and it's not fast food."

I tugged on my bottom lip. "Dinner plans? Is this...is it a date?" Dread tugged at my chest. Even though I'd accepted their separation, I still wasn't ready for my parents to date unless it was each other.

"Squirrel, I promise I'm not in the market for your stepmother." He chuckled.

"I don't want to know if you are." I bit back the smile I knew matched his. My indifference fooled no one. "Besides, last I checked you were still married to Mom, so unless that's changed, I can't have a stepmother." I held my breath.

"The status has not changed, but I'm a grown man who, believe it or not, is fully capable of taking care of himself and, in fact, enjoys it. *Capisce?*"

"Understood," I muttered, duly chastised by his uncharacteristic stern tone. "Enjoy your dinner."

We ended the call, and I returned my attention to my calendar, but it was no use. Then my phone pinged a text.

Jude: Come over after work. I have something to show you.

It was like he was an empath and knew I needed a distraction. Maybe he'd finally read through the restaurant material.

> **Molly:** On my way.

I logged off my computer, grabbed my coat and purse, and headed out.

Chapter Thirty-Six

When I arrived at Jude's building, I waved at the doorman on my way to the elevator bank without stopping. He knew me by now and would either announce my arrival to Jude or not. As soon as I stepped into the hallway on his floor, I heard the music coming from inside his apartment. When I reached his door, I recognized the song as "Take Me Home, Country Roads" by John Denver, but it was definitely not John Denver singing. And it wasn't Jude, who had perfect pitch, which left Alex or Jerry, unless they'd invited someone else over.

I knocked three times. When no one answered, I knocked harder. "Hello? It's Molly."

From the other side, muffled voices called, "It's open!"

I turned the knob and entered the apartment.

Yogi ran right over to me, the bell on his bowtie collar ringing. I bent to pet him and greeted the guys over the sound of Alex singing (if you could call it that) into a microphone.

I joined the two of them in the center of the room.

"Check it out!" Jude said, with a soft kiss to my lips. He pointed to a small portable speaker with a computer screen attached to the top. "One of our neighbors sold us his karaoke machine for a song. Pun intended. Grab a drink if you need to loosen up before you're up."

With a palpable need to loosen up, I went to the kitchen and poured most of a half-empty bottle of red wine into a glass before flumping onto the couch. "Is there a songbook?"

"Whatever's on YouTube," Alex said.

"Let me think." A challenging feat considering I couldn't stop replaying my meeting with Michael in my head. In theory, getting a promotion was *goals*, except in practice it hinged on me continuing to do things Michael's way, at least publicly, which meant more overtime at home. It was for a good cause— a symbiotic working environment for my clients—but it sucked for me, who enjoyed her life outside of work, now more than ever thanks to Jude.

"We're gonna do a duet and then you're up, Mole."

I let my head fall back. Was there a song about hating your boss? "Is 'Nine to Five' on there?"

"I'm sure it is," Jude said.

I took a large sip of wine, not bothering to swirl and sniff first. It was a shame because Jude, being a sommelier, didn't skimp on wine even at home. His restaurant would have a stellar wine list, I was certain. If he ever opened it. "Did you ever read the restaurant materials I gathered for you?"

He couldn't hear me over whistling the opening notes to "Wind of Change" by the Scorpions. I studied him...singing like he hadn't a care in the world. I had smaller shoulders yet seemed to carry the weight of all the stress in our relationship. It wasn't fair.

"Have you read the restaurant articles yet?" I repeated, this time in a much louder voice as Yogi danced at my feet.

"What?" Jude shouted over the music.

"Turn it off a sec!"

The music stopped.

I stood. "The restaurant. The one you want to open. How do you expect to launch a restaurant if you spend all your time singing power ballads from the eighties?" My chest tightened. The question came out a lot more forceful than I'd intended. I sounded angry—like someone who'd been wronged, even though Jude hadn't done anything to me.

Jude stared at me in silence.

"It's actually from 1990," Alex corrected.

Tossing the microphone to the side, Jude said, "It's all yours" to Alex. Without another word, he walked to his room and sat on his bed.

I followed him inside and closed the door behind us.

"What's up *your* ass tonight?" Jude said.

I knew this was where I should come clean about my crappy mood and apologize for taking it out on him. But I was too far gone and genuinely curious if he'd finally read any of the articles. They weren't exactly Jack Reacher novels, but you'd think a person who dreamed of opening a restaurant would want to gain as much knowledge on the topic as possible. I'd made it so easy for him to do just that. I glanced around the room. "Where is it?"

"Where is what?"

"The binder I made you."

"It's..." He averted eye contact. "It's still at the restaurant."

"You never even brought it home? I put so much time and care into searching and printing articles to help you, and you don't even appreciate it." I had these visions of us reading it together in bed with Yogi napping at our feet.

Jude stuffed his hands into the pocket of his hoodie. "I never asked for your help."

"I know. I did it to make you happy. The way my parents stopped doing for each other. It's what broke them. Did I tell you what my mom said about that? I was trying to show you I cared."

"So why do I feel like shit instead? Like I'm on some sort of timeline and if I take too long, you'll add me to your end-of-the-year naughty list?" He ran his fingers through his hair.

"Don't be silly." My fingers itched to smooth down the silky tufts that were now askew, but he wasn't finished yet.

"You realize you sound like my parents when you nag me about it, don't you? It's bad enough they're disappointed in me...something you've witnessed firsthand. When you stuck up for me at the party—before we even hooked up—something inside me shifted. I'd been fighting my attraction to you because...me and *Molly Blum*?" He wrinkled his nose like he'd inhaled rotten milk. "But it felt nice to have you on my side." His shoulders dropped. "Obviously, it was just for show. Maybe they even put you up to this. You heard my mom in the basement."

I flinched. I hated the way his parents had talked to him at the anniversary party—like being a bartender wasn't good enough. "I never meant to make you feel that way. I'm sorry. But do you seriously think I'd collude with Randy and Laura? Unlike them, I had no issue with your current career as long as you were happy. But you *told* me you had bigger dreams. I just don't get how you expect them to come true if you don't put in the work."

"Who said I wasn't going to do the work? But do I have to do it right now?"

"You're pushing thirty. If not now, when? I was only trying to help you plan for your future—"

Jude leaped to his feet, nostrils flaring. "You and your fucking plans!"

I jerked back, banging into his dresser. Rubbing my spine, I said, "Why are you screaming at me all of a sudden?"

In a normal voice, he repeated, "You and your fucking plans." He raised a finger. "You're killing yourself working overtime behind your sleazy boss's back because your *plan* doesn't allow for changing jobs yet." He lifted another finger. "You were offered a dream job and you won't take it because switching careers doesn't fall neatly into your *plan*." A third finger went up. "And you refuse to take a temporary pay cut because the *plan* is to make more money, not less, even if you're miserable. So, tell me, Molly, how are those *plans* working for you?" He shook his head in a show of disgust.

"What is so wrong with plans? *You* seem to think your restaurant is going to magically open itself." I muttered, "Although with your luck, it probably will."

"Well, actually, *my* plan was to be a baseball player, but that didn't happen and—oh yeah, whose fault was that?"

I gasped like I'd been punched in the gut. He'd sworn he forgave me...that he had no regrets.

Jude's face crumpled like he instantly regretted the words, but he didn't take them back.

Hurt quickly turned to anger. "I never would have spontaneously messed with your bike if I'd stuck to my precious planning routine, but I acted without thinking. Speaking of which, maybe if *you* ever thought before you acted, you wouldn't have been stupid enough to ride the damn bike in the first place!" I instantly regretted these words, but didn't take them back either.

Jude huffed out a laugh. "It's like the fog has lifted and I remember why I couldn't stand you for most of my life. You, Mollyanna, were a type-A bore with a stick up your butt then and you still are."

The blood rushed to my head. "And you're still an arrogant and mean..." I pursed my lips. Where were all the powerful insults when you needed one?

"What? You didn't have time to plan your insult?" He smirked before opening his bedroom door with force and joining Alex on the couch. Yogi promptly jumped on his lap.

With tears brewing, I watched the two of them for a moment—man and his best friend. Then I left, having no idea what had just happened.

Chapter Thirty-Seven

My whole body was shaking as I walked toward my apartment. Twice, I turned on my heel to go back to Jude's, but both times I realized I had no idea what to say or even how I felt.

I accepted the blame for initiating our fight. It was me who'd interrupted Jude's fun karaoke night with repeated questions about the binder I'd made for him. But he took it to a whole other level by screaming about my "fucking plans."

While it killed me to think I'd made Jude—always sure of himself and confident Jude—feel "less than" like his parents did, to accuse me of forming an alliance with them and insinuating what I'd done for him—out of love—was part of some sort of intervention was over the top. He was not blame free, and a large portion of my guilt was dulled by the cruel things *he* said that could never be unsaid or unheard.

I pulled the hood of my turquoise bubble coat more securely over my head. It was cold. The revulsion in Jude's eyes and the cruel timbre of his voice at the end. *I couldn't stand you for most of my life.* Did he mean it? Were we back where we'd started? I choked on a sob.

I approached Esther's building and headed up the ramp to her entrance and through the front doors without hesitation. There were benefits to living so close to your best friend.

I knocked on her door. *Please be home.*

From the other side, a voice shouted, "Pizza's here!" and the door flew open.

My jaw dropped at the shirtless man in front of me. "Jerry?" *Jerry in his boxers!*

"Molly." Jerry's blue-gray eyes widened, color rising on his fair cheeks. "We thought you were the delivery guy."

Esther slid into view, wearing a long t-shirt and nothing else. "Sustenance!" Our eyes locked, and she stopped short. "Molly!" She glanced at Jerry and back at me. "Oh my, this is awkward."

"I can...um...come back if you're busy." I darted my gaze over their heads, unable to make eye contact with either of them. It didn't take a genius to determine why Esther needed *sustenance* and Jerry was...well, Jerry was wearing only boxer shorts. I never imagined seeing his bare chest and...*gulp*...what if I accidentally looked at his bulge? My face burned.

Esther stepped closer and peered at me. "Are you crying? Why are you crying? What happened?"

"Someone ordered pizza?"

I turned my head toward the delivery guy, grateful for the interruption.

Jerry and I stood at the open doorway, not acknowledging each other, while Esther signed the credit card receipt. If the guy wondered why we were all huddled at the front of the apartment, two of us practically naked, he played it cool. Doing deliveries in New York City, this was probably tame.

Esther thanked him, and with the pizza box in her arms,

kicked the door closed with her foot. "Jerry, you need to go so I can talk to Molly."

Jerry looked at her with sad eyes, reminding me of Yogi when Jude said that playtime was over. "What about the pizza?" He slid his gaze to me and did a double take as if finally *seeing* me. "Whoa. What's wrong? What happened? Does Jude know?"

I mumbled, "Jude knows."

Esther squeezed his bicep. "Go get dressed. I'll make you a to-go bag for the pizza."

"Or I can walk around the block until you're finished and come back." The sad-puppy-in-boxer-shorts pouty face had returned.

I pressed my fist to my mouth. The comic relief was *everything* right now.

Esther pointed to her bedroom. "Go!"

Jerry scurried away.

When we were alone, Esther widened her eyes at me as if to say, "Well?"

"Later." I pointed in the direction of her bedroom.

"Understood," she said, flicking her bangs. "Jerry! How long does it take to put your legs through pants?"

"Sorry, sorry." Jerry shuffled into the living room with this shirt untucked, his shoes untied, and his face red from exertion. When he reached the front door, he turned around and cast a lingering gaze at Esther. "Thanks for . . . um . . . will you call me?"

Sympathy curled around my heart. Esther was a man-eater and Jerry was . . . *Jerry.*

He turned to go.

"Wait!" Esther jogged to the door.

Jerry turned around.

I watched the exchange with interest.

Esther grabbed him by the collar and planted a kiss on his lips. Then she slapped him on the ass. "Now go." She locked the door and faced me. "Why are you staring at me like the world turned upside down?"

I blinked at her. "Hasn't it? What is happening?"

The apples of her cheeks turned pink.

"First she giggled, then she blushed, and then the earth exploded."

"Fuck off." She laughed. "We'll get to me later. You first. Just let me put on pants."

"Please do."

Not long after, I curled on one corner of her red leather couch with Poppy dozing on the arm and caught her up. "I know I initiated it by asking about the binder when, really, I was just upset about Michael, but then Jude started yelling at me like what I did for him—something meant to be nurturing—was an insult to his very being. That I was a nag who was disappointed in his level of adulting. And then he made fun of my personality again...like he used to. He said all my planning did was make me miserable. He called me a bore! What's so wrong with planning for my future? *Our* future? Maybe I shouldn't have tried to plan for *his* future without asking, but it's certainly not a crime worthy of his level of anger."

Esther took a bite of pizza. She'd offered me a slice, but I wasn't hungry. "Is he right on any level? If he never follows through with the restaurant, would you be okay marrying a bartender or having one as the father of your children?"

"Whoa." I sat up straight. "Who's talking marriage and kids? We haven't even been together three months." I closed my eyes and imagined. Maybe we'd have a double-backyard wedding. We could have the ceremony at the Starks' and the reception at my childhood home. I didn't need anything fancy.

"Molly!"

I opened my eyes.

She squinted at me. "Where did you go?"

"Nowhere." I coughed. "The answer is yes, I'd be more than okay with it. I swear it wasn't about that. I only wanted to help make his dream a reality. I thought I was being selfless and sweet, trying to make him happy." I shared what my mom had told me about the little things she and my dad used to do for each other.

"Is there some truth to what he said, though? About your plans? You *have* complained about your job a lot lately. Are you staying because leaving doesn't fit into your plans? The way you described your lunch with Rosaria... I was almost jealous of how well you bonded. She'd be the ideal boss for you. Is changing the plan such a terrible idea if it means you'll be happier?"

"Whose side are you on?" I asked, only half joking. "Leaving Gotham is one thing, but taking a job with Ceiling Crashers is a whole other ballgame." I winced at the accidental baseball reference. *My plan was to be a baseball player.* "I don't know much about Manhattan real estate these days except a one-bedroom apartment in a doorman building with private outdoor space would be way outside my budget if I worked with Rosaria. I'd have to sell."

"Should I be insulted? I live in a doorman-less building where the closest thing to à balcony is the fire escape and I'm quite happy with it," Esther said.

"No! I love your place," I insisted, glancing around her apartment. It was the truth. "But I also have student loans. All I'm saying is it's not the easy decision Jude thinks it is." I brought her throw blanket to my chin. "Am I a type-A bore, Esther?"

My best friend studied me fondly. "Would you be my bestie if you were?" She tapped my leg through the blanket. "You, my dear, are just very bad at letting things happen."

"With good reason. Case in point, Jude's bike tire. Even tonight, I hadn't planned to yell at him. It happened because I let my anger and frustration with Michael get the best of me. Whenever I act spontaneously, things go wrong, unlike when I follow a carefully constructed plan."

Esther's expression was dubious. "Maybe it's less about planning and more about learning to control your emotions."

I sniffled.

"What are you going to do now?"

"No idea. I tried to explain my motives to Jude, and he didn't want to hear it. And he…well…if he can't stand me again, there's not much I can do about it. Either way, it stung. I think I need to cool off before I do anything. But…" I shoved her lightly. "How did Jerry wind up in your bed?"

A smile crept out in the seconds before she pressed her lips tightly together. "After my date the night we had drinks at Sachi, I went to Duane Reade for snacks. Bad dates and cocktails make me crave sugar. Jerry was in the candy aisle staring between the Twizzlers and the Swedish fish like he carried the weight of the world with his decision."

She cocked her head to the side while remembering. "I told him to buy both, and he stumbled at my voice into a display of protein bars." She chuckled. "Something tugged at my heart-strings, and I asked him to come out with me for a drink. We went to Ted's, and I'm not sure if it was the disappointment from another bad Tinder match, what you said about giving Jerry or Alex a chance, or just plain old horniness, but I invited him back to my place." Her gaze went distant.

"And how...how was it?" It wasn't lost on me it was two days later. "Did you invite him back, or has he been here the entire time?"

"He hadn't left until you arrived." Her lips curled up. "It was the biggest surprise of my life. Pun intended."

I snorted, then buried my face in my hands and lost it. Esther joined me, and we laughed until my belly ached. It hurt so good. I took a deep breath and let it out. "Thank you. It was just the distraction I needed."

"I can say the same about Jerry." She whistled through her teeth. "Who knew the boy was so agile?"

I shuddered. "I don't need the racy details. Just like I don't tell you about Jude." My face fell. *Jude.*

I pressed my palms onto the couch and pushed myself to a standing position. "Thank you for taking a break from your sexcapades for me, but let me go so you can call back Mr. Agility. I wouldn't be surprised if he's been loitering outside your door this entire time."

"Anytime." She pulled me into a hug.

I fell into her embrace wishing I could stay there, safely cocooned, a little while longer or at least until I knew what to do about Jude.

Because right now, I hadn't the faintest idea.

Chapter Thirty-Eight

lmost a week later, I was on my follow-up call with Romero, who'd just reported his second interview with Pro City Sportswear had gone well. "I'm so glad. Hopefully, they'll decide soon," I said.

I placed my office phone on speaker and slid my iPhone closer to me. It was already open to my text exchange with Jude. The last messages were the ones we sent right before our fight, when he told me to come over because he had something to show me. I hadn't spoken to him since I left his apartment in tears.

"I'll be waiting by the phone," Romero said.

I pulled myself back to the present. "Who did you meet with?"

I was dying to reach out and apologize for pushing Jude about the restaurant. I was desperate to encourage him to take all the time he needed—not rush on my account because of some imaginary naughty list. But why should I beg forgiveness from someone who called me a "type-A bore"? Someone who threw my biggest regret in my face—the loss of his baseball career—after claiming to have forgiven me. And sure, what I'd said about him stupidly riding the bike wasn't much better, but to channel my eight-year-old self, he started it.

I clicked out of the messages and back in before flipping the phone over with a sigh. My arms ached from the need to hug him, my lips were cold from missing the heat of his, and my brain was full of all the wacky observations it had stored to share with him if we ever reconciled. In simple terms, I missed him. I even missed our pre–anniversary party hijinks. He was the most fun I ever had. He'd been right all those months ago when he said I liked fighting with him. But I enjoyed getting along with him way more.

Unaware of my inner turmoil, Romero was answering my question. "...the senior legal counsel, and Maxine Posner, the vice president of legal."

I snapped to attention. "Did you say Maxine Posner?"

"Yes. Do you know her?"

No. No. No! My stomach lurched at the memory of her criticizing me, copying my entire department and hers, for not warning her of a potential conflict of interest in a deal. She'd conveniently deleted said warning from lower down in the email string, but it would have looked worse for me, not to mention petty, to forward the original correspondence in my defense rather than simply apologize. My fingernails bit into my fisted hands. "She's not at Sole Balance anymore?"

"She's relatively new to the company, so she must have quit there recently."

I placed my palm against my forehead. How did I not know about this? I gasped, remembering how I'd sent résumés to the company right after Michael first chastised me about my recruiting practices over the summer. Since Pro City Sportswear was a repeat client, I'd relied on my previous due diligence that had raised no red flags. If I'd trusted my gut, I'd have done my research again then, and then again when they resumed the hiring process more recently. But I hadn't. And now Romero might have to pay the price for my negligence. I squeezed the pink-and-purple crocheted stress ball Nicole had bought me for Hanukkah to release some aggression.

"How closely will you guys be working together?" I asked. *Squeeze.* Maybe they'd just be casual colleagues, only seeing each other at department meetings and staff parties.

"My direct report is the senior legal counsel, but since Maxine is her boss, I'll ultimately report to her too."

Squeeze. Squeeze. Squeeze. It was possible Maxine was nicer to people in her department than outside counsel. I chewed my lip, recalling a conversation with her former in-house paralegal after Maxine had driven her away from Sole Balance, which suggested otherwise. I could warn Romero right now. Except it had to be breach of...*something*...to badmouth a client or discourage a candidate from taking the job after being the one to set up the interview in the first place. My heart thumped wildly.

Fuck. Since I wasn't ready to come clean to Romero about my personal experience with Maxine, I promised to be in touch as soon as I heard anything, and we concluded the call. Under different circumstances, I'd be proud of how well I had maintained my cool. Jude would be impressed. *Squeeze.* It was best to leave Jude out of this entirely and figure out what to do about my candidate.

I closed my eyes and blew a breath of air out of my lips. A decent interview didn't automatically result in an offer. Maybe Pro City Sportswear would extend it to an applicant working with a different recruiter, and I could just remove myself from the equation altogether. I hated myself for hoping my candidate and friend didn't get what he thought was his dream job, but I might hate myself more if he did.

After work that night, I hung my purse on the storage bench by the front door and went straight to my bedroom to change into running clothes. The sun had set, but it was a relatively mild day for January and the wind chill wasn't too bad. The fresh air would clear my head and, if I was lucky, lead to an epiphany regarding my next steps with Romero and maybe even Jude too.

With my Taylor Swift mix playing in my ear, I jogged east to an area of the FDR Drive well-populated with other runners and walkers, where I felt safe despite the dark. Three miles and zero epiphanies later, I walked up and down the East River Esplanade, a wide two-block segment of space overlooking the water, for my cool-down. My heart surged at all the dogs out. A white labradoodle stretched out on its leash and licked the bare skin on my calf where my cropped black running pants ended.

I removed my earbuds and bent to scratch his ears. "Aren't you cute?"

"I think so."

I straightened my back and smiled at his owner, a guy somewhere in his late twenties or early thirties.

He returned my grin.

I ran my palm along my ponytail and subtly checked him out, from his dark messy hair peeking out from under his baseball cap to his stubbled jaw and his laid-back attire of a black windbreaker over baggy jeans. He was adorable. At least Jude hadn't destroyed me for other men. I was still capable of feeling attraction and getting my flirt on.

My eyes widened. *Oh.* I sucked in a breath. I recognized this man—or at least his type—right down to his taste in dogs. This one wasn't a *golden*doodle, but close enough. My stomach roiled in understanding of the habit playing out before my eyes as it had done so many times before, only this time with my knowledge. I felt my face drain of color.

"Okay, bye!" I said before running as far away as possible from Jude version I-can-no-longer-keep-track as fast as I could until my ribs cramped and my lungs begged me to stop. At the water's edge, I leaned over the railing and caught my breath as tears stung behind my eyelids. My phone rang, and I jumped in surprise. Maybe it was Jude. With shaky hands, I glanced at the screen.

"Hi, Nani." I wiped my eyes.

"I was sitting in my living room playing solitaire on my iPad when your pretty face popped into my head. I had this eerie feeling you needed me. Is everything all right?"

"Not even a little bit." I fell onto the nearest bench and hugged myself. "I do need you. When can I come over?"

Chapter Thirty-Nine

That Saturday, I took the train to Riverdale, the residential neighborhood in the Bronx where Nani lived. The scent of cookies wafted through the air as I made my way from the elevator to her apartment down the hall. She was waiting for me at the door, as always, and had pulled me into her arms before I even said hello.

She let go and scanned the length of my body. Finally, she looked up at me. "Did you get taller?"

I wiggled my nose. "Nani, I'm twenty-seven. I stopped growing about ten years ago."

"Well, it can't be because I'm shrinking. Absolutely not." She winked. "Coffee?"

I was about to decline her offer—I'd already had two cups that morning—when she said, "I have Bailey's."

I giggled. "Then the answer is a resounding yes!" Nani was especially darling when she was buzzed, and a shot of Bailey's in her coffee would do the trick. "Do you need help?"

She waved me off. "Make yourself comfortable."

While she headed to the kitchen, I retired to the living room and sat on the taupe paisley-printed fabric couch. Liquid warmth infused my body within seconds as I took in the familiar surroundings of the space Nani and Papi had called home since I was born: the armchair, upholstered to match the couch, where I'd sat on Papi's lap countless times when I was a little girl; the glass candy bowl on the small wood end table from which I'd plucked hundreds of individually wrapped caramels, Hershey's Kisses, and strawberry bonbons; and the beige-and-gold area rug atop the hardwood floor where my sisters and I played with dolls and Legos while the adults did their grown-up things. Through the years, the apartment had been upgraded with new furniture and modern appliances, but even with the addition of a stainless-steel refrigerator, granite kitchen countertops, and new tiles in the master and guest bathrooms, it still felt the same—homey, cozy, and safe—just like Nani herself.

She handed me my personalized "Molly" mug then went back to the kitchen for her own cup, along with the bottle of Bailey's, in case one shot wasn't enough. "I forgot the cookies!"

Insisting she sit down, I retrieved the platter of homemade mandelbrot, which was basically the Jewish version of biscotti, and placed it on the round glass coffee table.

From the armchair, Nani jutted her chin toward me. "Are you ready to tell me what's troubling you or do you need more liquor?"

Since my career was less sensitive than my love life, I started with my current predicament at work. After I summed up the situation, I said, "I always check who else works at any company I've taken on as a client. Except the one time I let Michael into my head, I got lazy and sent out résumés relying on old information and now I don't know what to do about Romero. Do I tell him about my experience with Maxine after cheering him on through two interviews, or do I feign ignorance and take the risk he either won't get the job or she'll be nicer to him than she was to me?"

Nani sipped from her mug. "What does your gut say?"

"It says it's a huge risk." I plucked a cookie from the plate. "I get that not everyone is going to love their jobs. It's why it's called work, blah, blah, blah. But at bare minimum, they should have a hospitable workplace, not one where they're so tense, they look just as forward to an offensive co-worker or client's vacation days as they do their own." I took an aggressive chomp of my mandelbrot.

Nani nodded in sympathetic understanding. "It must have been awful for you at the law firm."

My mouth full, I said, "It was!" before my good manners intervened, and I chewed and swallowed. "As a recruiter, I'm responsible for matching employer with employee and have some control over where my candidates gain employment. I'll be damned if I knowingly place Romero in a bad situation without his knowledge and then pocket the commission."

Nani leaned back in her chair. "There's your answer."

I glanced around the room. "Where?"

She chuckled. "You said it yourself. If you refuse to profit from putting your client in a bad situation without his knowledge, what *can* you do?"

My breathing slowed. "I can tell Romero about my experience with Maxine, acknowledging it might not be *his* experience with her, and let him decide for himself?"

Nani's blue eyes twinkled. "Are you asking me or telling me?"

I giggled. "The latter." I beamed at her. "I think I needed to talk it out, so thank you for listening."

She regarded me with obvious affection. "You're a shaina maidel, Molly Blum. Always have been."

My face warmed at the compliment. "Thank you. I only wish being a good girl was always enough." I took a gulp of coffee too fast to relish the chocolate flavor from the liquor and frowned into my now-empty mug.

Nani knitted her brows and extended the bottle of Bailey's toward me. "Enough for what?"

I raised my mug for another shot. "To keep my parents from separating, for one. Like the last time."

Her reaction was a blank look.

I sighed and slunk into the couch cushion. "Right before Dad moved out when we were kids, I overheard them fighting. It wasn't about him not helping around the house enough or how much sex they weren't having…" My cheeks burned like I'd guzzled a package of Red Hots candy, but Nani didn't blink. "It was about us—their daughters—basically how difficult we were." I gave her a knowing look. "Especially Michelle and Nicole."

Nani snorted.

"When he moved back in, I was afraid to be naughty or rock the boat in case it caused more fighting and he moved out again, maybe permanently. Basically, I tried to make up for Michelle and Nicole's clueless transgressions by being as easy to parent as possible so they wouldn't fight about us."

"Oh, honey!" Nani placed a hand against her heart. "It wasn't your responsibility to keep your parents together, nor was it you or your sister's fault they separated in the first place. Then or now."

"But it's been twenty years and it never happened again." *Until now.* Until I'd let my guard down.

She shook her head of short silvery blond hair. "Not because their youngest child was an angel, but because deep inside, they weren't ready to give up back then. It's different this time. Trust me. I was there."

I sat up straight. "So essentially I did it for nothing?" All those times I cleaned my room when I didn't want to and volunteered to help Mom with some annoying chore. Or when I pretended not to care when my sisters called dibs on riding shotgun or dictated what TV show we watched because I didn't want to make Mom moderate or break up a silly fight we wouldn't even remember the next day. It hadn't made an ant's crap of difference.

Nani reached out and patted my leg. "It wasn't for nothing. You were a delightful child then, and your parents are very proud of the woman you've become."

"Even though I quit the law? I had my career all planned out. All I had to do was follow the path I carefully set for myself and everything else would seamlessly follow. Instead, they paid half my tuition for law school for me to switch careers after only one year." My throat thickened from the shame.

"You were miserable. It takes chutzpah to do what you did. I mean it. In my day, if a woman chose to have a career, she lived with it no matter what. Overworked? Treated badly? *Pfft*. Suck it up." She slammed her coffee down.

I squeaked out a laugh.

Nani relocated to the couch next to me. "I'm so sorry you felt responsible for your parents' marriage and for keeping your family together for so long." She squeezed my hand. "But there are things we can't control no matter how methodical or well behaved we try to be. You need to let go of the notion mistakes can be prevented and try to focus on your happiness in the present, like with Jude." Her cheeks brightened. "I always suspected there was a fine line between love and hate where you two were concerned. I'm glad I'm alive to see love win the day."

I blinked back tears and sank into her side, inhaling her floral-fruity Nina Ricci perfume, originally purchased as a gift from her three granddaughters because it shared her name. "You might want to hold your horses on that one." I told her everything.

"He took my kindness and used it against me, claiming I was boring and incapable of functioning without a plan. I didn't cheat or cause him bodily harm. All I did was push a bit too hard, and he lost it on me! Not for nothing, but he's a grown man and some planning for his future *is* in order unless he's truly content in his current situation, which he told me is not the case." I paused to catch my breath. "Does he think ownership papers and a key to a venue is going to magically show up at his doorstep along with financial capital and a business plan?"

"He's Jude, so he might." Her mouth lifted on one side. "This is one of the reasons you two work. You rein him in and he helps loosen you up."

My stomach tightened. "You think I'm boring too?"

She frowned. "Not at all, bubaleh. I just think sometimes it's okay to color outside the lines or change colors altogether. I know you think progress is linear, but sometimes the zigzags are not only necessary and healthy but more fun and lead to even better things. There's nothing wrong with writing to-do lists and having bullet-point plans, but if you fail to leave room for revisions, you're often hurting yourself. Sometimes you just need to follow your gut and see where it leads. Or just do it and if it doesn't work out, no harm, no foul."

You regret the things you don't do.

She waggled a finger. "It should go without saying, do not follow your gut if it tells you to let the air out of someone's tires."

"*Tire!*" I laughed despite myself. "Maybe he *is* good for me in that respect." Even when we fought, it was fun. "Except there's no way he would agree I'm good for him the way you seem to think. He said I remind him of his parents—not exactly sexy—and basically told me he can't stand me again."

I hadn't recovered from the sting. Part of me had feared all along that Jude's attraction to me was temporary. Was it even love on his side? We'd never said the words. Were we back where we'd started? Only this time, rather than mutual hate for each other, one of us—me—had a nasty case of unrequited love?

"Oh, honey." Nani shook her head, frowning. "I'd bet the pool of my next mahjongg tournament Jude only said that to get under your skin. Unintentionally or not, you tried to push him out of a comfort zone he wasn't ready to leave which, in his mind, was akin to you not accepting him for who he was. He was hurt and reverted back to old habits, attacking you where he knew it would sting the most."

"Well, I absolutely accept him for who he already is." All the adjectives I'd used to describe Jude over the last six months lined up in my head like words on a Scrabble board: evil, shrewd, cocky, protective, caring, bashful, generous, sexy, loving, hurt, *back to evil again*. But I could forgive that last one. "I think he's extraordinary, Nani."

She smiled softly. "I think he feels the same about you, sweetheart."

"Really?" If she was right, it didn't have to be over. My skin tingled with hope.

"There's only one way to find out."

Just then, my phone pinged. Under normal circumstances, I wouldn't check my text messages while spending time with Nani, but these weren't normal circumstances, and it was Jude.

Jude: I'm sorry for the mean things I said. I was out of line.

A cocktail of happiness and relief swirled in my gut. I looked at Nani. "Would you be terribly insulted if I left early? I need to see Jude."

Nani's smile split wide open. "What are you waiting for then?"

Chapter Forty

I took the train back to Manhattan in much better spirits than I'd left it. Now that Jude had expressed remorse for the hurtful things he'd said during our fight, I would apologize again for pushing so hard on the restaurant opening, and we'd be back to our regular fabulously coupled selves.

There was so much to say. I pulled up the notes on my phone and jotted down my bullet points, which turned into...well, I was hesitant to call it "poetry" for fear Emily Dickinson and Maya Angelou would turn over in their graves, but hopefully Jude would appreciate my spontaneous effort to creatively express my feelings.

When I got off the subway at 33rd Street, I began the ten-minute walk to Jude's apartment. He didn't usually work on Saturdays, but just in case, I stepped to the side and replied to his text.

> **Molly:** Thx for the apology. I'm sorry too. On my way to your apartment now.

He responded within seconds.

> **Jude:** OK.

I doubled my stride. I couldn't wait to see him... to *kiss* him!

The doorman stopped me this time, but it was all good. It was his job to protect Jude in case I was a murderous ex-girlfriend who was stalking him. I was impressed he took this responsibility seriously. *My* doorman often let delivery guys up without calling first, never mind they could be on their way to chop me up into a million pieces and tuck my body parts into empty pizza boxes.

When he gave me the go-ahead, I refrained from saluting him on a job well done and joined the queue for the elevator before stepping inside along with several others.

Jude was waiting by his open door when I arrived a minute later. I studied him across the threshold, letting reality replace what my memory had kept alive since the last time I'd seen him. It had been weeks, not years, but time did *not* fly when you missed someone so much it hurt. I took a steadying breath even though I wanted to go full Yogi on him and lunge. "Hi!" He was blurry. My eyes had filled with tears.

An impressively more composed Jude gestured inside. "Come in."

I trailed behind him, immediately noticing his jeans were less snug in the butt than I remembered. *Is he eating enough?* Loss of appetite was a symptom of heartbreak. I hated the thought of Jude being heartbroken.

To his back, I said, "I've been thinking about you constantly, and when I received your text, I came straight here from Riverdale."

He turned around. "Nani?"

I nodded. "Thanks for making the first move and apologizing. Consider it accepted. We're much too good at hitting each other where it hurts. Lots of practice, I guess."

Jude gave a barely-there smile. "Truth."

I cocked my head. He was strangely placid under the circumstances. I cleared my throat. "Can we talk..." My words dropped off, and I did a double take as Jerry and Esther rounded the corner from Jerry's bedroom behind the kitchen. I knew they'd slept together, but Esther hanging out at his place with his roommates was altogether different from hiding him away in hers.

I regarded her with a *look*, and with the nonverbal language known only to best friends, asked all the questions.

She shrugged sheepishly, color painting her cheeks, as Jerry tugged her toward the couch.

Fascinating. I returned her shrug with a "to be continued" expression of my own.

Jude said, "Should we go to my room?"

Turning toward him, I said, "Yes" before thinking better of it. "Actually, no."

He jerked his head back. "No?"

"I didn't plan to do this before a crowd, but I'm changing the plan."

Jude blinked.

Ignoring the sweat building under my arms, I nodded. "You heard me right. This is Molly*plana* changing the plan!" I faced the couch where Alex, Jerry, and Esther were watching television. "Can I have your attention, please?"

Alex muted the TV. "The room is yours."

I turned to Jude. "Can you sit with them?"

He squinted at me, clearly confused. "Okay?"

When he was settled, I said, "I have a few things I need to say to Jude, and I'd like you all to hear it." I looked at Jude, and saw for a split second the four-year-old boy I played with in the sand at the Jersey Shore, followed by the thirteen-year-old teenager who wowed the audience at his bar mitzvah with the singing voice of an angel. (He later told me in no uncertain terms his parents forced him to invite me.) And finally, the seventeen-year-old almost-man, who lost his chance of becoming a professional athlete in no small part because of our antagonistic relationship.

"When I was five or six, I slighted Jude in front of the other girls in my class, and unbeknownst to me, the boy who had previously been my first and best friend decided then and there he hated me. So began a rivalry that lasted another twenty years. Now I want the world...er...the room...to know how I feel about him." My voice was shaking, and I took a moment to regroup.

"When we were first thrown together to plan our parents' party, I thought a forced partnership between Molly and Jude was the worst idea since the Yankees signed Jacoby Ellsbury." I paused while Jerry chuckled. "I was right. We disagreed on everything and put more effort into our pranks than on planning *anything*."

I licked my dry lips and talked directly to Jude. "But then we became friends. Sort of. And then I lusted you, even when I thought I was dying of the flu. And before I knew it and without my permission, I fell in love with you."

I looked as deeply into his eyes as possible from ten feet away. "I love you, Jude." I took a deep breath. The old Molly would have waited to declare love until Jude said it first, but this version-in-progress refused to regret the things she didn't say.

"I wrote a poem outlining some of the reasons I love you and the way you make me feel." I turned to the others. "I wrote it on the train in five minutes and it's probably horrible, but I'm reading it anyway. I'm spontaneous like that." I dared a knowing glance at Jude, who looked like a moose in headlights—an exceptionally sexy moose in black jeans and a red Henley rolled up to expose impressive forearms. I opened my phone to the notes and cleared my throat.

I love the way you make me laugh.
I love the history that we share.
I love the way you protect my friends.
I love the messiness of your hair.
I love your dog. Oh yes I do.
I love him so much it should count twice.
I love that you make me feel adored.
Even when you're not being very nice.
I love the way we are together.
Both when we get along
And when we fight
But between getting it done
And battling it out
The former wins out every night.
I never meant to push you.
I couldn't care less what you do.
Athlete, mailman, bartender, doctor
I do truly love you for you.

I lowered the phone and faced my public—four sets of dropped jaws.

"Interesting rhyme scheme," said Alex.

"Thank you!" I beamed with pride, though I suspected it wasn't meant as a compliment.

Esther reacted first, clapping slowly. Jerry and Alex followed her lead. Only Jude remained still and silent as if gagged by an invisible muzzle.

I scratched the back of my neck. Unnerved by his lack of reaction, I pressed on. "I never intended to hurt you or make you think I needed you to be some other version of yourself. I was just so ecstatic you'd truly moved on from baseball and wanted to support your actual dreams in any way I could. I see now I pushed too hard, but I was never disappointed in you. I think you're perfect just as you are. Well, perfect for me, at least. And I promise to always have your back against bratty girls who think you have the cooties, against your parents, against anyone."

"Beautiful." Jerry wiped a tear from his eye.

While Esther, Jerry, and Alex's heads swung back and forth between the two of us like they were at a tennis match, Jude was quiet. It was his turn now. I bit down on my lip on excited tenterhooks for his return monologue, which I fully expected to be better than mine despite being completely off the cuff.

Finally, he stood, his eyes a little wet. "Thank you for the speech and…" He coughed. "Poem. I did not see that coming. Like I said, I'm sorry too. I was out of line. I know you were only trying to help me. I shouldn't have overreacted and said what I did. But…"

My spirits soared. This was how it was done. Compromise. Owning up to our individual mistakes. Wait. *But?* "But?"

Jude dropped his gaze and visibly deflated. "No matter how you look at it, we're so different, Molly."

Molly. My heart pinched like someone had pierced it with a ten-inch sharp needle. Since when was calling me by my true name a reason to panic? But I was panicking.

Jude walked slowly toward me, his expression softer. "This break hasn't been easy for me either, but each time I thought about calling you, doubts crept in."

Why was he talking like we weren't about to kiss and make up? He was the one who'd initiated the apology. My poem/speech? They were like extra credit.

"Regardless of how we feel about each other now, I'm not sure if we're…" He looked over his shoulders at our friends. "If we're right for each other."

As nervous laughter bubbled through me, I said, "Is being different so bad? Would you rather date Timothy?"

That caused a chuckle from someone in our small audience.

"I'm not saying it's bad, but…well, you kind of sprung this on me…in front of an audience."

"You put him on the spot like a proposal at Yankee Stadium. The recipient is always pressured to say yes," Alex said.

Jude twisted his neck. "What he said. I'm sorry, Molly."

"I was trying to be less buttoned up…" *Less boring.* "You sent me that text apologizing. I thought—"

"And I meant it! I said some shitty things and I couldn't let them stand whether or not we stayed together. But if I'm perfect for you?" He licked his lips. "I need more time to think it over on my own. To make sure it's right."

"You need…" I swallowed. "Time?"

I had poured out my heart in front of his roommates. I used

the L word many, many times. I'd showed how unprepared I could be. He was supposed to drag me to his bed. Not... *this*. My lungs instinctively filled with anger—my go-to response when we were at odds.

He nodded. "Yes. Time." His hazel-with-blue-flecks eyes begged me to understand.

I was desperate to argue with him... to share what Nani had said about how our differences balanced us out. But letting my emotions get the better of me had never worked in the past.

"Absolutely. Take time. I'll just... um... leave." I looked pleadingly at Esther. *Do not cry. Do NOT.*

She jumped off the couch. "I'll go with you."

When I reached the door, I gave one final glance at Jude over my shoulder. He looked hesitant, regretful even, but surely not enough time had gone by yet to ask.

Instead I gave a pathetic little wave goodbye and followed Esther into the hallway.

Chapter Forty-One

After leaving Jude's, Esther and I headed straight to Joshua Tree, an eighties-themed bar around the corner. Rather than sports games, massive flat screens above the bar displayed music videos circa MTV 1984. Currently, Madonna's "Dress You Up" blared from the speakers while a throng of early twentysomethings danced in place, oblivious to the cheap house-brand alcohol spilling from their plastic cups onto the sticky floor.

"To thinking about it." I slammed the Jack Daniel's Honey shot down my throat, my tongue sticking out and head shaking involuntarily at the burn.

I signaled the bored-looking female bartender for another round. The mixed drinks here were weak and not worth the money. "I feel old," I said to Esther, while scanning the makeshift dance floor. "How are we only in our mid-twenties and I feel old?"

"More like *late* twenties." She smirked. "You, at least."

I flipped her the bird but laughed. "One month, my friend." Distraction over, I pounded another shot. "I'm such a simp."

Esther wrapped her fist around her shot glass. "Why are you a simp? I'm not agreeing or disagreeing, mind you. Just curious."

I didn't bother to feign offense at her failure to immediately argue I was not, in fact, a simp. "I serenaded him with poetry! All because I assumed his apology meant he was ready to kiss and make up, and I wanted to do something fun and unexpected. *Cringe*." I made a matching expression.

Esther downed her shot. "Your poem was adorbs. Textbook rom-com material with just a splash of cringe. I only felt an eensy bit of vicarious embarrassment on your behalf."

"Thank goodness." I made prayer hands sarcastically. "Name one rom-com where the grand gesture led to the love interest's need to *think about it*. What is there to think about?"

"Maybe it's exactly what he said. As moved as he was by your speech, he doesn't want to rush back into things without being completely sure it's the right move."

"But why would it be wrong?" I whined like a fourteen-year-old girl whose mom had just prohibited her from wearing a crop top to school. "Nani says I rein him in and he loosens me up. But maybe Jude doesn't want to be reined in. He apologized for losing it on me about my 'fucking plans,' but didn't actually take back what he said about my being a bore and a nag. What if my personality is a dealbreaker for him?"

Esther twisted her mouth as if contemplating. "Is *his* personality a dealbreaker for *you*? That he's so laid back about...well, everything, and you're..." She looked at me tenderly. "Not?"

"I love him. Jude wouldn't be *Jude* without his built-in confidence that everything will work out. Does it make me twitchy sometimes? Yes! And it probably always will. It wouldn't be *me* otherwise. We only work if he loves me as I am too—plans and all. But what if he doesn't?"

"I don't know, Molly. I don't know." Her eyes went soft. "You love him, huh?"

"I made that abundantly obvious." I slapped the bottom of the shot glass in an attempt to knock as much remaining liquid as possible into my mouth.

"Want me to try to get some intel from Jerry? I have methods of persuasion. One time—"

I held up a hand. "Please don't." I closed my eyes to wipe out the visual. "Imagine if you and Jerry go the distance while Jude and I implode? Although how much weirder is it for you to fall for adorable Jerry than I for my mortal enemy? Jude Stark. Jude *Desmond* Stark." *Desmond and Molly.* I smiled for half a second, then groaned. "Oh, God." I buried my head in my hands. "What if this has been a prank all along? His biggest one yet. Making Molly 'Mole' Blum fall for him so he could break my heart." Bile rumbled in my throat at the possibility. Or it might have been the numerous shots I'd done on a somewhat empty stomach. *Must cut myself off.*

"Stop it. You've been together three months plus a month or two of courting with chicken soup, kitty feedings, and hair accessories. He even pulled his family into it. It's a big commitment for a practical joke."

"Jude is nothing if not committed when it comes to making a fool out of me."

"I've seen the way he looks at you, even tonight. There's no way all of this has been a ruse, unless he's a talented actor, like Joaquin Phoenix talented."

Even though I knew she was right, I argued, "He can sing

and dance. But for his knee injury, he'd kill it on *Dancing with the Stars*. I wouldn't be surprised if he's a triple threat. Anyway," I said, wagging my finger at her, "I don't want you to try to get information from Jerry because it will sound like I'm pushing. And pushing him is how we got into this mess in the first place. So don't talk to him. Act like you don't care... like there's nothing to care *about* because you're so unconcerned about the Molly and Jude drama... because there's no drama to be concerned with in the first place." I gulped from the glass of water I'd ignored until that moment. "You know?"

Esther shook out her head. "Either I'm pissed or you're speaking another language."

"Just don't mention my name at all. Okay?"

"Got it."

My gaze dropped to my phone where a notification appeared for a voice mail. My heart somersaulted thinking it might be Jude, even though I *hated* him right now for putting me through this. But I didn't actually hate him. Not even a little bit. Not even at all.

Now I was really channeling a rom-com. *Thank you, Kat Stratford.*

Then I saw the call came from Pro City Sportswear. I had my office voice mail automatically forwarded to my iPhone. I stuck my finger in one ear to drown out the background noise and listened. I only heard every few words. "*Bleep* is Kevin from Pro City *Bleep*. I'm sorry to *bleep* you on *bleep* weekend, but I'm on vacation all *bleep bleep* and wanted *bleep* offer the legal counsel position to Romero Vasquez. In my absence, call *bleep bleep* for negotiations."

I saved the message to listen to again in quiet and when I was sober. But the gist was clear. The job was Romero's if he wanted it. Which meant I had to tell him the whole truth. I whimpered. It was too much. Jude, Romero. Love. Work. It was all too much. I lowered my head onto the bar, shouting, "Ouch!" when I was yanked upright by my hair.

"You might catch a disease." Esther looked at me with a mixture of disgust and pity. "We should call it." She whipped her head behind her and back to me. "Unless you want to pick up a Jude lookalike for the road."

My lips trembled and shoulders heaved. "Too soon!"

Chapter Forty-Two

The following Thursday, my eyes were on my computer, but my mind was elsewhere when there was a knock on my office door. I blinked myself to attention and swung my head to find Michael leaning against the frame. I gave him a stiff smile to disguise the irrepressible revulsion I always felt in his company. *Same as it ever was.* At least it was a distraction, albeit a greasy one, from wondering where Jude was right now and what he was *thinking* about. If God created the world in seven days, surely Jude could decide what he wanted in five.

Michael approached my desk. "I heard your candidate turned down the Pro City Sportswear position. Too bad."

"Too bad," I repeated with as much sincerity as I could fake. Why Michael insisted on keeping tabs on my every account was forever a mystery. None of it affected his bottom line.

He tossed my stress ball in the air and caught it in his palm before squeezing twice. "Any idea why he changed his mind?" *Squeeze.* "I thought you said he wanted more of a work-life balance?" *Squeeze. Squeeze.*

I willed him to release the ball from his clammy hand and considered my response. Being honest would result in one of his patronizing misogynist speeches—how I was naïve to the ways of the world or too maternal for my own good.

So I lied. "He wants to start a family in the next five years, so he's pushed back his move in-house until he's saved up enough money for a place in the suburbs." The truth was, after I told Romero he got the job, simultaneously divulging my personal experience with Maxine, he asked for a few days to think about it. Notwithstanding his unfortunate choice of phrasing, I told him to get back to me when he made a decision, promising to negotiate on his behalf with all the enthusiasm he deserved if he accepted it and keep searching for another position if he declined. To my relief, he ultimately turned it down.

But my fib today could be the truth next month. Romero wasn't married yet, but a lot could change in five years. Also, it was the only excuse I could think of to get Michael off my case.

He returned the ball to my desk. *Finally.* "You win some, you lose some."

I thought I was off the hook, but he wasn't done.

"Next time this happens, emphasize the resurgence of in-house stock options and deferred cash." With a rap of his knuckles against my door, he was gone.

I closed my eyes as a feeling of dread washed over me. My life at the moment sorely lacked joy. Every night this week after work, I'd watched mindless television in bed until I fell asleep. Sex was off the table, and I lacked the energy to take care of myself. Either Jude wasn't done thinking about it or we were over. At this point, I questioned whether I even wanted him anymore. I still loved him, *madly*, but Molly Blum wasn't about to sit around indefinitely waiting for a man to decide he wanted to be with her.

My phone rang, pulling me out of my pity party. Letting the call go to voice mail was enticing, but what if Mom was lonely in that big house all by herself? As long as she didn't mention Jude or work. Which left absolutely nothing to talk about.

It became quickly clear my reluctance to discuss my love life or career was irrelevant. Mom's agenda, while rambling and difficult to follow, had little to do with me. First, she'd complained about the two-day loss of internet due to an ISP service outage, then moved on to Eris's winter concert at the preschool the following month, followed by her book club's latest selection, and now we'd arrived at her recent shopping spree. "Bed Bath & Beyond had a winter clearance sale so I bought new bed pillows for every room yesterday."

Before I could question why she'd spend money on pillows when most of the beds in the house went unslept in, she was on to the next topic.

"Do you like candles?"

"It depends on—"

"Yankee candles were forty percent off, but they didn't smell that good and I couldn't remember if you liked them and anyway, have you heard of Body Holiday?"

I jolted at the weird non-sequitur. "Is it a brand of candles?"

"It's a resort, Molly." She sighed impatiently as mothers did so well. "We've booked a trip there for the spring."

"Who's we?" *Dare I hope she'd say, "Me and your father"?*

"Some girlfriends, all newly single."

My shoulders slumped at her comfortable use of *single*. I reached for my stress ball until I remembered who'd held it last.

"It's an all-inclusive resort and spa in St. Lucia devoted to wellness."

"It sounds fabulous." It wasn't a lie, but the forced cheer in my voice was.

"Do you know I've never been on vacation with a non-relative? First it was my parents, then I married your father, and then it was the five of us. This is my first girls' trip!"

I couldn't help but smile, and this time it was genuine. Her excitement was infectious. "You sound happy, Mom."

"I am. It wouldn't be true to say I'm happier than I've ever been, because raising you girls was the paramount of joy . . . most of the time." She chuckled. "But life doesn't end at sixty. My world is full of opportunities and I want to take advantage of as many as I can while I'm still of able mind and body. This is the time. I'm retiring soon. My girls are out of the house and don't need me—"

"I always need you!"

"You sure you don't have it backwards?"

"What?"

There was a brief pause before she spoke again, her voice soft and tentative. "Are you sure you're not confusing needing us with needing us to need *you*?"

"Nice awkward phrasing, Mom," I teased, already knowing where this was going.

"You know what I mean."

"I do." I frowned into my lap.

"I'll say this once. I'm *fine*. I'm better than fine, and so is your father. Take care of *you*. Focus on your own joy and let us worry about us."

"I will." This time I meant it. First Nani and then my mother had urged me to focus on my own happiness. In a single moment, it had finally sunk in. It was so obvious. "Mom?"

"Yes, sweetheart?"

"What would you say if I told you I wanted to leave recruiting to be a career coach?"

She only hesitated for a second. "I'd say I trust you to know your own heart. You are, of course, the most practical of the Blum sisters."

I smiled. "I gotta go. I love you."

"Love you too."

We ended the call, and I took in the 150 square feet of my office. It was a nice space—decent size, with my diplomas and framed drawings from my niece lining the walls and a great view of the East River—but I hadn't been happy in it for quite some time. I put so much effort into helping candidates find their perfect job, but this wasn't *my* perfect job, even with the possibility of a promotion to director in the not-so-distant future.

I wanted what Rosaria had…what she had offered *me*. And I'd turned her down because of an arbitrary plan…because I felt some sort of obligation to stick with it…like it was my punishment for leaving the law.

Working for Ceiling Crashers came with a substantial pay cut, but Rosaria said it might be temporary. As the company grew, so would my salary. And if it didn't? So what. I'd allowed what I brought home to count for more than my happiness and job satisfaction. I used my apartment as another excuse to say no, but it was just a place to live. I could find another one. I had far less confidence I'd be offered another dream job.

I spent most of my life trying to be perfect, planning all my moves to avoid missteps. But sometimes even the best-laid plans fell apart or came with unexpected results. Sometimes you had to follow your heart, come what may. I'd followed mine from

Riverdale straight to Jude's front door and embarrassed myself with my silly, impromptu poem. Had he taken me in his arms? No. But at least I'd spoken my truth. No matter where the two of us went from here, I wouldn't have to wonder what would have happened if I told him I loved him. I would not regret the things I didn't do when it came to us.

Mom and Nani were right—it was time to be my own fairy godmother and make my own dreams come true. Maybe I'd get another chance with Jude and maybe I wouldn't. But in the meantime, there was another significant relationship I needed to focus on.

I found Rosaria's name in my contact list and pressed call.

She answered on the first ring. "Molly! Nice to hear from you."

I spun my chair. "About that job offer..."

Chapter Forty-Three

*L*ater that night, my smile couldn't be contained as I descended the elevator from the Ceiling Crashers headquarters to the lobby. I'd begun the day as an unfulfilled and sometimes secretly insubordinate legal recruiter with a dream and was ending it with an accepted offer as CC's newest career counselor and director of member relations—a title Rosaria and I had brainstormed together during our two-hour meeting in her office, soon to be down the hall from mine.

Bad things came in threes, they said, but they *also* said the third time is the charm. The first time, I was a lawyer. The second time I was a recruiter. Recruiting, while temporary, had been a necessary pitstop on the way to my third (and hopefully final) destination: career counseling. And if it wasn't? That was okay too. Even more satisfying than creating the perfect plan was changing it to create the perfect life. (But who was I kidding? Rome wasn't built in a day, and Molly Blum loved, and would always love, a good plan.)

For the love of fresh sushi, crisp wine, and deep, hot kisses, please let this one stick!

Without warning, a lump settled in my throat, and my nose

tickled as I walked through the revolving doors of the office building. I froze in my individual partition. What happened today—the huge change I made—was too momentous to keep to myself, but the person I most wanted to tell was Jude. The surprise on his face at my unexpected 180 would be even more priceless than his "I can't believe I fell for one of Mole's pranks" expressions. But more than the surprise, I yearned to see the genuine joy I knew he'd feel reflected in his beautiful hazel eyes.

Another person pushed the door behind me with force, and I jerked forward and stepped out into the cold air. I wrapped my ombre coral oblong scarf tighter around my neck and wiped my damp eyes. *No. Just No.* I might be in some weird relationship purgatory, but this was a good day—a *great* day. I wished I could share it with Jude, but I wasn't alone. I had a best friend. Esther would be so happy for me and insist on immediate and excessive celebrations involving a lot of alcohol. I smiled, weeping fest successfully averted, and retrieved my phone to call her. But she'd beaten me to it with a text:

Esther: Call me ASAP. 911.

The following day, I loosened my seat belt and glanced over my shoulder at the empty seat behind me in Esther's car. "Who's feeding Poppy while we're in Connecticut?" Her uncle had suffered a breakdown of sorts—a burst of renewed grief about his wife and panic over raising the girls by himself. Esther had offered to babysit so he could get away and regroup for a few days. But then she'd freaked out too. Caring for the twins alongside him was one thing, even being alone with one girl at a time was doable, but was she capable of taking care of both toddlers by herself for a long weekend? What if she killed one of them? I told her she was being ridiculous, but agreed to join her. Then we had a proper squealing session when I told her I had (very) belatedly accepted Rosaria's job offer.

"Jerry's taking care of it."

I smirked. "I'm surprised you didn't invite him to help you out instead of me. You could pretend the girls were yours. It would be like playing house." I giggled at the look of pure terror on her face. "Seriously, though, minus the kids, it has the potential for a romantic getaway for two. Unlike me, you have that option." I felt her piteous stare on me and gazed into the side-view mirror.

She patted my hand in silent understanding without commenting on Jerry. Either she didn't want to rub it in or wasn't comfortable admitting they were a real thing yet.

It was time for a subject change. "We can celebrate my new job when the girls are asleep." I'd taken a few vacation days and would give my two weeks' notice to Gotham City Recruiters when I got back. I didn't want to abandon Romero and would continue to scope out in-house positions in my free time. Cindy could take over negotiations from there, and we'd split the commission.

"I've no doubt there will be celebrations," Esther said.

I stared out the window, watching the cars pass by on I-84, and contemplated my bittersweet accomplishment. The sky was an ugly winter gray, but the snowcapped mountains in the distance were beautiful. "What's it going to be like the next time the Blums and Starks get together and every time from now on? We should have given more thought to how a breakup would affect the general dual-family dynamic."

I tried unsuccessfully to find humor in the fact that my parents were in a somewhat similar situation, navigating how to move forward in their friendship with the Starks in their new normal. "The stakes are way higher than when a typical couple splits. But, *no*, we were too starry-eyed to imagine anything beyond exploring every inch of each other's body and having make-up sex for days to correct twenty years of fighting."

I pictured Jude naked, simultaneously wanting to permanently ingrain the image to memory and banish it from my brain forever. I turned to Esther, my mouth dry. "What happens now? Will we act like strangers or revert to our old tricks? I'd rather be his rival than have him look right through me with no emotion whatsoever." My voice cracked. "I don't think I can bear it."

"Why are you assuming it's over? Have you officially broken up?" She glanced at me for a beat before quickly facing the road.

I frowned. "No, but we might as well have. It's been almost a week. At this point I can't think of anything he could say to justify needing so much time to *think*. The damage has been done."

Esther turned away from the wheel, her brown eyes wide. "You mean you don't even want to get back together anymore?"

"I don't know what I want," I whined. Out of the corner of my eye, I saw traffic slow down ahead of us. "Watch the road!"

Esther whipped her head forward and slammed on the brakes.

I stopped talking. I might be heartsick, but I didn't want to cause an accident and kill us both.

Eventually, she pulled off at an exit. "What does Mrs. Hughes want me to do next?" she asked, referring to her British GPS woman.

"Make a right on Trout Brook Drive." I laughed. "You'd think you'd know how to get there by now."

"I'm bloody awful with directions."

I pursed my lips. "Since when?" We'd taken countless drives to the Jersey Shore and the Hamptons as well as day trips to various amusement parks and wineries over the years, and she'd never gotten lost. Pointing at a sign on the road, I said, "Talcott Mountain! Nicole and Dean hike here every year. I had no idea this is where your uncle lived."

Esther peered carefully out the windshield without commenting.

I zipped my lips so she could focus on the road. Assuming her uncle lived in a residential neighborhood not unlike where I was raised, I was surprised when, following several right and left turns up country roads, she drove up a gravel path and pulled up to a log cabin. I inched forward in my seat. "Is this where your uncle lives? Why did I picture a ranch or colonial like my parents' house?"

"Because you lack imagination?" She stopped the car. "Trunk's open." She gestured to her phone. "I'll be right out. I need to return a text first."

I exited the car and removed my small polka-dot wheelie suitcase from the otherwise empty trunk. Where was Esther's bag? The hair on the back of my neck prickled like needles. Something was off. "Esther?"

She popped her head out of the open window. "Please don't be mad, but you've been Starked."

"I've been..." My head jutted back. "Huh?"

"Toodle-oo." Before my eyes, the window went up and she peeled out of the driveway.

I watched her car disappear from sight with my mouth hanging open until a bark followed by the sound of bells captured my attention. I regained my bearings, clapping in delight at the sight of Yogi running toward me. "Yogi!" I bent down, and he put both paws on my shoulders, licking my face, while I scratched his ears. Oh, how I'd missed his wet kisses and doggy smell.

Wait. Jude's dog was here, which meant...I gulped and lifted my head...*he's here too.*

My breath quickened, and my stomach tangled with knots.

He leaned against a tree and flashed his cocky Jude grin, but not before I saw the question in his eyes.

I had questions of my own. What was he asking? What did he want? Why was he here? Why was *I* here?

He approached, a blush on his cheeks, and wordlessly took over possession of my suitcase and walked it toward the cabin, Yogi at his heels.

My skin zipped with electricity where his hand had brushed with mine. I pressed it to my face.

He reached the door and turned around. "You coming?"

Chapter Forty-Four

On unsteady legs, I followed Jude inside the cabin, gasping upon entry. *Little House on the Prairie* it was not. The walls and vaulted ceiling were wood-paneled, and the stone brick fireplace was lit. Aside from a red suede couch, all the furniture, including cabinets and tables, was wood and appeared handcrafted. A candlelit table was set with two wineglasses, and a bottle of red had been uncorked. The mood was utterly romantic.

But wowed as I was by this rustic, charming, and luxurious cabin, I needed Jude to explain why he'd tricked—make that *Starked*—me here. "Either you've summoned me to this cabin to kill me, woo me, or sell me a timeshare. Which is it?" I hugged myself to still my shaking torso. The unexpected appearance of my estranged boyfriend had me chilled with nervous excitement.

"Definitely door number two." He licked his lips. "I'm sorry."

I dropped my arms. "Sorry for what?"

He stepped closer to me. "Needing time. Not being prepared to immediately move forward as a couple after your speech last weekend."

I nodded. "I get it." But I didn't. "Actually, I don't. You always knew we were different. Suddenly it was a dealbreaker all because I pushed a bit hard?"

Jude gestured to the back of the room. "Can we sit?"

Once we were settled on either side of the couch, he continued. "Our relationship went from zero to a hundred so fast—"

"Twenty-seven years is fast?"

He laughed. "No. But once we got together, it felt serious. Did it not to you?"

"It did." Serious enough to daydream about our double-backyard wedding.

"I started to worry that maybe what we had was just pent-up sexual tension or hate fucking, and once the novelty wore off, we'd regret it. Not to mention what a breakup would do to our family dynamics." He leaned back as if preparing for an attack.

I'd said the same thing to Esther on the drive over. I slouched against the couch cushion, not bothering to argue on the assumption he had more to say.

Jude rubbed his hands down the leg of his jeans. "It wasn't only about me feeling pressured by you this one time. As you know, I'm more of a 'do things when the mood hits' person and you're on a bullet-point schedule with everything. I was afraid you'd continue to get frustrated with my tendency to wing it and eventually we'd combust. I went on the offensive and blew first this time, but even though I apologized, I still worried that these major differences in our personalities meant we were doomed."

It was time to argue. "Only if we let them doom us. We could try to meet in the middle." Something I was willing to do, but I could only speak for myself. I looked around the wood-furnished room. "What happened to wooing me? This feels like the opposite of being wooed."

He cracked a smile. "Because then it occurred to me whatever this is has already passed the test of time. I realized it's not new. Even when we went months or years without any contact, we were subconsciously seeking each other out. Every guy you've dated has been a substitute for me and every girl I've been with has been an imitation of you. For years. Which means it's real, right?" As if emphasizing his point, Jude pulled a throw pillow from underneath his butt and drummed his fingers along the velvet, just like Timothy had done.

I tore my gaze from his moving fingers and raised my head in cautious hope he wouldn't add a "but."

He was grinning.

I melted...dazzled.

"I've been searching for a little..." He blushed. "*A lot* of Molly in every girl I date. And you did the same with me. We want each other in spite of...maybe *because* of those traits that make us so different."

"Well said." My voice cracked.

He shifted an inch closer to me. "We have staying power, Mole. We're not always going to agree. And we'll probably argue a lot. The likelihood of you getting frustrated with me over something I don't do and you driving me nuts over something you *do* are about a hundred percent. But it doesn't matter."

"It doesn't?" I slid to the center couch cushion, reducing our distance even more.

"No. When we're on the same page, we're fire. But when things go sour, we'll deal with it, and it will be okay. We can work it out." His lips quirked.

I snorted at the Beatles reference. Another trait he had in

common with Timothy. Or Timothy had in common with him. "We can and we will."

Jude nodded. "I just needed time to get here. Alex and Jerry, even Esther, throwing shade, sped things up a little." His hazel eyes were soft and pleading as they traced a small circle around my face. "I'm sorry I left you hanging, but when I finally came to my senses, I wanted to go big...like you did with your public declaration and amateur poetry."

The affection behind his teasing wrapped me up like a warm blanket. I placed my hand on his.

He squeezed. "I tried to implement my plan as quickly as possible, but true greatness takes time."

I was halfway onto his lap before I dropped back. Moved as I was by his grand gesture, I'd spent the last week miserable and heartbroken thinking we were over permanently. Could he have put an end to my pain earlier and chose not to? I stood before him. "You left me hanging for days because you wanted to one-up me?"

"No. Definitely not," he said assuredly before joining me on the floor. "I promise I'm not that cruel. It just worked out that way. The one-upping part, that is." A cocky grin appeared half a second before he dipped his chin in typical coy Jude form.

"You!" I shook my head in disbelief, knowing I should be furious, but not quite getting there, thanks to irresistible "bashful" Jude making a convenient appearance. "You're infuriating. You always have to be better than me! You're so *Jude*." But my angry cover was blown by my laughter. I was also impressed he *planned* this weekend at all. It was so not like him, but I refused to ruin this moment by emphasizing our differences again.

Jude smiled with every muscle on his face. "And you're so

Molly. And I love that about you. I love how much effort you put into pulling one over on me when I always emerge the victor." He thrust his tongue into his cheek. "Except for the one time you lost your mind and didn't think at all."

I opened my mouth to apologize...again, but he raised his hand in a stop gesture. Wincing, he said, "Pretend I didn't go there. There's more I want to say."

I nodded. "Continue. At the very least, I deserve a prolonged monologue of all the reasons you love me." I stilled. He hadn't said he loved me yet, only that he loved *things* about me. "I didn't mean...I don't want to presume..." My hair clung to the back of my neck. *Could it be any hotter in this cabin?*

"I love you, Molly. Of course I do." He wore his heart on his face, and I knew he meant it. I smiled shyly. Jude Stark loved me.

His eyes glistened. "It used to bother me that everyone saw you as this sweet 'most likely to subtly remove toilet paper from your shoe' girl when I knew you were capable of being hardcore ruthless. It infuriated me that you were the apple of everyone's eye at home while I was always the troublemaker."

This was a frustration I understood. None of the girls in our class who crushed on Jude had any idea what a jackass he was either, and at home, it didn't seem to matter how much trouble he caused. Sure, he got punished more than I did, but with an impish grin, he had all the grown-ups wrapped around his finger without ever having to actually lift one to help. But I wasn't about to counterattack. I had a feeling his speech was going to get much better soon. *He loves me.*

"There was so much more to you than making good grades, planning for your future, and ensuring your parents' marriage didn't implode that no one else knew. You were also so determined to keep up with me and my"—he shrugged—"let's just call it assholery. And as much as I rejoiced in getting you flustered when you were otherwise so poised, I also secretly gave you props. You were a worthy opponent." He reached out and stroked my cheek.

I closed my eyes against the sensation.

"Rather than wanting to expose your less-than-squeaky-clean reputation like I did when we were kids, I realize how lucky I am to see a side of you no one else does. I'm special. I'm not just shrewd Jude. I'm the one." His voice trembled with emotion. "I didn't mean what I said about remembering why I couldn't stand you for most of my life. I was angry and hurt, but the truth is I can't even recognize the version of me who wasn't anything but desperately in love with Molly Blum."

Zing zing zing went my heartstrings. My history of boyfriends flashed before my eyes, like the long line of bridesmaids at the end of *27 Dresses*. None of them had been right, because looking like Jude, working in the same industry, even loving the same breed of dog didn't make them Jude. Jude was the original. The first. I'd known him my whole life, but I'd finally found him.

Jude *was* the one. The one who knew me, really knew me, who *saw* me for everything positive and negative I encompassed. I didn't have to toe the line with him. We could just *be*. He knew all my secrets and had forgiven all the bad. I'd mess up again, and so would he, but we'd get through it.

"I have a serious question for you." I looked him deep in the eyes knowing if I peered hard enough, I'd see the reflection of my own desire. "Is there a reason we're not kissing yet?"

Jude's head flew back in laughter. "None at all," he said before rectifying the situation. We remained on the couch making out for what felt like hours. I kissed him with the desperation of a skydiver with a faulty parachute or a death-row inmate on his final appeal. Like I was drowning and only Jude's lips could save my life. I kissed him until it was no longer enough. Then I took a breath and held out my hand. "Is there a bed in here?"

Jude's swollen lips twitched. "Yes. Did you want to take a nap...or something?"

"Or something." I couldn't wait any longer. Not breaking eye contact, I grabbed the bottom of his t-shirt and hitched it over his hips.

He raised his arms.

I stood on my tippy toes and pulled the fabric over his head. The relief that I didn't have to memorize what he looked like with his shirt off was palpable. It wasn't over. It was only beginning. "Let me look at you." My eyes lingered at the trail of hair disappearing under his jeans. I wet my lips.

"Take all the time you need." His voice was strained.

I ran my hands down his torso from his shoulder blades lower, lower, and lower still, lavishing the taut muscles below my fingers, until I reached the waistband of his boxers peeking out from under his jeans. "So warm." His skin was a furnace compared to mine. I rubbed my thumb along his nipple.

Jude groaned and pushed my hands down just long enough to help me remove my shirt. His fingers shook as he touched my breasts over my bra—my boring nude one since I was expecting a girls' weekend—like it was his first time at second base.

I shivered as my own nipples rose to his touch.

"We never had the 'over the bra' groping stage. We went

straight from our first kiss to our first bang in the same night," Jude said.

"Touching over the bra is overrated," I responded.

"In that case." He reached behind my back, unclasped my bra, and slid it over my bare shoulders and onto the floor so we were chest to chest. Warm to cool.

He pulled my jeans down to my hips. "Don't trip," he teased while I awkwardly stepped out of them.

I chuckled.

He rubbed his palm over my already-wet thong.

I moaned, taking a hold of his hand and rubbing harder. "Jude," I said a few minutes later through bated breath. "Either take me right here or carry me, because I'm not sure I can walk to the bed."

He dropped to the floor and hitched his thumb in my panties before pulling them down my thighs.

"The couch is an option too..." My head fell back as his tongue swept right through my pleasure center. "*Jude!*" I writhed under his mouth and grabbed onto his hair as he took me right to the brink...and stopped. "Don't stop. *Please.*"

He picked me up and carried me down a short hallway. "Not sure I feel right getting you off on someone else's floor."

I groaned. "Oh, *now* you have principles."

He laughed deviously.

I vaguely noted the décor of the bedroom. More wood paneling, wood ceiling, wood dressers. But I was blinded by lust and more focused on *Jude's* wood straining against his jeans.

He placed me on the bed and removed his pants while I watched, trying to piece together how the boy I hated had grown into the man I loved. I suspected it would take a single session for a therapist to diagnose my childhood disgust as pent-up affection, but it was a theory I'd never share with Jude. *Cocky Jude.* Amusement returned to want as he hovered over me in a forearm plank.

I gripped both of his biceps. *Mine.*

"Where were we?"

I pulled him to me. "I want you closer."

He reached under the pillow and flashed a wrapped condom. "Abracadabra!"

I snorted. "And we didn't even need to leave a tooth."

"I thought I might get lucky. There's one under a couch pillow, too." He tore open the packaging.

"I'm the lucky one."

The first time we made love, there was hesitation—an unvoiced question hovering in the air we breathed as to whether the unexpected electric attraction between us was a fever dream and we'd regret giving in once the fever broke. I didn't trust Jude, and further, was holding onto a momentous secret. And Jude, well, Jude just didn't *like* me.

Today, there were no second thoughts. We were stripped clean, both literally and figuratively, and we were good...better than good. We were loved.

There was power in that. I took possession of the condom and straddled him, stopping to kiss the beauty mark I'd discovered the first time we were together, before rolling it over him. Then I sank onto him. Almost as much as the pleasure of the act itself, I enjoyed watching Jude unravel—first he seemed to marvel at the sight of me rocking above him, but then his own bliss took over and his jaw clenched in his effort to maintain control. Finally, ecstasy made it impossible to focus on anything but finding my own release. I moved faster. My breasts rubbed against his chest hair. His hands cupped my ass. I tightened around him, shuddered, and came, crying out his name. He flipped me over and drove into me, growling mine, before collapsing on top of me.

Yes. Jude loved me and I loved him—for the kind, the wicked, and everything in between.

Much later, I rested my head on Jude's chest. "How did you find this place anyway? It must have cost you a fortune."

He played with my hair. "Working in the restaurant industry has its benefits. One of the managers rents it out, but it was unoccupied this weekend, and it was his way of thanking me for taking on so many extra shifts."

"Nice. This is way better than babysitting twin toddlers." My mind drifted to my best friend. At some point—meaning after the weekend—I'd ask how Jude and Jerry had suckered her into this plan. Driving to and from Connecticut went above the call of best-friend duty. I sent her a silent thank-you, hoping she'd receive the message by mental telepathy. Returning my focus to Jude, I told him about my change of heart over Rosaria's job offer with Ceiling Crashers.

His mouth hung open. "Way to bury the lede." But then his face changed and there it was: the expression of pure, unadulterated surprise and delight I knew would be there. *I knew it.*

"We had more pressing matters to attend to, like kissing and making up."

"I'd say we did a lot more than kiss." He pressed his lips to my wrist.

"You were right. When the plan stands in the way of true happiness, you have to chuck it. I'll need to put my apartment on the market and find a more affordable place to live, but I'll worry about that tomorrow." I kissed *his* wrist. "Or the next day."

Jude let out a breath. "I know I gave you a lot of shit for your fucking plans." He winced. "I was right in *your* case. But you were right in mine. Plans aren't always a bad idea."

"Six words I never thought would come out of your mouth in that particular order." I smirked. "I didn't want to say anything before, but this cabin took some...*ahem*, planning. You said it yourself."

He grinned, but then turned serious. "I've had a lot of time to think..."

I glared at him. If I never heard the phrase "think about it" again, it wouldn't be long enough.

His lips quirked. "*Ponder*...and my restaurant isn't going to open all by itself. I think I was afraid to put real effort into it in case I failed, but I read through your binder of articles."

I slapped a hand to my mouth. "You did?"

He tickled my arm. "Yes. It's here in case you want to read it together in bed later."

"Be still my heart!"

He turned on his side and rested his head on his forearm.

My gaze drifted to his arm. Lucky head.

"I've already looked into business classes and started scoping out potential partners and investors. I'm thinking it won't be in Manhattan, probably, because who can afford that, but maybe in the suburbs or New Jersey."

If I loved this man any harder, I'd need another heart to keep it from leaking out of me. "Wherever it is...*whenever* it is...I'll be by your side as you make your dream a reality. And you'll be at my side to do the same for me."

He stroked my neck. "I can agree to that."

"We agree on something again! I also promise to fly my mean flag only with you."

His face shined. "And I promise always to be just slightly meaner than you."

"Of course you do."

I kissed his shoulder to seal the deal and sighed in contentment. It was romance Jude and Molly style, and I wouldn't have it any other way.

Epilogue

Eight Years Later

1 lurched as a surge of cold liquid splashed me in the chest. "Jude!"

He laughed, a deflated red balloon dangling from one of his fingers. "Relax, Mole. It's just water."

I shook my head at him in a combination of adoration and exasperation. "Don't you think you enjoy water balloon fights a little too much for a man pushing thirty-five?"

Esther, who sat next to me on a wicker loveseat, used her hand to shield her face from the sun. "Jerry brings out the little boy in him."

I chuckled. "So true." It was a warm Sunday in June, and Esther and Jerry had come over from the city to our house for the day. The guys' idea of unwinding was running around the backyard with the kids, getting their heart rates up, while Esther and I took the opportunity to chill on the patio, nursing glasses of wine and catching up. "I should be glad he hasn't tried to set up a basketball net in the living room."

The men joined us on the pair of matching oversize wicker chairs situated on either side of the sofa while the kids played quietly in the makeshift sandbox we'd set up on the lawn with a senior Yogi as their dozing guard dog.

Jerry removed a beer from the cooler and clinked it against Jude's. "This is the life."

I sighed contentedly in agreement. The three-bedroom ranch-style house where Jude and I lived with our five-year-old son, Billy, in Teaneck, New Jersey, was small, but the covered patio and huge, fenced-in backyard sealed the decision for us, making it the go-to destination for barbeques with our friends. Once it was safer for children, we'd build a pool, something all the Blum and Stark siblings had wanted growing up but never had.

Jerry and Esther didn't believe in marriage but were fully committed to each other and still lived in the city with their four-year-old daughter, Lucy.

"I don't wanna go to work tomorrow!" But for the British accent, I might have mistaken Esther's petulant whine for Lucy's.

"Not much is guaranteed, but you can always count on the Sunday night blues." I plucked a tortilla chip from the bowl on the tile-topped wicker coffee table. I'd go inside soon to refill the salsa and guac. The cheese plate was also getting a little melty.

"Don't listen to Molly. She loves her job."

My lips spread into a smile. My husband spoke the truth. The third time had been the charm after all. Over the last eight years at Ceiling Crashers, I'd taken on the bulk of the counseling while Rosaria focused more on the business end. I commuted to the city twice a week to meet face-to-face with Rosaria and local clients. The rest of the time, I worked remotely from home and had virtual sessions with our members from outside of the area. Helping them turn their skills, interests, and passions into viable, lucrative careers, from personal shopping and fundraising to professional house staging and more, fulfilled me in a way recruiting never had.

Jerry pointed at Jude. "Like you're one to talk."

"True, true, true." Jude grinned and took a pull from his beer.

I patted his knee. Jude's pub, aptly named Jude's, had opened three years earlier and was located in the town of Montvale, less than twenty minutes from our house. Jude's, whose tagline was "We Make It Better," was a laid-back, no-pretenses restaurant-tavern serving five-star food that had received accolades from food critics at *New Jersey Monthly*, *Jersey Bites*, and the *Bergen Record* as well as from diners on Yelp, Foursquare, Tripadvisor, and more. Because his schedule was flexible, Jude was able to stay home with Billy on the days I went into the city.

"You can all feck off because I'm the only one whose job actually feels like work." Esther turned to Jerry. "When are you and Alex going to come up with a billion-dollar app so I can quit editing dry medical journals?"

Jerry kissed her cheek. "Any day now, your highness. Any day now."

I watched them affectionately, loving that Jerry still looked at my best friend with googly eyes. Their dynamic was so different, at least outwardly, from mine and Jude's, which hadn't changed much over the years either. We still mocked each other endlessly, and while the pranks had ceased, small competitions were a part of our everyday life—our son's first word was "Mama," but he took his first step into Jude's waiting arms—something Jude reminded me of often. But it was no longer about who won or lost, but how we played the game. And we were compatible playmates. Most important, our relationship occurred against a backdrop of safety, passion, and trust beyond my wildest dreams. And, of course, all four grandparents got along splendidly. My parents never reunited, but they were both happy in new partnerships and enjoying retirement.

Life is good. I watched Billy and Lucy playing in the sandbox, so fortunate my best friend fell in love with Jude's best friend and we had our first baby around the same time. With any luck, they'd be, as Esther so charmingly referred to it, "mates" for life.

Just then, the children's voices increased in volume. I sat up straight and put down my wineglass.

A red-faced Lucy stood and pointed a pudgy finger at Billy. "Where is it?"

Billy looked up from the sandbox. "I don't know where your dumb doll is, Lucy Goosey," he said calmly before returning his focus to his sandcastle.

While the adults looked on, not wanting to intervene unless absolutely necessary, Lucy's eyes shot arrows at Billy's head he didn't see before she took a running leap toward the sandbox and kicked Billy's tower to the ground.

While Billy remained frozen in apparent shock, Lucy plucked the doll, now in full view, from the pile of sand and yelled, "Liar!"

Billy moved slowly, like a snake waking up from a nap. He stood, grabbed the heavy-duty water pistol either Jude or Jerry had left on the grass, and aimed it straight at Lucy.

Lucy, holding her doll tightly to her torso, stepped back.

Billy pressed the nozzle.

Lucy used her doll to shield her face from the force of the water and screamed, "Stop it!" before slipping butt-first onto the grass.

Esther bolted up and rushed over to her daughter.

Jude stood. "Billy!"

Our son dropped the water gun, turned to us, and rounded his large hazel eyes as if just realizing we were there.

"Apologize to Lucy right now!" his father demanded.

"Don't want to." Billy scraped a hand through his unruly head of dark hair and shrugged before doing a laughing dance in place. "I can see her underwear!"

I pressed a fist to my lips. Getting a kick out of my son's impish behavior was not something I was proud of, but he was *such* a mini-Jude. I'd never loved anyone so much in my life.

Jude shook his head and pointed at our designated "time-out" chair in the corner of the patio. "Take five. Now."

Billy's lips trembled as he did as directed. "She ruined my sandcastle. Where's *her* time-out?"

Lucy ran over, her faded-red tie-dyed dress soaked, tears streaming from her blue eyes, and jumped onto her dad's lap.

"It's okay, Lu. Daddy's got you." Jerry patted the back of her blond, nearly platinum, hair in a soothing motion.

Lucy turned her head to the side and stuck her tongue out at Billy.

Esther gasped. "Lucy!"

Lucy pressed her face into Jerry's shirt and continued to cry. "I hate him!"

Billy continued to mumble from his chair, "Why is it always my fault? How come no one ever yells at Lucy Goosey?"

I locked eyes with Jude.

His widened.

I gritted my teeth, but it was no use. We burst out laughing.

Jerry peered at us over Lucy's head. "What about my daughter's crying do you two find so amusing?"

Jude's eyes sparkled with mischief. "Private joke. You wouldn't understand."

I linked my arm through his. "It will all make sense in about twenty years."

Acknowledgments

As I write this, I'm still riding the wave of the release of *As Seen on TV*. I haven't gotten over the thrill of seeing my book on shelves and am so blessed for the opportunity to repeat the experience with *Someone Just Like You*. I have so many people to thank for this.

To my agent, Melissa Edwards. Throughout this experience, you have been so levelheaded, business savvy, informative, and kind. You probably have no idea how many times you talked me off the ledge without even realizing it. Thank you for believing in me.

To my editor, Leah Hultenschmidt. Your ideas during our brainstorming session helped me polish *Someone Just Like You* and its characters into something I'm so incredibly proud of. You spot issues and opportunities for depth and humor that I often lack the objectiveness to see on my own. I cannot thank you enough for making me a better storyteller.

To Estelle Hallick. Each time you've called me a "star," it has made my day. I'm so grateful for your expertise, marketing savvy, patience, and kindness. (And for organizing such a special event for me at the flagship Barnes & Noble location. Dream. Come. True.) *You* are a star.

I'm so appreciative of the entire team at Hachette/Forever, including Beth deGuzman, Dana Cuadrado, Sabrina Flemming, Rebecca Maines, Luria Rittenberg, and Elece Green for everything you do to turn my dreams into reality and my stories into books in all formats.

To Libby VanderPloeg. We were messaging on Instagram when I learned you were creating my cover again, and I literally whooped with joy. I love it, I love it, I. LOVE. IT. Thank you for making my covers so delicious and eye-catching.

To Ann-Marie Nieves at Get Red PR: I'm so thrilled to work with you!

Thank you to my critique partner, Samantha M. Bailey, and beta readers, Josie Brown and Margot Ryan, for taking time out of your busy schedules to read and provide honest (and sometimes brutal) feedback. Your individual strengths have allowed me to write a better book.

I'm so grateful to Lori Weiss for answering my questions about legal recruiting. Readers: in my twenty-five-plus years as a paralegal, I've worked with many recruiters and none of them were slimy like Michael. He was a figment of my imagination, and I meant no disrespect to all the wonderful recruiters out there, several of whom have helped me find jobs!

This book was loosely inspired by my family and our neighbors across the street growing up, the Solons. Doris and Howie were my second parents; Mark teased me like an older brother; and Jill, the oldest, was too cool to pay me any mind, but I always coveted her pretty pink bedroom. And Ronni, my forever friend and third sister: despite us both being the youngest of three, we share none of the animosity of Molly and Jude! Thank you all for the inspiration and for so many memories of evenings playing running bases and SPUD in our backyards, dual family dinners at Chicken Unlimited, garage sales, and so much more.

Thank you to the producers of *Friends*. I was watching "The One with Russ" when I came up with the doppelgänger hook for *Someone Just Like You*.

The publishing journey comes with so many emotional highs and lows, and I am so grateful for the many friends who have provided a safe place to celebrate, cheer, worry, vent, and freak out:

Samantha M. Bailey: The fact that you were with me the first time I unexpectedly saw *As Seen on TV* in a bookstore the week before it was published was nothing short of magical. I love you so much. I'm so glad we are on this journey together and can't wait to see where the future brings us both. Keep soaring. Never stop dreaming. Keep taking those risks!

All my love to my fellow Beach Babes, the above-mentioned Samantha M. Bailey, Josie Brown, Eileen Goudge, Francine LaSala, Jen Tucker, and Julie Valerie. At this very moment, I am counting down the days until our "beach baby" in Florida while also manifesting a seven-person reunion in 2024. Let's do this, bitches!

I am indebted to #TeamMelissa for so many things, including providing excuses to procrastinate doing the work, but also for the commiseration and exchange of information, book and TV recommendations, tweet decoding, and so much laughter.

Thank you, also, to the NYC Writer Commiseration Station. I love getting to know you all through our Discord and look forward to more in-person afternoon coffee chats, Friday happy hours, and reading all your amazing books.

I owe much of the success of *As Seen on TV* to the many book influencers, bloggers, podcasters, booksellers, and avid readers who continuously shared their love with reviews, multiple posts, stories, and reels, and/or provided podcast/interview opportunities, including but *definitely* not limited to: Andrea Peskind Katz (Great Thoughts; Great Readers), Suzanne Weinstein Leopold (Suzy Approved Book Reviews), Suzanne Fine, Craig Kennedy (Fairfield University Bookstore), Liz Donatelli (Reader Seeks Romance), Anna Mercier (Basic Pitches), Hannah Mary McKinnon and Hank Phillippi Ryan (First Chapter Fun), Elle Greco (Steam Scenes), Dara Levan (Every Soul Has a Story), Eden Boudreau (The Lonely Writer), Kris Clink (Kris Clink's Writing Table), Jacqueline (@Purposelyunperfect), Janet (@purrfectpages), Jamie Rosenblit (@BeautyandtheBook), Kate Rock (Kate Rock Book Tours), Erin Branscom (@mylevel10life), Tiffany (@TiffanytheReader), Joanna (@Lifewithprinceman), Jocelyn (@JocelynRobinsonAuthor), Melissa Amster (Chick Lit Central), Sarah (@Bookish_Sbe), Courtney (@courts.book.nook), Lianna (@getlitwithlianna), Gabriella (@reads.withgab), Linne (@cozypagesss), Stephanie (@theespressoedition), Cee (@celiarecommends), Shay (@Booksaremagictoo), Michelle (@nurse_bookie), Julia (@chicklitistheshit), Haylee (@haylsbookshelf), Paige (@nycturnthepaige), Megan (@alspawreadsitall), Scott Silverman (@BookConvos), Kathy Lewison (Books and Booze), Courtney (@Booksarechic), Kelly Perotti, Ashley Williams, Bethany Clarke (@books_with_bethany), Kaley Stewart (Books Etc.), Lindsay Lorimore, Erin Pullman, and Rebecca Moore.

So much gratitude to Abby Jimenez, Helena Hunting, Farrah Rochon, Kate Spencer, Dylan Newton, Devon Daniels, Lacey Waldon, Stacey Agdern, Melonie Johnson, Jean Meltzer, Lizzie Shane, Jenny Holiday, Kerry Winfrey, Kristin Rockaway, Sophie

Sullivan, Maddie Dawson, Ashley Winstead, Sonia Hartl, Kelly Siskind, Sarvenaz Tash, and Amanda Aksel for taking time out of your busy schedules to read and endorse *As Seen on TV*. I'm so honored and humbled!

My parents, Susan Goodman and Michael Schorr, are my biggest fans. Thank you both for telling everyone you know about my books without charging a publicity fee. And, Dad, thanks for accompanying me to every Barnes & Noble within a fifty-mile radius so I could sign stock. I hope you'll do it again with this one!

Special thanks to Megan Coombes and Vanessa Williams for being so unbelievably supportive of my debut. Your generosity astounds me, and I love you both.

Thank you to Ronni Candlen Nee Solon (mentioned above), Shanna Eisenberg, and Deirdre Noonan for being among my closest friends for so long!

Deborah Shapiro and Phyllis Porter: you make the day job fun!

Last but not least, I will always…*always*…thank Alan Blum for his unflagging belief in me (and for the use of his last name for the main character of this book)! I couldn't have come this far without you, and I miss you every single day.

About the Author

A born and bred New Yorker and lifelong daydreamer, **Meredith Schorr** fueled her passion for writing everything from restaurant reviews, original birthday cards, and even work-related emails into a career penning romantic comedies. When she's not writing books filled with grand gestures and hard-earned happily-ever-afters or working as a trademark paralegal, she's most often reading, running, or watching TV...for research, of course.

To learn more, visit her at:
MeredithSchorr.com
Twitter @MeredithSchorr
Instagram @MeredithSchorr
Facebook.com/MeredithSchorrAuthor